To my best
artistic peer
RL

Super Bowl
2012

THE VAN

By

Lee Irby

PUBLISHED BY BROKE DOWN PRESS

ISBN 0615591159

Hanover, West Germany
1964
00000

We here at the Hanover factory produce 14,000 Type II Transporters each month. Think about that. An amazing feat, no? Twenty years ago our country was in ruins. The Volkswagen "miracle," some call it. To this company I literally owe my life, and that's why from me Volkswagen always gets an honest day.

But sometimes the line shuts down and production stops anywhere from a few minutes to an hour. I try to find things to do, but on certain days the storm clouds in my head start to gather, and that's when I need to laugh. To dream. To forget, the hardest trick of all. So much to forget. So many faces. So many graves. My mother. My baby sister. The boy down the street who loved kites. Uncles. Aunts.

So I go looking for Holgar, who is very amusing. In no time he'll cheer me right up. He is a strapping lad, an eager young pup with no bad memories of the war. His birth came after Hitler's death, the lucky bastard.

From the Inspection well I head over to Holgar's station. He grins when he sees me coming. A wide gap sits between his top front teeth. Sometimes his tongue pokes through it when he smiles. A curious face. Skin the color of mud. A broad nose. Protruding, pointy ears, like a fox's.

"Hello, young friend," I call out to him.

"Weiss! You're still alive?"

"Barely."

"You had me worried when I didn't see you for a week. They say you were sick. In the hospital."

"Oh, it was nothing too serious."

Behind Holgar, suspended at eye level, stretches a long line of Type II bodies. Each has the rear hatch propped open, because Holgar's job is to help install the engine. Then he bolts down the muffler to the exhaust manifold. Hardly exciting work, and very tiring. We all must start somewhere, I remind him.

We step over behind the big tray of bolts and washers where Holgar squats down and lights a cigarette. "Well, good, because let me tell you, Weiss, I almost died myself last night," he sings out merrily, waving the burning cigarette like a baton. Then he adds with much satisfaction: "I got no sleep, not a wink, and I'm bone tired. Get it?

Done tired."

"I do." Already I feel my spirits lifting. "What was her name?"

Holgar snorts like a racehorse at the starting gate. "Greta. I think. I'm no good with names."

"Was she pretty? You can remember that, can't you?"

He shrugs indifferently and thinks for a few seconds. "She wasn't bad. I don't remember much, though. Things got a little blurry. A little foggy."

"You're lucky, Holgar. I remember too much about everything."

"Try drinking more beer, Weiss. Works for me."

"It doesn't help. If only it did. How easy the world would be then."

Another long drag, and then he's back up on his feet. He can't stay still for long. He springs up from his haunches and goes over to the line. He pats the exposed rear wheel of the microbus facing him, rear hatch open like a yawning mouth. "So, Weiss, who do you think'll drive this one?" he asks.

It's a game we sometimes play. Holgar likes to imagine the lives of the Americans who are going to buy our transporters. This might seem ridiculous, but it soothes me. And others, too. Because over comes Vadst, and Benneker, followed by Schegel. Veterans like me. Men who saw too much and can't forget. They gather around and listen with thin smiles, thumbs jammed into their blue overalls, faces covered with grime and sweat. "Ah, good question," I answer, glancing at the vehicle for clues. "Let's see. It's a standard model, not a deluxe. This one will belong to a New Yorker who listens to Frank Sinatra."

"No, a woman will buy it. A beautiful woman."

"Is there any other kind, Holgar?"

"A beautiful woman with a long, delicate neck and curly blonde hair."

"You sound very sure of yourself."

"From California. Malibu Beach."

"An actress?"

"A fashion model."

"An exotic creature."

"Oh is she ever! And she'll drive around picking up strange men. Men she's never met before. Because she likes danger. She likes almost getting caught. It turns her on."

"Really? Like an exhibitionist?"

A bell rings, and voices cry out. The line starts to lurch back to life. The microbuses will begin to move once more. My heart sinks. We were just getting to the good part, where Holgar describes the things this woman will do. But Holgar must return to his position before his supervisor sees him idling.

Too late.

Marcus Anker is already on his way. He's a fussy little Swabian, and they say his wife dresses him each morning and gives him an allowance each week. He stands holding his clipboard against his chest. Somehow he always manages to smell like fresh-cut flowers. His thin lips are red, almost as if he was wearing lipstick. "Is something the matter?" he asks.

"No," I say cheerfully.

"Is there a problem with the engine installation?"

"No, no. Nothing of the sort."

I have to return my own inspection duties, but Marcus Anker won't leave my side. He trails behind like a dog hoping for a bone.

"I heard you were sick," he says quietly, talking to me like I might collapse any second. "I hope you're feeling better."

"I am, thanks."

"You got some rest, I hope."

"Not enough."

"Listen, about Holgar. I know you are friends with him, but there's been a few issues, and I'm gonna have to write him up unless he gets his ass in gear."

"Like what kinds of issues? Performance?"

"No, not performance. He's displayed a piss-poor attitude toward his co-workers, for one thing."

"I've never seen that."

"There've been complaints. Several, as a matter of fact. It's all documented." He taps the clipboard for emphasis.

"Really? He's a friendly kid. Cheerful. Works hard."

"He's awfully full of himself, is his main problem."

"Which means what?"

But Marcus Anker doesn't have to spell it out for me. I can see into that pumpkin-shaped head of his. It's because of Holgar's background, being the son of a local woman named Marta Koblenz who in April 1945 slept with an American soldier. A member of Patton's army sweeping through Lower Saxony. A negro, apparently, judging from

Holgar's dark complexion and tightly curled hair.

"Which means he acts like a son of a bitch," Marcus Anker tells me, voice straining against the anger rising in his throat, "and he needs to learn how to respect his superiors."

Marcus Anker had been a member of the Nazi party, and in some twisted way he must blame Holgar for the humiliation of defeat. He'd deny it, of course. We shouldn't dwell on the past, he'd say. We've had enough trials, he'd claim. The guilty have been punished, he'd insist. Isn't this the Week of Brotherhood? On TV, channel ZDF is showing a slew of documentaries about the war. Just last night there was a program about the valuable contribution that German Jews have made over the past three centuries. Very informative, he'd offer.

"Let me talk to him during lunch break," I say, playing the peacemaker. "Maybe I can pound some sense into him."

"He needs it. You'll be doing him a big favor. But I doubt he'll listen, because I've tried setting him straight a hundred times already. He might be a lost cause, Weiss. Which is too bad, because I know you two talk and joke around."

A subtle threat. He's accusing me of malingering. Of being a shirker. Because I want to forget and laugh and dream. "I'll try my best. But he's a grown man. He'll do what he wants, regardless."

Marcus Anker has heard enough, and he's holding all the cards. He gives me a hale pat on the back. "And take care of yourself, how about it, Weiss? No more trips to the hospital!"

I hurry away to return to my post. As soon as I can, I'll warn Holgar to watch his back, as they say. I'd hate to see him get fired. I'd miss his stories of the Americans driving our Type IIs. Holgar has boned up on America inside and out, and one day he hopes to visit and look for his father. That won't be easy, because he doesn't even know the man's name or where he grew up. Nothing.

But will he listen to me? Will he heed my advice to go easy on Marcus Anker? Probably not, because like many West German kids today, Holgar despises people such as Marcus Anker, those who allowed the madness of Hitler to occur. The generation of culprits. And why should Holgar respect the likes of Marcus Anker? He shouldn't. He won't.

The way I see it, one day soon, very soon, all the bitterness and resentment boiling inside these kids will gather into a huge bomb and just explode. And maybe that's just what this world needs.

National City, California
1964
00005

You never forget your first sale. It was my second day on the job, a Tuesday. I was the only salesman on the floor. I was nervous as hell. A wreck. I kept circling the showroom and stealing hopeful glances outside for some customers to come along. But there weren't any. I felt like running down the sidewalk and tackling the first person I saw and dragging him back here. I couldn't go home empty-handed again. My wife wasn't sure about this job. Selling German cars? She thought I was nuts. *That's why we moved out to California? So you could sell German cars?* She was pregnant, and we were broke. Talk about tense!

Still, I was real excited about my chance with Fortune Motors. Mr. Fortune was one of the first car dealers in San Diego to land a Volkswagen dealership, and VWs were all we sold. When I was a kid back in New Jersey I used to look at these strange German imports like they were from outer space. They were so small compared to the powerful American hot-rods, and they did look like bugs. Like little insects. But I was convinced they were the future, and so I quit my job selling appliances and came over here. I planned on making it big. I wanted to be number one in sales by January 1965. So I soaked up every word Mr. Fortune said.

He told me I needed to know my customers. The Volkswagen Corporation of America had done studies about who owned their cars. I could recite the results by heart. The typical VW buyer had graduated from or gone to college, lived in the suburbs, worked a white-collar job, went for outdoor sports more than indoor ones like bowling, and were younger than other car buyers. They were the kinds of people who responded to the funky VW ads like "Why Won't Your Wife Let You Buy This Car?" and "Think Small," or in other words grown-up beatniks who liked to be different. I had a cousin like that. Lit major at Brown, schoolteacher, and he drove a Beetle. The hard sell would never work with eggheads like my cousin, so there was no point in even trying.

It wasn't easy keeping all this inside dope straight. For eight hours the day before Mr. Fortune had given me advice, pointers, tips, suggestions, hints—you name it, and he had a story about it. He'd been selling cars on National Boulevard before it became famous as the "Mile of Cars," back when there were just a few dealers and some rundown Navy housing and Keith's Drive-In. He knew the business backwards and forwards. And what he'd learned over the years boiled down to this: if you can't sell cars in California, you're one sorry son of a bitch. And you wouldn't last long at Fortune Motors.

He said he'd hired me because I looked honest. He even gave me a nickname, Choir Boy, which was hilarious because back then I would've slit my best friend's throat to make a buck. I was twenty-three but I barely needed to shave every day. Mr. Fortune said I'd go far if I did everything he told me. Dress nice. Be polite. Don't budge.

*

When the businessman in gray pinstripes came in, I went over and greeted him, doing it the way Mr. Fortune told me to do. Kept my distance, looked him in the eye, low but firm voice: "Let me know if I can be of assistance," I said respectfully, wishing I'd had a breath mint to hide the smell of that tuna fish sandwich I'd eaten for lunch.

"Yes, as a matter of fact, you can," he spoke up right away. "I'm interested in that Volkswagen out front. The blue one. What's it called? Station wagon? Minibus? I've heard both."

"Either name is fine. But it's a beauty, isn't it? A marvel of German engineering. And practical. You could fit an army in the back."

"I want to buy it."

I almost couldn't believe my ears. "Of course," I muttered, trying not to smile. Mr. Fortune had said that the Type II Transporter (that was the official name) wasn't selling much these days, because of what was called "the chicken war." Because Europeans had raised the tariff on American chicken meat, we'd responded by raising the tariff on imported trucks and buses by something like 25%. That caused the price of the Type II to go up 10%, to around $3000. It had hurt sales, said Mr. Fortune. Then the VW marketing people had started calling the Type II a "station wagon" to attract buyers. But Detroit was waging a "Buy American" campaign, too, and that didn't help.

So the fact that this guy was willing to pay more for the Type II than a Detroit wagon made me kind of suspicious, and I started wondering if I wasn't getting set up. Were the boys pulling a fast one on me, since it was my second day on the job? Did they find this bum at Balboa Park and pay him ten bucks to razz me?

"It's for my son," he explained. His voice was trailing off into a quiet sadness. "He's turning sixteen."

"Well, he'll be very happy to get this as a present. Every kid in San Diego wishes they had one."

"He saw one down at the beach. We used to do a bit of surfing together. Before he moved." He must've realized he sounded downbeat because he added very quickly: "I know I'm spoiling him rotten, but my old man never bought me anything."

"You can say that again."

We shared a forced laugh as we walked out into the sunlight. I kept waiting for him to mention the price, but he seemed happy just loping around the minibus. I pointed out a few of the features I'd read about in the pamphlets Mr. Fortune had given me. The air cooled engine, which meant it would never overheat. The spacious storage capacity. The handsome design. This boxy contraption wasn't my cup of tea, but you couldn't tell by the way I laid it on thick. Everyone always said I could sell snow to an Eskimo.

"This is exactly what he wants. I just wish I could deliver it to him in person."

"Where does he live?"

"Dallas, Texas. I have to ship it to him. Will that be a problem?"

"No, of course not. We can arrange something." I had no idea what or how, but I was hoping the girls in the office might know what our options were. It would cost an arm and a leg, but this guy didn't seem to care. He was dressed nice, with freshly polished shoes and silver cufflinks and a silk band around his fedora. I made him for an engineer at a big defense contractor like Lockheed. Those bastards pulled down good money and they spent it too.

"Let's go inside and get started on the paperwork," I said, trying to maintain my poise.

"Yes, we should do that. His birthday is next week."

I wrote down the information I needed into a notebook just like Mr. Fortune had shown me. I wrote fast, just in case this guy decided to change his mind. I was also calculating my commission in my head: twenty bucks! I couldn't wait to call my wife and tell her. Maybe she'd ease up on me. I wasn't going to spend my life selling refrigerators and stoves. I had bigger dreams than that.

It turned out I'd made the right decision, because over the next two decades I sold thousands of those Type II Transporters to every kind of long-haired hipple and surfer in Southern California. Mr. Fortune said back in the Fifties VW couldn't even find people to open dealerships. They recruited anyone with two dimes to rub together, including this shady Swede masseuse and this old rancher. But Mr. Fortune had seen VWs during the war in Germany and he knew the Krauts built them to last. To run forever.

Dallas, Texas
1964
00008

Good Vibrations

When Mother saw the van parked in the driveway, she turned white as a sheet. "We're sending it back!" she barked at me like an insane phys ed. teacher. All she needed a whistle and a stupid haircut.

I didn't know what to say. She was a little drunk because I could smell the gin on her breath and see the pinkish clouds swirling in her slightly bloodshot eyes—she'd just returned from lunch at the club. The Dallas Country Club. On Mockingbird Lane. Which meant three martinis with olives, on the rocks.

But it was love at first sight. I loved my van. And no one was taking it away from me. Ever.

"No way," I protested. "You can't do that. It's mine and ownership is ninety-nine percent of the law." My voice was as flat as west Texas. I was a real cowboy now, and cowboys came to a duel with guns blazing. I was standing my ground, no matter what she said, and she could say plenty.

"Has your father lost his mind? What on earth was he thinking? He actually had this thing delivered here without asking me? The nerve of that man." Mother always got worked up when recounting Dad's flaws, especially after a few drinks. Then her tongue would really start to wag and she could remember spats from years ago as if they'd happened yesterday.

"It's what I wanted. I asked him for it."

"That excuses nothing. He should've consulted with me first. But that's typical of your father, always going off half-cocked. I don't intend to demean him, Norman, because I know you love him because he's your father, but this is very upsetting to me. I don't like rudeness and incivility. This is boorish of him."

"I don't see what all the fuss is about. It's just a car. I need a car. Problem solved."

"The problem is not solved. It's the principle of the thing, that he thinks he can just buy you whatever you want. Is that even a car? It looks like some sort of small bus."

It was aqua blue and white, with a split windshield and a big, round chrome VW emblem affixed in the middle of the flat nose. With California plates. My real home. The only thing missing was a surfboard strapped to the roof rack.

"It's not a bus. It's a van."

She didn't buy what I was selling. "It looks flimsy for a van."

"Well, it's not. They're very handy. There's acres of storage space. The back seats come out. A person could live in one." I'd seen the commercials on TV showing just how roomy these vans were. If you put a sleeping bag in the back, you could drive down to the Baja and live like a king.

"Don't get any wise ideas, Norman."

"I'm not saying I will."

"Good." We both gazed at the van, and I could almost hear the gears grinding in her mind. She hated it because Dad had sent it to me. She hated it because it looked unusual. She hated it because it was foreign. But I loved it, and I told her why.

"It reminds me of home," I said, but then stopped myself. I could feel her withering glare, hot like a bare 100-watt bulb.

"This is your home."

"My old home."

She winced like I'd just jabbed her in the eye with a pencil. She'd promised to make it up to me, but I wasn't ready to forgive her. Because, honestly, I'd never forgive her for making me move out here. "Ted promised to buy you any car you want. Why must you be so difficult? Can you answer that question?"

"I don't need for Ted to buy me a car. I have a car." I jingled the keys in my pocket for emphasis.

"Then you'll need to get a job to pay for the gas."

"No problem."

"Because we won't give you one red cent to keep that thing running, agreed? That misshapen German abhorrence is your responsibility."

"Are you finished yelling at me?"

She sighed in exasperation and went inside to check on Rosa, the Mexican cook and maid. The last I'd seen her, Rosa was pickling cucumbers in the kitchen, which was filled with glass jars and salsa music. I didn't have to ask Rosa what she was doing, I already knew—she was preparing food for our new fallout shelter, the deluxe model offered by Lone Star Steel of Dallas, which had been installed in the backyard about three weeks ago. Ted, my stepfather, was convinced that the Soviets would stop at nothing to destroy our country, and he personally wouldn't get caught with his pants down. To Ted, getting caught with your pants down was the ultimate no-no for a man. "Caught you with your pants down, didn't I?" he'd growl and pretend to grab me when I wasn't looking, making me flinch. His point was that he could destroy me at any moment, which I didn't dispute.

I hated Ted. I hated the smell of his Hai Karate cologne, I hated the squeak of his Bass loafers, I hated the thin cigars he smoked, I hated his John Birch politics, his lack of imagination, his endless stock of clichés, his beer gut and his booming foghorn voice—and he knew I hated him. We understood each other perfectly.

And Ted eventually got his revenge last May: a transfer to Dallas, Texas.

I Get Around

I stood staring at my new van, and it felt like I was floating on cloud nine. I couldn't believe Dad had actually bought it. I had to thank him—although I had no idea where he was. He traveled a lot on business trips, so I'd have to write him a letter, and he'd eventually get it. Maybe this summer I could drive the van out to California and never come back.

Drive. Exactly. That's what I needed to do. Drive.

I went inside to tell Mother I was heading out. She was on the telephone, and by her hushed tone I figured she was talking to Ted. She had to be telling him about my birthday present, delivered just that Wednesday afternoon, September 12. My official birthday had been last week, when Dad had called to tell me to expect a "big package" to arrive soon. He wouldn't tell me what it was, only that I'd be "very surprised." A new surfboard? I didn't have much need of one out here in the landlocked heartland where it got as hot as an oven in the summer: no cool breezes from the Pacific, no mountains, no escape.

She held her hand over the receiver. "Yes, Norman?"

"I'm taking my new car for a spin."

Her eyebrows arched suspiciously. I returned her stare with one of my own. I wasn't backing down. "Where are you going?"

"For a drive."

"When will you be home?"

"Before dinner."

"Have you finished your homework?"

"We didn't have any."

"Oh, really?"

"We didn't. Honest injun." It was true. My high school was a cakewalk compared to the one in California. We were doing stuff that we'd covered in eighth grade, and it was a real yawn fest so far. Not that I was complaining. I had no desire to cram my brains out. I figured I'd coast for the next three years and then go to college somewhere far, far away.

"Be careful," she told me, sounding almost maternal. "I don't know if that thing is safe to drive. Ted says that the engine is in the rear and should you collide head-on with another car—"

She stopped and gathered herself. Displaying emotion wasn't in her bag of tricks. "It wouldn't end well," she finished tersely. It touched me that she cared. But I was going anyway.

"I'll be fine," I assured her. "I'm a careful driver. You said so yourself."

"Precisely, when you were driving a Cadillac. Not that German bandbox."

"Bye!"

I skipped away, feeling giddy and strangely content for the first time since arriving in Texas. I got inside my new Volkswagen van and marveled at how clean and perfect the interior was. It felt a little disorienting being so high off the ground, but I quickly grew to like the feeling. I was lord of all I surveyed, an exiled prince from an exotic land who'd been sent to the sterile, arid hills of middle America, where all dreams came to die.

I started the engine and then pushed down hard on the gear stick to get the van into reverse. When it began to drift backward, I hit the brakes and stalled out. First attempt, aborted. I'd never make it as an astronaut. For lots of reasons. But I did finally manage to back out of the driveway without running into anything.

And then I was on the move, so close to the windshield that the asphalt seemed to be leaping up at me—and Mother was right—if I ever got into a head-on collision, I was history. Finished. Caput. I wouldn't stand a chance. But I felt alive, alive and terrified and thrilled, and I was driving very, very slow. Like a tortoise with a barbell strapped to its shell. Eventually I got used to the feel of the van and decided what the hell—let's go on a little adventure.

I drove two blocks and then went right on Mockingbird Lane, a busy road with lots of traffic—most of the cars were destined for Highland Park Village, a fashionable shopping center built to resemble a Spanish mission. But first I passed by the entrance to the country club, a fancy playground for rowdy petroleum executives still stuck in their SMU frat boy days—yet, at the same time, how convenient for Mother, who had within reach all that she required for happiness: snobs to have lunch with and stores to spend Ted's money.

Next came Highland Park Village. The church people were still picketing in front of Volk's, a spiffy department store. They were holding hand-scrawled signs and marching in a line along the sidewalk. *We Protest Topless Suits in the Name of Christ*, one sign read. I'd seen the same group out last week when Mother drove me to shop for new clothes. I'd grown three inches during the past year and nothing fit anymore. So we had to slip past the outraged church group, dismayed that somewhere in America, certainly not in Dallas, women could buy what was called a topless bathing suit.

Topless bathing suits, the ruin of civilization.

There were a few girls I would've loved to see try a topless bathing suit on for size. Mary Rogers, Dede Funson, the varsity cheerleaders— none of them knew I existed, of course. I didn't play on any sports teams and I didn't hang out with the in-crowd—I was the new kid who was a bit of a loner by nature, a fish out of water in the one city in the world I actually despised. When Mother had first told me about Ted's promotion and transfer, I was sure she was joking. Dallas? The city where our president could spend approximately 52 minutes without getting killed? It was a miracle he'd made it that long.

Where the hell was I going on this maiden voyage of mine anyway? My options were limitless. I could go wherever I damn well wanted, and no one could tell me different. The record store? There was a Sam Goody's close by. I could buy some new LPs and then grab a bite to eat.

Or what about Dealey Plaza?

I'd only been to downtown Dallas once. Ted worked in the Mobil building, with the big Pegasus on the roof. We went to have lunch with him last month. But Mother had purposefully avoided Dealey Plaza, despite my begging her to take me there. "I don't know why you'd want to visit a place so steeped in tragedy," she told me. "A boy your age should have other interests."

"Like what? Football and girls?"

"I didn't say that, Norman. But I don't think spending hours each day thinking about the assassination is healthy for a boy about to turn sixteen. You could use a hobby."

"I have a hobby. It's called surfing. Do you see any waves around here?"

"Don't get smart with me, young man. You should branch out and try new things. What's wrong with enjoying a sport and dating a few girls? I don't see the harm in that."

"I don't like football."

She waited a few seconds before asking her next question. "You like girls, don't you?"

I almost said no, just to see her face drop, her thinking I was a queer. But that would've been too cruel. "I guess so."

"You guess so?" She sounded scared. "We'll have to introduce you to some of the young people around here. I've seen some pretty girls at the swimming pool at the club. You should come with me one afternoon to see for yourself."

I wanted to see Dealey Plaza with my own eyes. Just to say I did it. To get it out of my system. Then I'd hit every record store near my house. It wouldn't take long to get downtown if I went on the Stemmons Freeway. "Stemmons Freeway, Market Place of the South West." It had just opened, and now hordes of commuters could get to their boring jobs faster. What an improvement to the big D!

The entrance to the freeway was a few blocks away. I stepped on the accelerator and sped toward it. I had the radio tuned to a rock and roll station, though, so it wasn't all bad. The DJ even played a Beatles song, which I wasn't expecting. "Please Please Me." Mother detested rock and roll and wouldn't allow me to listen to it in her company. She dug the Lennon Sisters and watching *Bonanza* and laughing at the talking fist of Señor Wences on *The Ed Sullivan Show*, which just about drove me ape.

I got downtown in under ten minutes. I had a vague idea where I was going, and I tried to follow the signs for Houston Street, but I took a wrong turn coming off the Stemmons and before I knew it, I was heading over the goddamn Trinity River and into Oak Cliff, the neighborhood where Oswald had lived. Where he'd shot the cop. Where he'd gotten arrested at the Texas Theater. That was all I knew about Oak Cliff, but it was enough so that I didn't want to stop and ask for directions to *Dealey Plaza*, for God's sake. I didn't want to drive around like an idiot for ten hours, either. There were some tough-looking Mexicans eying me pretty close, like they knew I was in over my head.

So as soon as I saw a Rexall I pulled over. Parallel parking wasn't my strong suit, and it took a lot of effort to ease the van into the open space. I was sure I was going to crash—on my first drive in my new wheels! How typical that would be. How goddamn par for the course.

Dealey Plaza had to be close by. I looked over at the skyline of downtown Dallas in the distance and spotted in the foreground the orange brick of the Texas School Book Depository—hard to miss with the big Hertz Rental Car sign and clock on top of it. I almost jumped right back into the van, thinking I'd find the plaza eventually. But I was a little hungry and felt like grabbing a snack from the drug store. A candy bar. Maybe some Twinkies if the mood struck me.

I saw a pretty girl walk by and so I followed her inside and then down the Beauty aisle, ogling her finely sculpted rear-end, and then she stopped and looked at a bottle of shampoo and I scurried past, getting close enough to inhale her perfume. She would've looked great in the backseat of my van, naked.

Not surprisingly I found myself at the magazine rack and I went through the usual routine. First a quick perusal of *Sports Illustrated*, and then *Time*, until I was sure the coast was clear. There was a new issue of *Playboy*. October. Must've just hit the newsstands. The cover was a close-up of a brunette's face from a side view. A little too artsy for my tastes, and I didn't even pretend like I cared about the interview with Cassius Clay. I went right for the playmate buried inside. A blonde. Hefty-size boobs on her, too.

Before I could get a good look at the centerfold, this old geezer with an ivory-handled cane wobbled by me. He gave me a scornful look, and I felt ashamed, but why? What was so wrong with what I was doing? In defiance I stuck my chin out and folded the magazine under my arm and carried it straight for the front counter. I grabbed a Snickers from the candy display in front of the register and avoided making eye contact with the cashier.

"Eight-five cents," the guy said, putting the magazine and candy bar into a brown paper bag. For my own protection.

I dropped a dollar bill on the counter and hustled out of there as fast as I could, without bothering to ask for directions to Dealey Plaza. I had other things on my mind. Two other things, to be exact: the boobs of Miss October, which I feasted on as soon as I got back to the van. Miss October was pretty much of a dog in the face department, but she more than made up for her plainness in the torso region.

I slid the magazine back into the paper bag and started the van up again. Since I'd come down all the way down here, I figured I should make one more try to cruise by Dealey Plaza. I owed JFK that much. I still had nightmares about the assassination, and this would be my way of paying my last respects. I just had to go back over the bridge I came across and head for the orange brick building with the Hertz sign on top. Then, that taken care of, I'd zip back toward Highland Park and the record stores in my neighborhood.

Everything was going according to plan. Five minutes later I was waiting to take a left onto Elm Street, just like JFK's motorcade route. The Texas School Book Depository was right in front of me, and all around people were going about their business, oblivious to the hallowed grounds upon which they trod. Did anybody in Dallas care? Hell no, they were all happy he was dead. I wanted to stick my head out the window and start shouting at the top of my lungs, but then the cars ahead of me began moving. I put it in first gear and eased off the clutch, but stalled out anyway.

Cars behind me started honking. I tried again and this time gave the van so much gas that I tore off like a rocket and went speeding toward the Texas School Book Depository like I was going to plow into it. Not a bad idea, actually. I was so filled with impotent rage that I could barely drive. I was mad at the world, my mother, Ted, all these normal people walking around with stupid smiles plastered on their faces. My hands were shaking and sweat was poring down my face in buckets. A Kingston Trio song came on the radio and I snapped it off, preferring the silence as I took the big sweeping left onto Elm.

Then I heard what sounded like a gunshot. I froze for a second, thinking I was hit. My neck hurt. Had Oswald shot me? What was happening? Other cars were speeding past me, around the curve and down the hill by the Grassy Knoll where Zapruder had been standing with his Kodak movie camera.

Another shot. And another. I could see Jackie trying to crawl out of the convertible. She had to think they were all going to die. She'd watched her husband's brains get blown out, and she had two young children to raise alone as a widow. She had to live for their sake.

I made it to the Triple Underpass just as a big locomotive came thundering over me. Then I screwed up again and missed the turn-off for the entrance to the Stemmons Freeway. I had to keep going straight. Very quickly, though, Elm Street ended at Industrial Boulevard. I needed to turn around and get back on the Stemmons. I just had to find a safe place to do that first.

So I turned right on Industrial Boulevard and decided to pull into one of the desolate old stockyards that bordered this part of downtown. I put on my blinker like I'd been taught and turned right, and I must've cut it too close to the curb because I heard a loud bang and then the van started limping and lurching in a strange way. I stopped, killed the engine, and with my heart in my throat, I ran around to see what had happened.

It was awful. The right front tire was blown, and there was a big dent and long scratch along the quarter panel. The headlight on the passenger's side was busted out, the shards of glass glinting on the rocky ground like diamonds strewn carelessly.

"Goddamn it!" I screamed. I wanted to kick something. Myself, mostly. What a boob! Who wrecked a new car the first time they drove it? A boob, that's who.

But what the hell was I supposed to do now? Suddenly it seemed like I was the last person left on earth—no cars were going by. All I could see were the haunted facades of empty warehouses and the concrete banks of the Trinity River—and I could see an orange brick building off in the distance.

There had to be a spare tire. I had no idea where it was. Usually spares were in the trunk, but there was no trunk. Suddenly I wished I had a normal American car with a normal goddamn trunk, and not this alien German thing that made no sense.

I told myself to pull it together. Germans didn't build cars without spare tires. There was one, somewhere. I started crawling around the interior looking for a hatch of some kind, and my knees soon began to hurt from the rough metal floor. But in the back I found the well, and I lifted off the lid to uncover the jack and the spare. Triumph!

Miss Reynolds at Chula Vista High School had shown us all how to jack up a car so you could change a tire. She was the driver's ed teacher, a stern trout-faced young woman who wore purple-tinted eyeglasses and walked with her shoulders hunched over. I saw her once at Napoleone's Pizza House in National City, but she didn't recognize me. She was having dinner with another young woman and smiling in a way I'd never seen before. She'd only ever scowled at us. I'd heard she was a lesbian and maybe the rumors were true; but I didn't care because she'd made sure we knew how to fix a flat. I loosed the nuts first but didn't remove them. Then I found the spot where the jack was supposed to go, close to the front axle, and I started cranking and slowly, very slowly, the van began to lift up from the ground.

It was a miracle, a goddamn miracle. A Frank Capra movie.

Help Me, Rhonda

When I pulled into the driveway, Ted was waiting for me, as if he knew I'd return with the van busted up. He was smoking one of those long, thin cigars he liked, wearing plaid Dacron polyester slacks and a white polo shirt with the country club logo emblazoned on a pocket. His thinning hair was glued back off his forehead by a healthy dollop of Brill, and a second chin protruded beneath his first, as if someone had pumped his neck full of air.

I switched off the ignition and slid the brown paper bag beneath my seat, and then stepped out as nonchalant as a window shopper during the lunch hour. Ted was gawking at the damage to the front end of the van, inspecting it with a satisfied grin, the way he got when watching *The Flintstones.*

"I wrecked my first car, too," he said, looking me in the eyes. "It was a 1927 Packard. Damn nice vehicle. Collided with a delivery truck one block from my house. I wanted to crawl under a rock and never come out."

This admission caught me off-guard. Ted wasn't one to own up to mistakes. He was much more apt to correct yours than to examine his.

"What did you do?" I asked haltingly.

"Told my father and he laughed his rear end off. I was the butt of jokes for years to come. Don't worry. I'll never do that to you." He took a long drag off his thin cigar and knelt down to caress the broken headlight. "What'd you hit?"

"I don't know. I was turning right into a parking lot and I must've cut it too close and run into a fence post. I did that and blew out a tire."

"You put on the spare by yourself?" He didn't sound surprised or he was good at masking it. I'd never shown much in the way of mechanical aptitude. Tools frankly bored me, and Ted loved tools.

"Yeah. It was easy."

"You tighten the nuts?"

"As much as I could."

"Good man." He pointed to a dent by the headlight. "You grazed it. I'll bet that's exactly what happened. Where were you anyway?"

"Downtown."

"Dealey Plaza?"

"Near there."

"That's a shame. Brand-new car." He stood up and stomped out his cigar with the heel of his new boots. "You can't drive it at night with a busted headlight. You'll get a ticket."

"I know."

"We'll have to take it to a mechanic. They can pound that dent out, but you'll still have a scratch on it. A pretty big scratch."

"Can I drive it to school tomorrow?"

"I don't think that's a good idea." He could tell I was keenly disappointed, so he quickly came up with a suggestion. "I'll get the name of a place that works on Volkswagens. I'm sure there's one around here. My secretary at work drives a VW. She might know."

I almost hugged him. I'd never hugged him, ever. "I'll pay for it. I promised Mom I'd take care of everything."

Ted smiled and gave me a nod. "You damn sure will. You wreck it, you fix it."

I wasn't sure how I was going to pay for it, but I didn't care. Ted had never treated me this way before. We'd lived together for over ten years, but I hardly knew him and what I did know, I didn't like. But now he was talking to me like I was just another person. No lectures, no homilies on virtue, no sighs of exasperation. Just a pair of regular Joes talking about cars.

Ted walked around the van and looked in through the eleven windows. I followed behind him and stopped when he stopped. "This is strange-looking critter," he said. "Never seen one close up before. Bigger than I imagined. Roomy on the inside."

"It takes some getting used to, that's for sure."

"Well, what did you think about Dealey Plaza?" he asked matter-of-factly, standing at the rear by the tail pipe.

"It was spooky."

"I haven't been there. Too busy. Too much going on at work. One day I'll have to walk down and see it for myself."

"I thought somebody was shooting at me."

"Is that why you wrecked?"

"No."

He seemed satisfied by this answer and continued his tour, finishing up where he'd started, by the front bumper. "I hope it's out of your system now. It's been almost a year. You're worrying your mother to death."

"She doesn't have to worry about me. I'm fine."

"I almost turned this job down because she was so worried about you moving here. But I told her you'd snap out of it. I told her that you had a good head on your shoulders and you'd make friends and you'd like Dallas." Then he paused for a second waiting for my reply. There was none. "Dallas didn't kill Kennedy. Oswald did. He was a kook, Norman. He was off his rocker."

"What if it wasn't Oswald?"

"But it was Oswald."

"He said he was a patsy. Remember that?"

"He was a kook."

"Maybe. Maybe not."

"I think it's almost time for dinner."

Ted went back inside but I lingered there on the front stoop a little longer, gazing at my new van. I was mad at myself for wrecking it so soon, but apparently it happened sometimes, even to people like Ted who dwelled in certitude and never questioned the basic facts. Even people like Ted made mistakes. Next time I'd be more careful.

I grabbed the brown paper bag from beneath the driver's seat and ran right up to my room before Mother could get her two cents in.

California Girls

Ted found a garage in nearby University Park that handled Volkswagens. The place was near the SMU campus and apparently plenty of college professors drove them, which kept the garage real busy. I found out from the mechanic, a man named Dino who has tattoos all over his beefy arms, that VWs were easy to work on because the models didn't change much from year to year, meaning their parts were interchangeable. He told me about the story of a man who'd built a VW from a dozen different model years, and each of the pieces fit together perfectly. "Try doing that with an American car," he said, chopping at the air for emphasis. "An old Model T you could— and we used to change parts on Chevys—but that's about it."

The bill came to $136, which Ted paid. Now I owed him, and I promised to do odd jobs around the house until my debt was settled up. But at least now I could drive myself to school, which I'd been dying to do ever since we'd dropped the van off to get repaired.

Tomorrow was the big day, when I could pull into the student parking lot where all the varsity cheerleaders and jocks gathered before school to smoke cigarettes in secret and flirt in that blustery, boastful Texas way. No longer would I have to ride my bike like the pimply faced underclassmen, who by definition equaled zilch.

Nobody else had a car like mine.

That night I could barely sleep, I was so excited. And nervous. Because that Volkswagen was going to get a lot of attention. Everybody at my high school who didn't fit in got a lot of attention, much of it unwanted. I'd seen football players beat up a kid who spoke with a lisp, and they were rough on the few cool kids who wore their hair long like the Beatles. Like me. They didn't know me, yet, but my Pendleton shirts and my floppy blonde hair had gotten plenty of long, simmering looks in the halls. The one thing going in my favor was that I was pretty big. I stood over six feet and weighed one-eighty. I could do a hundred push-ups and a hundred sit-ups, and I knew I could hold my own in a fight. I didn't like fighting, though. I hated it. Sometimes I thought I could be James Bond, but he had a nasty right hook and I just couldn't bring myself to hit anyone. There were a few tough gangs around San Diego County, especially down around National City, which was a pretty gritty town where sailors on liberty liked to look for hookers or get tattoos at Iwo Jima Eddie's. Once I was in front of Escalani's Liquor Store with my friend Tom Waits and some Mexican kids drove past and yelled at us, and they circled back around and yelled some more, but we just put our heads down and kept walking. Tom was a music fiend. He was going to start his own band one day, and I was going to learn to play the drums.

In the morning I felt groggy. The alarm clock clanged like someone was beating my head with a hammer. But quickly I hopped out of bed because today was the big day. I already had an outfit draped over a chair, and my wallet and keys were carefully positioned on my desk, by a capped bottle of Lowenbrau beer Ted had brought home from a business trip to Europe five years ago. There was also a picture of my father and me surfing at Mission Beach, both of us wearing big toothy grins. "Thanks, pop," I said under my breath.

I took a quick shower and got dressed, but it was only seven-thirty. School didn't start for another hour and the drive was under five minutes. I walked downstairs to have breakfast. Rosa was making pancakes but I wasn't hungry. Ted was at the breakfast nook reading the *Morning-News* and scowling at the front page.

"There he is," he said, snapping the paper angrily and putting it down on the table. He'd just finished eating a soft-boiled egg, which he had every morning except Sunday, when he had waffles. "You ready?"

"I'm ready. Is Mom up yet?"

"She should be down soon."

"I kind of feel like getting a head start."

"I know she wanted to say good-bye and get a picture."

"She'd better hurry up."

"You're not late. Have a bite to eat. Read the comics."

I didn't want to eat or read the comics or wait around for a photograph. I wanted to go, to be on my way. My heart ran wild and filled my head with extreme ideas. Maybe I'd drive down to Mexico today. Tom Waits would go on long trips in Mexico with his father and they sounded like a blast, a real gas. He said he was going to drop out of school, because it was a waste of time. He'd do it, too.

I walked over to the stairs and listened for any signs of life from upstairs, but heard only a muffled silence, all noise being absorbed by the plush carpeting.

"Mom, I'm leaving!" I called out, not masking my annoyance. I was like a volcano ready to erupt.

"Wait, Norman! I want to get a picture!"

"Okay, okay. But hurry it up, if you don't mind."

"Are you planning on robbing a bank or something? What's the rush?"

I couldn't answer the question, which only pissed me off even more. Why couldn't they just let me go? Were they insane? I couldn't take it. I grabbed my school satchel, which was empty except for a few stray sheets of ruled paper, and headed out the door. Waiting was a form of torture. For weeks I'd been waiting to get my van back and do precisely what I was about to do.

"Norman, hold your horses! I said I wanted a picture." Mother was standing on the front stoop in her pink dressing robe, curlers still rolled in her hair. She meant business. She'd never show herself in public in that state unless she was dead serious, so I gave in.

"How's this?" I asked, posing by the front of the van, standing next to the chrome VW nose emblem above the bumper.

She held up the Kodak Instamatic that Ted had gotten her for Mother's Day. Each photograph developed right there on the spot, so no need to drop film off at the drug store. "Get inside," she ordered me. "Get behind the wheel. That'll be fun."

I complied, because taking pictures made her happy. She was the first person in her bridge club to own this new-fangled camera, and she enjoyed using it. So I posed while she took a shot, the flash exploding, but I didn't want to wait around for the film to develop—one minute.

"I'm leaving," I said, starting the engine.

"Drive carefully, okay?"

"I will."

And I did, because I was positive I'd never make it to school. Somehow, though, I managed to arrive at the high school without getting shot or running into anything. I was way early. No other cars were yet in the student parking lot, but I didn't care. I let the radio play and leaned back and closed my eyes, listening to Bobby Darin. In San Diego I probably would've swung by to pick up Tom Waits and Bruce Bones, and we would've hung around in the parking lot laughing and joking, hoping some girls would come over to talk to us.

But now I was alone. I didn't have anybody to share this moment with, one of life's great milestones. I just sat there in the front seat for what seemed like hours, years, decades, wondering if I'd ever make friends at this school. Most of them had been together their whole lives, insulated in the cocoon of Highland Park, and they didn't need any new friends. Maybe if I'd played football, it would've been easier. The sport was like a religion here; it was all anyone ever talked about. Today there'd be a pep rally and the whole school would turn out to yell and scream as the varsity cheerleaders leapt around, their skirts flying up just long enough so you could see their fleshy thighs. Then the players would come out, wearing their game jerseys that billowed on them without the shoulder pads, and they'd stand like the heroes they were, basking in the adulation.

I was big enough to play football. I just didn't like it. Basketball was okay, but you had to run a lot and it made me tired. But I needed a hobby, an outlet, since I couldn't surf. Table tennis? Maybe I'd ask Ted about putting a table in the fallout shelter so we wouldn't get bored waiting for the radiation to die down. A kid could only read so many comic books.

Finally, another car. A Chevy Corsair. I didn't recognize the driver. He looked older, a senior since he parked in one of the rows reserved for the graduating class. He got out and sat on the hood of the car, smoking a cigarette. He never even glanced in my direction. I wondered if I shouldn't get out, too, and stake a claim by my vehicle. Maybe playing the radio wasn't enough. I wasn't a smoker, though. Dad made me promise I'd never start, no matter what, and I'd kept my word.

I sat tight and felt pretty goddamn foolish. What was I trying to prove? Nobody cared about me here. It was possible that no one knew my name. This was pointless. I almost started the engine to drive off— to skip school, the ultimate dream—but something inside me could never do that. I was too afraid of getting picked up by the cops for truancy.

But then the parking lot became a flurry of activity: cars started streaming in, all makes and models, including a few old pickup trucks that were the envy of most everyone because those were driven by the most popular guys in school, such as Curt Henson, the starting quarterback, and George Filya, the starting running back. They were the center of the universe, and the rest of us orbited around them. I was Pluto, the farthest planet from the sun.

And the game was on, the before-school competition of who could attract the biggest crowd and the most attention. Curt Henson and

George Fliya parked right next to each other, and within seconds, like pigeons going for breadcrumbs, girls had flocked to them, two deep, smiles galore, makeup fresh and skirts neatly pressed.

A car pulled up next to mine. A sleek Ford. A girl got out and whistled as she inspected the van. She wasn't like the other girls. She didn't wear makeup and her brown hair kept spilling into her face and so she had to brush it away from her eyes. "Nice wheels, cowboy," she drawled in obvious parody of the Texan accent. "You sure could rustle some cattle in that wagon."

A girl, talking to me? I gulped and tried to think of something funny to say. But I couldn't. I was blanking. So I sort of grinned and nodded my head.

But luckily she gave me a side-wise glance and a friendly smile.

"You're from California, aren't you?"

"Me?"

"No, the guy next to you. Yes, you."

"I used to live in San Diego."

She seemed excited about that. She bounced on her heels a little, and her eyes got wide. "Do you know how to surf?"

"I can surf."

"I knew it!"

Now I was terrified. Had this girl noticed me before? I tried to place her face but couldn't. She was pretty but not gorgeous, not very tall, but slender, decent boobs—she would've been cast as Annette Funicello's friend, the one who kept secrets and stayed in the background as Annette and Frankie Avalon cavorted by the bonfire on the beach.

"What's your name?" she asked, getting out of her car.

"Norman Alehouse."

"Hi, Norman Alehouse. I'm Louise Hoffman." She pronounced my last name "ale-house," but we said it "all-haws" and I corrected her. She kind of rolled her eyes at me.

"I like ale-house better. It reminds me of London. Not that I've been, but I'm going to go one day. I'm saving my baby-sitting money and once I get enough for a ticket, I'm hopping on a plane. Forever."

"Really?"

"Really." Some of her friends came over and she talked to them for a few seconds. I didn't know what to make of Louise Hoffman. She spoke in torrential bursts, with words falling like hale, with a similar effect—you kind of felt like covering your head. She was wearing a polka dot dress and pink hose stuffed into cowboy boots, a striking ensemble in stark contrast to the staid country-club plaids and pleats. She didn't fit in here, that was obvious.

Louise and her friends looked me over and then they all started walking toward the building. "Well, bye, Norman," Louise called out just when I thought she wouldn't. She seemed one who liked surprises.

"Bye," I whispered, watching her go.

Be True to Your School

I was hoping I'd see Louise Hoffman again that day. Maybe she was in one of my classes and I'd just never noticed her. So each time I switched classrooms, I carefully checked out each girl, but Louise Hoffman wasn't in any of my classes. Nor did I run into her in the halls, because my high school had hundreds of students, and despite my best efforts, Louise Hoffman was nowhere to be found. I ate lunch alone again, but I kept my eyes out for her. One time I thought I saw her way across the cafeteria, and for a few seconds I sat immobile, paralyzed by a choking fear. I wasn't sure why I'd felt this way, but I vaguely understood that she liked me, and that her liking me meant something. What, I didn't know. I'd only kissed one girl, Bonita Ramirez, at a pool party last year. We'd dive underwater together and fondle each other in the privacy of the aquatic depths, coming back up for air, breathless and grinning and unsure why we were doing it. But she never told me to stop, so I didn't. Then the party ended, and I never saw her again.

In geometry class the teacher, Mr. Gangel, had us get out protractors and draw perfect circles, one after the other, and as I did, I couldn't help thinking of Louise Hoffman. Was she pretty? I couldn't remember. She might've been plain, with a healthy dousing of freckles across her face and stooped shoulders and stubby legs—but decent boobs. And she wanted to go to London, which meant she had to love the Beatles, which meant she wasn't like most of the girls around here, who seemed oblivious to the world outside Dallas.

Mr. Gangel stood over me and looked down at my work. "Keep a steady hand, Norman," he advised me sternly. "You're wiggling too much."

There were some twitters and I could feel my face growing red. I hated being the center of attention, which was why I always sat in back. I couldn't wait for the bell to ring so I could get out of here—and back in my van. I was thinking about getting a part-time job so I could save up to buy a new stereo. A hi-fi. Nothing was stopping me. It was as if I'd been given a new lease on life and I had to take advantage of it, no matter how much I hated Dallas.

And as Mr. Gangel circulated around the room, I even entertained the notion of heading over to Biff Burger, the after-school hangout popular among kids in Highland Park. I'd never been there but I'd heard plenty of chatter about it. There were lots of similar places in San Diego, pizza joints and beachfront greasy spoons, but the big difference was that I'd go there with friends like Tom Waits, and now I'd have to show up alone.

Unless Louise Hoffman wanted to go.

Did I even have the guts to ask her?

The bell rang and noise erupted spontaneously, the joy of a thousand juveniles released from prison at the same time. I hopped up from my desk and hurried to my locker, where I deposited my books and then headed out, no homework once again. I figured I might see Louise in the student parking lot, since she was parked next to me. I waded through the sea of strangers, faces unknown to me but with a few random acts of recognition—there was a kid from English class, and a girl from World History—and they even nodded at me and I nodded back. I started to think that in time I could make a few friends here, that the situation wasn't as hopeless as I'd imagined it.

I burst outside and stepped into the bright sunshine. I bounced down the set of concrete stairs like a beach ball, joining in the other upperclassmen who'd driven to school and were now migrating in a horde toward salvation.

The student parking lot sat behind the cafeteria, which entailed walking down a long sidewalk toward the rear of the campus. Off in the distance I could see the football team starting to assemble on the practice field, and mustard-yellow school buses sat in a long line as students embarked on their journey home. As I got closer to the parking lot, I found my van, at least the white top of it anyway, which was hard to miss.

There was a crowd of people standing around it, and right away I got worried. Why would there be a gathering around my van? My walk gave way to a trot and then a jog, and each step only added to my concern. I could see about twenty kids huddled around the van, gawking at it for reasons I couldn't fathom. Had they never seen a VW van before? Impossible. What was it?

It didn't take long to figure out the source of the attraction. When I got within ten feet, sweat dripping down my face, panting like a dog, I saw that someone had spray-painted a penis onto the side panel behind the driver's side door. Next to the cartoon phallus was the word "Faget," which I inferred was supposed to be "faggot."

Since no one in the crowd of on-lookers knew who I was, I mingled among them in savage silence, staring at the graffiti on my gleaming factory paint job.

"I heard it was a couple of football players," one said with some trepidation. He was gangly youth with a crewcut and big earlobes.

"Which ones?" I erupted, earning a look of horror. Everyone instantly understood whose van it was, and they began creeping away in furtive strides, leaving me alone with the handiwork of the vandals. My eyes burned from the unrelenting sun and the rivulets of sweat and the searing reality of the defacement, the black paint violently applied. The cock was anatomically correct, with testicles the size of baseballs perfectly rounded beneath an arching shaft. The letters were crudely rendered, sloppily executed, and barely legible.

I tried rubbing the paint off with my shirt, but the paint was dry. I stepped back and gritted my teeth, ready to punch someone, anyone. Kids were streaming by and I could hear snippets of conversation, and I was ready to fight them all.

"That's horrible," I heard someone say. A girl's voice. I spun around and saw Louise Hoffman, standing by her car. "I can't believe they did that, the dumb jerks. You must be going ape."

"Yeah," I sputtered, fighting back tears.

She came over and joined me, and together we stood and regarded my van. It felt like we were the last two people on earth. "It had to be football players," she quipped, "because of the spelling. Some of them are illiterate, I swear."

"I don't even know anybody at this school," I pleaded. "I just moved here. I don't have a beef with anyone."

"You're the surfer boy."

"I am?"

"And to some morons, that means you must pay."

I knew she was right, that the newcomers often got it for no good reason. And it was strange, within a few minutes, lots of people had gathered around and were giving me pep talks and apologizing, and then the assistant principal came out, and he was abhorred by the sight of my van and what had happened to it. He insisted on calling the police even though I begged him not to, but a crime was a crime and it had to be reported if only to prove a point. So I had to stick around school for another hour or so, talking to the cops and to the guidance counselor, who really wasn't a bad guy. They were sure they'd find out who did it—the usual suspects would be rounded up and one of them would confess in time.

Once we were done and I was free to go, I left feeling better about Dallas. Not everyone here was a John Birch fanatic who wanted JFK to die. Not everyone here was a dumb cowboy. And as if to prove this point, Louise Hoffman waited in the parking lot for me to finish. She was sitting in her car reading *The Portable Faulkner.* When she saw me, she put the book down and smiled.

"You should drive over to Biff Burger right now!" she cried. "You'll be the biggest hero in the world. I'll go with you."

"Really?"

"Really."

That's exactly what we did.

Grand Prairie, Texas
1965
1004

For years kids around here have been meeting up at a place called Yello Belly to drink beer and race cars, and so Sarge sent me over there one Friday night just to keep things under control. The weekend before there'd been a knife fight between rival groups and some boys from Dallas had been cut up pretty bad.

By the time I got there, though, things were just breakin up. I cruised along real slow so they all could see me, and that seemed to do the trick. Cars started streamin away, leavin behind only empty beer cans. I'd gone to races like this back in high school, and I seen a boy from Grapevine flip his 1955 Thunderbird and walk away without a scratch. Still couldn't believe my eyes. And sure, we'd scrap some, but not like they did nowadays at Yello Belly, which lately had gotten rough. Sometimes a gang of coloreds or Mexicans would show up and then all hell would break loose, like it did last weekend.

But not tonight. Things was quiet, so I kept on drivin, headin back to Main Street toward Arlington. I decided I might check on Mountain Creek Lake since that place could get a little rowdy on a Friday night, too. The football games was over now, and all the high school kids in Dallas and Ft. Worth would be out lookin for mischief—or lookin for a fight, dependin on the score of the game.

On the way I figured I ought to swing by the industrial park to make sure nothin was happenin there. We'd gotten some reports of vandalism in the area, mostly punks breakin windows and that kind of thing, and Sarge had reminded us to do a sweep while on patrol.

I pulled in and was a little surprised to see a car parked in an empty lot. Not a car, but a Volkswagen bus of some sort. What got me was the California plates, which made me suspicious. Just a hunch. Just somethin to check on. Probably nothin, but that VW stood out.

I parked and got out my flashlight and my gun and approached the vehicle. I could see the outlines of two people inside the Volkswagen. They was movin around from back to front. Then the driver's door opened and a young man staggered out. He had on a pair of pants, unzipped, and no shirt. He looked about sixteen years old, if that.

"Please, officer, everything's fine," he said, hands up over his head like I was gonna arrest him.

"Who's in the car with you?" I asked.

"My girlfriend."

So they were making out. I could see now that the girlfriend was still tryin to get dressed. I had to ask for ID anyway just to make sure his story checked out. The kid didn't argue at all. He reached for his wallet and then started pattin down his pockets, lookin like he was about to croak.

"Crap!" he groaned. "I can't find my wallet."

"Maybe it fell out in the car."

"Can I look for it?"

"Go ahead."

I tried not to laugh. The boy's face was red as beet now, and I was worried he'd start ballin like a baby.

"Louise," he called out, "do you see my wallet anywhere?"

He went back inside the van. I walked over so that they could use my flashlight. The girlfriend had most of her clothes on now, but she kept her eyes averted from mine. "I know I had it when I left the house," he explained as he looked under the front seats. "I paid for the pizza. And then I took it out so I could get the—"

He stopped. My flashlight was shining right at the condom wrapper on the floor in the back.

"It's in here somewhere," he said forcefully, on his hands and knees like a bloodhound picking up a scent. I told him not to worry about it and just let the two of them alone.

South Padre Island, Texas
1966
10,654

We all piled into Norman Alehouse's VW van because he wanted to go see this band that was playing across the bridge in Corpus Christi at a club no one had heard of. Us girls sat in front, so I squeezed in next to Louise in the passenger's seat, trying not to rub up against anything to protect my precious sunburn. But other than my reddish skin, you couldn't pry the smile off my face with a crowbar. I'd been looking forward to this week for a long time, ever since my older sister had told me of the crazy antics down here. The tradition at our high school was for the seniors to all rent rooms at a cheap hotel on the beach and then drink as much beer as possible and get a tan in time for graduation.

"I'm telling you, this band is great!" Norman shouted above the din. Everyone was already plastered, especially the boys in the back of the van, who'd spent the afternoon playing drinking games like Quarters, where you filled cups with beer and then tried to shoot coins into them. The loser had to chug.

"What's their name again?" Jimbo asked in a suspicious drawl.

"Zakary Thaks. They supposedly sound a lot like the Beatles."

"I hate the damn Beatles," Jimbo growled. "We should go to see a good ole Texas band, not some English fairies." He was a big football player who when drunk liked to pick people up and throw them around like rag-dolls. He'd already broken a lamp and a table using various people as projectiles, and the manager of the Sandy Central Motel had nearly kicked us out. But Norman had slipped him some extra cash to smooth over the hard feelings. That was Norman in a nutshell, the eternal peacemaker, the one with the good head on his shoulders.

"Jimbo, there'll be so many girls there that you'd think you'd joined a sorority."

"There'd better be. Because it's our last night on the beach, and I'd assume not waste it."

"You'll love these guys. Would I ever steer you wrong?"

Jim chewed on this question like a plug of tobacco, and in the silence I couldn't help myself. "And there'd better be some cute boys there, too!" I crowed, just to annoy Jimbo. We'd gone steady until last year when we broke up because he got so jealous of me all the time. And yet he was the one who ended up kissing Shirley Vreeland. What a two-timer he was.

"You liked those sailors last night, huh?" Louise asked me, only too glad to get Jimbo's goat.

"Did I ever!"

Cody's Volcano had been filled with recruits from the nearby naval air station, and we'd had fun dancing with them. One told me that he was shipping out to Vietnam in the morning but he was just trying to get something off me, and it didn't work.

"They were a bunch of homos!" Jimbo erupted from the back. "One tried to dance with me, swear to God!"

"Did you?" I shot back.

"Hell no!"

Louise and I both started laughing our heads off as we passed right by the entrance to the navy base and then rocked across the Oso Bridge. We could see the lights of Corpus Christi up ahead, glowing faintly against the sweep of the dunes. Norman seemed to know exactly where to go. He was always eager to try new things and go to different places. He wasn't like the other boys at our high school. He and Louise had gone steady for two years, and I was sure they'd get married and have three perfect children and buy a new car every two years.

*

We pulled into the parking lot and didn't see many other cars there. The sign, though, told us that we were in the right place, the Maison Rouge. And the exterior of the club was painted red, with faintly French trimmings. It didn't look like the kind of joint where they'd play rock and roll.

"What the hell is this?" Jimbo roared, thundering out of the van and scratching his big stomach, which was filled with a case of beer. The sun had turned his skin the same painful shade of red as mine, which was almost the same color as the building, and painful just to look at.

"Come on," Norman countered, unphased by Jimbo's bluster. "Let's check it out."

He led the way inside, and we followed behind. I stayed close to Louise, letting the boys go first. Norman, Jimbo, Bill Thomas, and Fred Galson, who basically formed a big wall as they walked in. The Maison Rouge was what might be called intimate. There was a small stage to one side, a bar in the middle, and tables at the far end. Potted plants flanked the bar, and strands of white lights were strung across the ceiling overhead. Open windows let a cool breeze in, and the usual Corpus Christi smells of spilled beer and stale urine were absent. The cozy darkness made it seem like the kind of place couples came to in order to get engaged or to break up.

The bartender gave us a curious look since we were the only customers. "Is Zakary Thaks playing here tonight?" Norman asked. The bartender nodded his head yes and kept on wiping down the snifters.

"Let's get a beer!" Jimbo said, and he ambled up to a stool and sat down, elbows propped up on the bar. The other guys followed suit, while I remained in the shadows with Louise.

"What is this place?" I asked her.

"I hope Norman knows what he's doing. Jimbo's right—it's our last night of beach week. Sometimes Norman gets these crazy notions and you can't talk him out of them, no matter what."

"I see some amps and a drum set on the stage."

"That's a good sign, I guess."

Then two guys came in and sat down at a table. They didn't pay us much attention, and kept to themselves in the back. Then three more came in and sat at the bar. Then two women, older and nicely dressed. With the place starting to fill up, we heaved a sigh of relief. Norman hadn't led us astray. The band came out and picked up their instruments and we headed straight for the dance floor, ready to shake, rattle, and roll. The lead singer looked a little like Paul McCartney, and I kept smiling at him hoping he'd notice me. I had a thing for guys who played in bands.

And Norman was right: these guys had a great sound, very British, with enough East Texas twang to make it interesting. We danced with each other, and only slowly did we realize that the men were dancing with the other men and the women with the other women. Louise noticed it first, and whispered in my ear to look around. We both started giggling, because now I understood why the Maison Rouge smelled the way it did. I'd heard about clubs like this, but never in a million years did I think I'd ever go to one. This was where homosexuals came to get together. Even Jimbo, drunk and sweating and waving his arms around, finally got the drift.

"What the hell's going on in here?" he said between songs. "This place might be for queers." He kept scanning the bar, eyes roving from one man to another, each smoking and talking and some even touching each other. "Oh hell no! We better get the crap out of here."

"Why, Jimbo?" I asked. "Are you a chicken or something?"

"The hell I am!"

"You should ask someone to dance, Jimbo. That guy over there is real cute. Just your type."

Jimbo got all flustered and I thought for a second he was going to pick me up and throw me through a wall. Instead, we all left and about busted a gut laughing, but when we got outside to the van, we realized that Norman wasn't with us. "I ain't going back in there," Jimbo vowed, voice trembling, like a dentist had vowed to do a root canal on him without anesthetic. "Somebody else go get him. Either that or I'm calling the damn Vice Squad."

Louise went back, and I volunteered to go with her. As expected, Norman was still right in front of the stage, dancing by himself. Louise went up and tugged on his sleeve, and then whispered in his ear. I couldn't hear what he said back to her, but he didn't leave. He just kept dancing, and then Louise joined him. And since the song was pretty decent with a good beat, I hopped over to them, and the three of us kept going. The lead singer smiled at me, and I felt my knees go weak.

*

We didn't get back to the motel until midnight. Jimbo made Norman stop and buy another case of beer, and now the boys were in their room drinking it. Louise and I went out and sat in the back of Norman's van. We were ready for a little break from their immature antics.

"Are you excited about heading to Austin in the fall?" I asked Louise, who like me was going to UT. Which was a surprise, because she'd always vowed to venture east for college. Vassar or Smith or Mount Holyoke. Norman said he was going to Harvard or Yale. Instead, they were both coming to Austin. No one was really sure why, not even I understood, and she was my best friend.

"I guess so," she said, dragging hard on a Virginia Slim. Her face was crimson from the sun, almost like she'd fried her skin on a skillet.

"You guess so? That's it?"

"I'm excited. At least I think I am. I don't know what I am, to be honest."

"I've never heard you like this before, Louise. You're always so happy."

The van was parked so that you could see the Gulf of Mexico, stretching off into a black infinity. We were supposed to leave in the morning. Graduation was Sunday, and my aunt and uncle were driving from Tulsa for it. Then Mom and Dad were going to throw a big party, catered by Dad's favorite BBQ joint in Fort Worth, Sonny's.

"Life'll never be like this again," Louise said, flicking her cigarette into the sand. "It'll never feel this sweet and easy. Never. And that scares me a little bit. What if I'm making a mistake? Maybe I should've gone to Vassar."

"You didn't get in."

"I was wait-listed. But that's not the point."

"I think we'll have a blast in Austin. And it's a good school, too. As good as Vassar. Who wants to hang out with a bunch of Yankees anyway?"

Then Louise reached over and hugged me. Tears came to my eyes and soon we were both crying but it wasn't from sadness. Or maybe it was, the most profound sort of sadness there is, the overwhelming melancholy of knowing the end is near. We weren't children anymore. The adult world waited for us, and with it all of the pressures—finding the right man to marry, the right sorority to join, the right this and the right that—while in the back of Norman's van we clung to our childhood like it was a life preserver, the only thing that kept us from getting swept away.

"We should be happy," I told her, brushing away tears. "We're graduating and getting on with our lives. It's exciting. Just wait till fall. We'll have so much fun in Austin."

"I'm drunk," she giggled. "That must be it."

"Me too!"

We went back inside where the party was still alive and kicking, but I never forgot what Louise had said about life never being that sweet again. Because she was right, in more ways than she could possibly know.

Dallas, Texas
1966
12317

I stand and watch the van pull away. Norman is going off to college, all his worldly possession stuffed into it. Except for one very important item. Something Norman said he'd never use and didn't want to have anywhere near him.

A gun.

Ted had bought him one last week. Nothing too fancy, a pistol that he could use for his own protection. Just in case. *In case of what?*

In case, Norman, a deranged man happens to start shooting innocent people for no reason whatsoever.

That was an anomaly, Mom.

Fourteen dead, scores more wounded. It still makes me go weak in the knees, just thinking about it. A sniper in the bell tower in the middle of the UT campus, shooting. Charles Whitman. After he'd strangled his mother and stabbed his wife in the heart. Just three weeks ago! I almost insisted that Norman choose another college, somewhere safer and closer to home. What was wrong with SMU? It's right down the street, for crying out loud. You could live here, Norman.

So Ted got him a gun instead. And Norman didn't take it with him. All his records and his books, they made it into the van, apparently. But what can you expect. Norman takes after his father, which is strange considering how little contact the two have had over the years. Two dreamers unable or unwilling to accept reality, heads eternally in the clouds.

I wave until the van disappears from my sight. It's Saturday morning, and I'm alone. Ted has already gone to the club because he had an early tee time, and Rosa isn't coming in because one of her myriad cousins is getting married today. A prolific brood, *la familia Santana.* A fertile tribe.

I walk inside the house. Shafts of morning light come slanting in through the Venetian blinds, creating bars across the white tile in the foyer. There are breakfast dishes left to wash. I'd made Norman his favorite, pancakes with maple syrup. But he was too nervous to eat very much. He was so excited to be on his way, in such a hurry that he barely hugged me good-bye.

I find myself walking up the stairs, with no idea where I'm going. Into his room. The bed unmade. Old clothes sticking out of the dresser.

Book shelves empty now, with a fine layer of dust revealing where the cheap paperbacks had once been. I'll tell Rosa to use some Pledge on them.

The posters removed from the wall. Good riddance. I tried never to come in here. I didn't want to see the inner workings of the teenaged mind. A boy needs his privacy, far from the prying eyes of his mother.

His desk. Where he worked so hard. Straight A student. But doesn't know how to change a light bulb. The bottle of beer Ted brought back from Germany. A plaque from the National Forensics League. Debater of the Year, 1966. One of his friends called him a "master debater" right in front of me. Like I didn't have ears. Or a sense of humor.

I sit on the bed. I told Ted last night that I wanted to try Jamaica. Some place different. He rolled his eyes and grunted something about being busy at work. I think he might be sleeping with his secretary. He's been staying later and later, without explaining why. Because he's busy.

There's a mirror by the closet. I gaze into it. Who's that old woman sitting on the bed? All those wrinkles from the California sun. I heard that in Switzerland there are special clinics where women go to have wrinkles removed. It costs a fortune, however. Ted would never indulge me.

I stand up. Too early for a drink? I won't watch the news tonight. My nerves can't take it. Since when did people just start shooting each other in this country? What's this world coming to anyway?

Austin, Texas
1968
20004

It was the night of the Spring Formal, and Norman Alehouse was supposed to drive. Every year Delta Delta Delta sorority rented out the ballroom at the University Club, which was very exclusive and honestly one of the highpoints of Greek life at the University of Texas. Those Tri Delt girls knew how to put on a swanky affair, despite the fact that most of them kept their legs crossed and wore diamond-studded chastity belts. The year before, the Tri Delts had actually black-balled a girl because the sisterhood had heard a rumor that she'd slept with one of our brothers, Dan Drew, aka Dan the Man, which was true, but the fact was, old Dan had bedded down three or four other Tri Delts who were all too willing to be total hypocrites about the situation. Norman and I understood all too well the largely insane politics of that sorority, since we were both dating girls who belonged.

It was a Thursday night, and I'd rented a tuxedo at a place near the Capitol for the princely sum of ten dollars, which to a poor college boy from Plano was a month's worth of groceries. But no way was I missing the Tri Delt Spring Formal, the most sought-after invitation around. Not that I had much affection for my date, Miss Trudy Hixson from Houston whose daddy owned five oil refineries and a yacht the size of Delaware. Trudy was saving herself for marriage, despite my best efforts to convince her that virginity was as old fashioned as a pocket watch.

So I didn't have the highest of hopes, but I was more than looking forward to rubbing elbows with the smart set, the sons and daughters of the football boosters and Austin politicos who ran things on campus, and since I was thinking of law school one day, I figured a few contacts wouldn't hurt, since my own daddy owned a hardware store and hated football.

Then around six o'clock Norman called and said he had some bad news to tell me. "I'm not going to the formal tonight," he croaked, sounding like a dang bullfrog.

"What's shaking, Daddy-O?"

"It's Louise. She quit the sorority."

"Quit? Why?"

He heaved a great lamentable sigh. Norman was a get-along sort of guy, not one to cause a ruckus. He studied hard and when he got

59

drunk, was fond of doing the stupid dance moves he used to watch on *American Bandstand* as a kid. He and Louise had gone to high school together, and everybody was waiting for the engagement announcement.

"Because," he said, "she thinks the sorority should cancel the formal."

"What on earth? Why should they cancel?"

"Because of the King assassination."

"That was three days ago."

"She thinks it's disrespectful. So she's inactive and not going and so I can't drive you. I mean, I will if no one can give you two a ride. I'll be your chauffeur."

"Hell, Norman, I'm sure Trudy knows someone with a car."

"I hate standing you up, and I won't leave you in the lurch."

"That's good of you, buddy. So Louise is taking this King thing pretty hard, huh?"

"Yeah, she is. We both are. It's very upsetting. But not at all surprising, when you get right down to it. I tried telling her that, but she just won't hear it."

I found another ride after all, and never did get to go in that rust-bucket VW van to the Tri Delt formal. I regretted that very much. I'd been hoping that the old VW van might've loosened Trudy up a little, give her a taste of the wild side of life. Instead we went with Rick Davis and his date in a Plymouth that smelled like a chemistry lab. The dumb sumbitch had sprayed Lysol all inside it and Trudy started having an allergic reaction and breaking out in hives, and we ended up in the dang emergency room, me in my rented gorilla suit in the lobby with an expectant father who let me drink a pint of Jim Beam with him.

So it wasn't a total waste. And I ran into Trudy Hixson five years later at a UT football game and we ended back at her hotel room, and she wasn't a virgin anymore, I promise you that. Hook 'em Horns!

Ennis, Texas
1968
21119

I got as far as a truck stop outside of Ennis and it was getting dark. No one ever gives you a ride at night, so I was thinking I needed to find me a place to bed down where the fuzz won't bother me none. Didn't have a dime to my name, only a knapsack with some sandwiches and a sleeping bag. It was still 150 miles to go to Huntsville, and I probably wasn't getting there until tomorrow.

Then I seen this VW pull in to get some gas. I watched the kid fill up the tank. He was wearing a Texas Longhorns t-shirt, but he had long hair he kept in a ponytail. A hippie. They was always good for picking you up. Maybe he wasn't headed south, though, but north on I-45 back to Dallas. I was fixin to ask him but then I saw a cop roll up and park by the diner. Ellis County Sheriff's Office.

I kept my head down and walked out toward the on-ramp of the interstate, which led me out to where some cows was grazing. Maybe I'd spend the night in a barn, because I didn't need no trouble, but trouble always had a way of finding me. I guess I wasn't very good at hiding from it. I started to think that visiting little brother wasn't such a great idea after all. But I hadn't seen him in a year and he was just twenty and still looking at another sixteen months behind bars. He needed to know we still cared. I did at least.

I looked back one more time. I could still see the VW van. The kid was just about done. He put the gas cap back on and then went inside to pay. The sheriff's deputy was leaning against the counter talking to the waitress. His fat ass wasn't goin nowhere soon. "Come on," I said to myself. "I need a miracle."

The kid paid for his gas and got in the van. He started it up and I could tell by the sound of the engine that the head bolts was real loose and the cylinders was loosing compression. The thud-thud-thud gave it away.

I stuck my thumb out and waited. The VW sputtered toward me, and then the kid must've seen me because he swung over onto the shoulder. Across the road the cows looked up in disbelief. Even they couldn't believe my good luck.

"Need a ride?" the kid asked me.

"Sure," I said. "I'm heading south. To Huntsville."

"Hop in."

"You going south?"

"Sure, why the hell not?"

A strange answer, but he was a hippie and that's how they talked. I slid into the front seat and he barely got that thing up the ramp to the interstate. I told him about the head bolts and he kind of shrugged.

"It never breaks down," he said. "I've had it four years and never had a problem."

"You will," I told him.

"Just my luck."

"How far you going?" I asked once we got a mile or so down the highway.

"Far? I don't know. How far is Huntsville?"

"Three hours."

"Maybe that's where I'm going. I can't say. I just can't say. Because I don't know where I'm going, man. I'm just driving, dig?"

With the windows rolled down I couldn't hear him too clear. I didn't feel like talking much anyway, and so I closed my eyes and tried to act peace-loving. No reason to spook him. If I just sat there peaceful, maybe he'd drive me the whole way. Because now we was in the middle of nowhere. If he let me out here, I'd be stuck.

"What's in Huntsville?" the kid asked nervously, like he was having second thoughts. Maybe he'd never picked up a hitchhiker before. That's how he was acting.

"My brother."

"Yeah?"

"He lives there."

"I can dig that. I've never been to Huntsville. Drove through it on the way to Galveston, that's about it."

"Yeah. Ain't much to see there." I didn't want to tell him my brother was in the big house, because he'd sure as hell toss me out then. But he was a hippie, so maybe he'd dig why my brother was there, serving three motherfucking years, all because he got caught with a joint of grass. One joint, and the Amarillo pigs busted him. The judge lowered the boom on his behind, and there he was, doing hard time for gettin high.

Ten minutes of quiet went by. I thought about eating a sandwich but I wanted to save as much food as possible. I could get hungrier.

"Have you ever had a woman break your heart?" the kid asked me out of the blue. He seemed serious, like he really wanted to know the answer. It caught me off-guard. No one I knew ever asked questions like that. I had to think about it a minute. Back in seventh grade there'd been a honey who wouldn't give me the time of day. No matter what I did, it wasn't enough and it drove me damn crazy. So the answer was yes. What the hell, I was man enough to admit it.

"Once. A long time ago."

"A woman just broke my heart. My high school sweetheart. I thought we were going to get married. I guess that makes me a sucker, doesn't it?"

"No it don't."

"It does, too. You don't have to sugar-coat it. I'm the biggest sucker in the history of the world."

"Hell no! You can't think that way. Never let no woman break you down. Never, ever, ever. You'll find another one, trust me."

"Not like her."

"Bullshit. How old are you?"

"Twenty."

"Man, you got plenty of time to get all kinds of poontang. You go to college, don't you?"

"Yeah, in Austin."

"Tell me there ain't a load of poontang at that big ole university. You know there is. Shit. You're lucky she broke it off, man. Now you're free as a bird! You can cut a fool all you want and get some trim."

He chewed on what I told him, like he really was listening hard. He was biting his lower lip and shaking his head, and I didn't know what else to say. So I just sat there, watching the miles tumble by.

"I know I'm being ridiculous," he finally said, "but it just happened an hour ago. I got in the van and started driving to clear my head. Because it doesn't make any sense. She's the one who's crazy, not me. She's fallen in with this group of so-called radicals—it's nauseating. It is. If you only knew. We were watching the Democratic convention on TV—the cops were just busting heads all over Chicago—and we ended up in a fight. It was so stupid. We never fight. I'm not kidding, either."

I just let him talk and talk, because them miles kept tumbling by, getting me closer to Huntsville. And that boy could talk. Now I didn't understand much of what it was about, Martin Luther King this and Bobby Kennedy that, but I knew enough to nod my head and agree with him. And damn if we didn't get all the way to Huntsville by midnight. By then we'd become pretty good pals, old Norman and me. He felt real bad about my brother and predicted that in five years grass would be legal on account of everyone he knew in college smoked it.

He even slipped me a ten so I could eat. Then he got back on the interstate and headed on back to Dallas, Big D. Before he left, I told him he should look up a friend of mine there, Lulu Wilson. She danced at a few clubs around town. She'd mend his broken heart real fast.

Bethel, New York
1969
43732

We were pretty sure we were going to have to walk home. No one had seen Norman since the rains came back yesterday afternoon during Joe Cocker's set. We'd finally gotten dry from Friday's downpour, and then the skies had darkened again and despite our best efforts to repel the deluge with chants and incantations, we were soaked once more. Winds had gusted to what felt like gale force, and someone thought that the speakers on the stage were going to topple over.

I suggested we drop another hit of acid.

Norman had never tried acid before. He'd smoked some grass, but until we convinced him to drive to Woodstock, he'd never tripped. August in Dallas is brutally hot, and on an atlas I showed Norman that the area of the big musical festival was in the Catskills, where it was sure to be cooler. "You won't sweat your nuts off for three whole days," I said to him. Norman perspired like someone had doused him with water.

"I seriously doubt that."

"Come on, man. You like history, right? Dig, this concert is going to be historical. Unforgettable. The Who. Jefferson Airplane. CCR. Crosby, Stills, and Nash. Sly and the Family Stone. Hendrix, man! Joan Baez."

"Oh please. I can't stand her."

"You love The Who. Admit it, Norman. You wish you were Roger Daltry."

"I like the Stones better."

"What's going on in Dallas you can't miss this summer? Huh? Bingo night at the club?"

That was a veiled reference to his old girlfriend. They'd split up last year and Norman still was hung up on Louise, which he was ashamed to admit. I knew that was his weak spot and took full advantage. But he owed me. I'd been his roommate since freshman year and I'd heard all I could stand about Louise Hoffman. The ups, the downs, the ins, the outs. His miserable broken heart, the poor bastard.

So I had him cornered and he knew it. "I'll drive under one condition—that we spend a couple of days in New York. I want to check out Greenwich Village. Deal?"

So we had a ride to Woodstock after all. In a VW van no less, meaning we could crash in it, the four of us, Norman, myself, Dan the Man, and Lars. We bought three-day tickets to the festival for eighteen bucks, which seemed a little expensive but then you had to consider the line-up—never before had any show put together acts like these, all on one stage in the middle of a farm in upstate New York.

And now we were going to have to walk home. A thousand flipping miles. It was 10:30 on Monday morning, and Hendrix had just finished the last song of the event, his encore of "Hey Joe," but everyone was still grooving on the mind-blowing rendition he did of the National Anthem, which honestly was the best song he did for the two hours he played, two hours where we stood amid the huge piles of garbage and the discarded clothes and the shredded tents and battered blankets, shivering and stoned out of our minds—I hadn't slept. Literally. Not once did my eyes close. I stayed awake and if I started to feel tired, I just took more acid. Not the blue acid, which gave people the creeps— this one guy was writhing around so badly that it took five people to subdue him and get him to the medical tent up the hill.

But I wasn't tripping anymore. Saturday night there had been several hundred thousand of us, and Jefferson Airplane didn't finish until after sunrise, but now, Monday morning, only a fraction of the horde remained. Many had left, including our trusty driver, the one and only Norman Alehouse, who said he was wet and cold and hungry and tired. He should've taken another hit of acid. But instead he'd wondered off down West Shore Road, and now we were stuck.

We weren't the only ones. Dozens of people stood motionless holding signs announcing their hometowns. Ann Arbor. Cape Cod. Miami. That was a hoot. But then again, someone would probably give the guy a lift. For three days we'd all shared everything we had. People passed around boxes of Cocoa Puffs, watermelons, sunflower seeds, joints, hash pipes, beers, sodas, anything you could think of— and there were no fights, none, not a single confrontation, but instead true togetherness, the freaks of the country all gathered to form our own island of sanity. The pigs saw us getting high but were powerless to bust us because they would've had to bust all of us. People danced naked, made love in public, helped those who took the bad acid, made room in tents and under blankets and in cars—hell, they even stopped charging people money to get in—they just opened up the gates and we all grooved, even if we couldn't hear the music.

"Where do you think he is?" Lars asked, pupils still dilated, stubble covering his long face and mud caked on his skinny legs.

"The van," I answered. "He's sitting in that van reading a book."

"Do you think he split the scene?"

"Son, he wouldn't leave us up here like that. He knows if he did, I'd hunt him down and kick his ass."

Dan the Man was still bidding farewell to his latest chick, some little blonde from Pennsylvania who looked fetching in her cut-off jeans and see-through blouse, and they were in her tent but it was time to go. Even I was ready. I took one last look at the stage down below us. The roadies were already at work, breaking it down. A kid came by asking if anyone would volunteer to stay behind and help clean up Max's farm—Max Yasgur, our hero, who'd let the concert be held here when no one else would—the good people of White Lake and Bethel had brought in free food and water for us, had done all they could to keep us alive, and for a second I thought about staying back to lend a hand. Why did I have to go back to Texas so soon? Why did I need to go to college at all? Why couldn't I just do this the rest of my life? The Hog Farm commune had set up a big festive area over by a pond, and they'd prepared a mean gruel they passed out to the hungry for free—and they appeared to be making it in this world just fine. Little naked babies running around, the Grateful Dead playing concerts at the Free Stage—it seemed like bliss to me.

Of course, had I dropped out of college, I'd lose my deferment and would have been eligible for the draft. Unless I burned my draft card and went underground with the Hog Farm.

"Come on," said Lars, "I'll get Dan. He's got to be finished by now."

"Yeah. He's had enough peace and love for one man."

And so I turned around and walked with Lars up the hill toward the camping area. Exhaustion was setting in. These crazy thoughts kept bouncing around in my head, and I figured it was the remnants of the acid. I wasn't going to drop out of college. I had one year left. We all did. Lars was going to be an accountant, Dan was going to work for an oil company, Norman was going to become a history professor, and I was going to—do something with my degree in Psychology. Maybe work with kids in the ghetto. Try to make the world a better place. I knew it could happen. This weekend had proved that we could live together in love and harmony, without squares or pigs or fascists.

We crossed over Hurd Road and passed by an old school bus

painted DayGlo, and a pretty girl in a blue dress was leaning out of one of the windows and she waved at us. It was love at first sight. Smooth skin, bright smile, long brown hair. I wanted to ask her if she'd like to go swimming at the pond. But then her old man came up and grabbed her. Good thing, too, else I would've married her on the spot.

Miracle of miracles, we found Dan the Man in the chick's tent, huddled behind an RC Cola truck some hippies had turned into an apartment building on wheels. Lying on the ground was a pair of sneakers someone had left behind. I tried them on and they fit perfectly, so I wore them, despite the fact that they were muddy. I needed a souvenir.

"Come on, sonny boy," Lars yelled at Dan. "We're blasting off."

I kept digging the scene, the wreckage really, the acres of refuse. Groups of people now were sweeping through and setting fires to burn the junk that remained. I kept thinking that all kinds of treasures were sure to be had buried beneath the mud. The mud, the glorious mud we'd played in, sliding through it like snow, smearing our naked bodies with it so that we resembled brown swamp creatures. And then the pond, the cleaning up, and all the beautiful naked people down there, unashamed, at peace, natural.

Finally Dan emerged, the girl from Pennsylvania still clinging to him. "I swear I'll write you," he told her. She made him promise again and so he did, meaningfully and with all his heart. Chicks loved him. No one in our fraternity got more action than Dan, the pretty boy from Abilene who looked like Rock Hudson. They all fell for his lonesome cowboy routine, especially the naïve ones like this blonde. I was jealous as hell.

"I'll miss her," Dan said as we started walking. "She was insane. I mean, damn. She couldn't get enough."

"Yeah? In what ways?" Lars egged him on, always wanting the details. Dan didn't mind describing the various acts, although I wasn't in the mood. I kept glancing at every one of the girls who remained, the fellow die-hards whose hair was as nasty as mine, grimed and gnarly and smelly—I loved them all and wanted never to leave them, their long skirts billowing, many still dancing, hearing music no one else could, still in the moment, not wanting it to end.

The van was parked a good six miles down Route 17B, past White Lake, where on Friday Norman had abandoned it in the pasture of somebody's farm, along with about a hundred other cars. The traffic had come to a complete stop. It had taken us two hours to get from the town of Monticello to that spot, with miles still to go, and everyone else had started pulling over and walking, so we did, too. All we had with us was a couple of blankets to sit on and a cooler of beer. We thought we could get food inside the show, so we didn't laden ourselves down with too much. No one was opposed to sleeping on the ground under the stars—I'd pictured myself finding a comfortable place in a field of alfalfa, which was what Max Yasgur fed his milk cows.

But three hundred thousand people and torrential rain had turned the alfalfa fields into mud pits, and sleeping on the ground didn't seem like a good idea. Norman had tried to find some place dry, and eventually he crawled into a big teepee and got some rest, while I just kept on keeping on.

"Does anybody remember which field Norman parked in?" Lars asked after we'd walked for about an hour. The fields we passed by all looked about the same, bucolic and filled with tire tracks and mud and a few stray cars.

I tried to remember. Friday seemed like a long time ago. Eternity. But I had faith that all would work out. I was convinced that higher powers were watching out for us. Not just us three, but everyone who'd come to Woodstock. "We'll find it," I vowed. "Don't even worry about it. It's all taken care of."

"My foot is killing me." Lars had stepped on something and sliced his heel open. A nurse had applied a bandage, but he needed to rest it.

"So what?" Dan snorted. "My dick is killing me."

"Do you walk on your dick, smart ass?"

Up ahead I saw a pig's squad car. It was stuck in some mud, its tires spinning. Normally I would've laughed at the sight, the futility of a pig trying to get back on patrol, but all weekend we'd helped each other. We'd all shouldered the burdens, lending a hand whenever we could.

"Come on," I said, "let's give this cop a push."

Soon enough about ten of us were over there, flashing the V peace sign as the cop grinned at the spectacle of ten long-haired and filthy dirty hippies getting him unstuck. He nodded thanks to us and then got back into the long line of cars streaming down the road. I hoped that the next time he saw one of us hippies, he wouldn't be so quick to judge us on our appearance. He'd give us the benefit of the doubt, remembering how we'd pitched in when he'd needed assistance.

"I can't take another step," said Lars, sounding very fatigued. "I'm getting dizzy. And I've got to eat. Did we eat anything today yet?"

"Does anybody have any food?" I called out. We were surrounded by a big group of fellow travelers but no one had anything to share; the weekend had depleted us all. This was the bitter end, and we still had a long drive back to Texas.

"Crap," Lars spit. "I'm starving. And my foot!"

"There it is!" Dan stopped and pointed. Off in the distance, parked on a gentle slope in the middle of a muddy field, was Norman's VW. We all started hooting and hollering and punching each other as we jogged like gleeful children over to the van. It was worth it, all of the rain and the cold and the hunger, the exhaustion and the hassles of getting here—the best time of my life.

When we found Norman, he was sitting in the back of the van having an intense discussion with a guy with a long beard wearing overalls and no shirt or shoes. They both stopped talking when we arrived, yelling crazily and hopping around. Norman looked on bemused as always, one leg crossed over the other, his thinning hair pulled back into a ponytail.

"You missed Hendrix!" I cried at Norman. "He pretty much stank except for when he played *The Star-Spangled Banner.* It blew us away, man."

"This is Chester," Norman said, introducing the guy in overalls.

Chester flashed a peace sign and then started rolling a joint. It was a most welcome sight.

"You're absolutely wrong about Johnson," Norman said, going back to the discussion he was having, oblivious to us. "He never cared about Vietnam. He wanted to end poverty. That was his ultimate goal, his true passion."

"Let him roll the joint, how about it?" Dan interjected. He had little patience for political talk. In that way he was like most of the other brothers in our fraternity, who were largely apolitical if not conservative. Norman and I stuck out because of our outspoken antiwar stances, although we were hardly radicals. We weren't willing to blow up the ROTC building and we didn't burn our draft cards but we hated the war. We hated the war and it seemed to me, based on what had just happened at Woodstock, that we were going to become a force to be reckoned with, and Nixon would have no choice but put an end to the madness. Six months tops and it would all be over, as long as we stayed together.

Austin, Texas
1970
56832

At the last minute our ride backed out on us. It was Saturday morning, and we were stuck. We needed a car big enough to get all the brothers and sisters to Fort Hood who wanted to go. There was a march planned for "Armed Farces Day," and six or seven of us were determined to make it come hell or high water. There was no question about it: we needed a van. Fast. Today.

"Ask him," Quinn said to me.

"Who?"

"You know who. The frat boy."

"I don't think he'll go."

"Come on. I've seen the way he looks at you. Just ask him. He'll do it."

Quinn was talking about Norman Alehouse, my ex-boyfriend from Dallas, who was a wishy-washy pathetic liberal, satisfied with the system and his place in it. He was a Eugene McCarthy-Bobby Kennedy "children's crusade" sellout who wanted the war to end but wouldn't do much about it except complain, even with Nixon invading Cambodia—even with the pigs killing us now, picking us off one by one. First Kent State, then Jackson State—we had to make a stand, to show the pigs that we weren't beaten.

"I don't know," I said, rolling over and pulling the sheet over my head. Thinking about Norman always got me confused.

"Just call him."

I threw the sheet off of me and looked over at Quinn, who was lighting up a roach. "He's not like us," I said. "Can you dig that? He's got his 2-S deferment and a nice comfortable life and he won't do anything to upset the apple cart. He's going to grad school so he won't have to burn his draft card. He's not like us. He's a chickenshit liberal."

"We need a van, sister. Call him." He offered me the roach but I wasn't into getting high just yet. Then I felt Quinn's arm snake around my stomach and he pulled me close. He told me that our love was holy, a sacred force of goodness in a world rotted with lies. Neither one of us believed in marriage, and so we were liberated from the shackles that tied down those who couldn't think for themselves. I wasn't interested in becoming somebody's little doll-wife, and Quinn had no intention of making me his property. We were both free to do whatever we wanted with whomever we wanted, knowing deep down that our love was a fortress no one could surmount.

"Come on, sister." He nibbled at my ear, and then kissed me on the neck. "It's for the revolution."

"He's a total square. You dig that, don't you?"

*

There was a long list of phone numbers on a tattered sheet of paper taped on the wall by the phone, and down at the bottom, scrawled in tiny letters, was Norman's. The only reason I'd added his phone number was the van. I always figured it could come in handy one day. Everybody always said I was practical.

I dialed the number and waited, expecting the operator to tell me the number had been disconnected. Instead Norman answered on the second ring, sounding very groggy. "Hello?" he croaked. Caught off-guard, I suddenly had no idea what to say.

"Hello?" he tried again.

"Norman?"

"Louise?"

"Yeah, it's me."

"What's wrong? Are you in trouble?"

"No. Do I sound like I'm not in trouble?" Norman always assumed the worst about everything, fretting from the moment he woke up till he closed his eyes at night, sure he'd die in his sleep.

"I suppose not. What time is it?"

"It's nine."

He tried to stifle a yawn. "I'm still in bed. I was up late reading. But you didn't call about that, did you? Or did you?"

I had to laugh. Norman had a dry wit, one of his best features. "No, I didn't. What're you doing today?"

"Today?" The question puzzled him. I could almost hear him scratching his head. I never called to ask him what he was doing. I was the one who'd broken up with him, so he was probably confused. "I was thinking of spending some time in the library. I've got a huge paper due next week, on George Creel. He's the guy who invented Uncle Sam."

I had to cut him off. He could talk for hours about his history papers. "I need to ask you a favor."

"A favor? What kind of favor?"

His voice didn't express suspicion but more curiosity. Norman never got mad. He was too analytical for that, too far removed from emotion, head in the clouds, living in a fog of academic hairsplitting. He'd get passionate when talking about the Civil War or Andrew Jackson, but get him on the subject of the Vietnam War, and he'd drone on with the usual liberal platitudes. *Light at the end of the tunnel...victory right around the corner...*

"I need a ride to Fort Hood."

"Why do you need to go to Fort Hood?"

I thought about lying, but I knew he'd sniff it out, so I really could only tell him the truth. "I have to deliver some newspapers and there's a march today."

"A march? Really? At Fort Hood?"

"Yeah, the GI's are staging it to protest the war. They're calling it Armed Farces Day, instead of Armed Forces Day, which the war pigs cancelled because they were afraid of people protesting. I really want to be there because of what happened at Kent State—I just can't believe they'd gun down innocent people like that. Were you in the march at the Capitol last week?"

"No." He sounded ashamed to be admitting this to me, but I wasn't surprised. He was never comfortable with my radicalism—my decision to take a more aggressive stance in opposing the war, which in turn led me to reject Amerikkka and all it stood for. "But it was necessary. I can understand why people are upset. I'm upset. Sickened, actually."

"You are?"

"Yes, I am. You don't believe me, but I'll prove it to you. What time?"

"What time what?"

"What time do you want to go?"

"Go? You'll go? You'll drive us to Fort Hood?"

"Sure. I think it's important to keep the pressure on Nixon at this juncture. There's momentum in the Congress to end the draft, and the more large-scale demonstrations there are, the more newspaper articles there'll be. The tide is turning. I can feel it. We can end this war."

It was the same liberal claptrap he'd been spewing for years, his unblinkered belief that the System Would Eventually Work. But there wasn't time to argue with him. I told him to come by as soon as possible.

*

I got ready as fast as I could, throwing on a granny dress and leaving my hair uncombed. I had to shake Quinn out of bed but finally he got up and put on the same jeans he'd been wearing for a week. We really needed to do a trip to the Laundromat, but there was never time. The last two weeks had been a blur, ever since the murders at Kent State. In some ways I still hadn't come down. Rage boiled inside me, and hatred seethed like molten lava inching up my throat. I couldn't wait to march today. I couldn't wait for the pigs to come at us again.

Fifteen minutes later I heard a strange noise, a kind of mechanical *thump-thump-thump-thump*. It was loud and sickly, and I ran outside to check it out, arriving just in time to watch Norman pull up in the VW van and park in the dirt of the front yard. He got out and gave me a tepid wave, and I noticed that he'd lost even more of his hair. He'd be totally bald before he was thirty, which was a shame because he used to have such nice California blonde surfer hair.

"You guys ready?" he asked.

"Yeah, just about." I kept looking at the van, which was scraped and gnarled and ragged looking. The hot Texas son had faded the aqua blue to a pale, grayish hue. Two hubcaps were missing. A layer of dust fogged the windows, and it needed a good scrubbing. I could remember the day Norman first drove it to high school, how shiny and new it had been. Six long years ago. A world ago. "Are you sure that thing can make it to Fort Hood?"

"I guess so," he replied flatly, same as always, unconcerned about the everyday matters such as maintaining a vehicle. "It made it to Woodstock and back."

"It did?"

"Somehow. Even though the head bolts are stripped out, whatever that means. I'm selling the van after I graduate. I won't need it in New York."

"New York?"

"Yeah. I'm going to grad school at Columbia."

"Oh. Far out."

"It should be a trip."

Quinn came out, carrying a cooler full of beer. He'd already taken some mescaline and soon his pupils would dilate and he'd get real quiet and into his own thing. He'd asked me if I'd wanted some, but I didn't partake because I'd wanted to talk to Norman, stupid as that sounds. Sure, he was a total square but since he was doing me a favor, the least I could do was make sense for a few hours.

"Nice VW," Quinn chirped. "What year?"

"1964."

"Right on. I dig it, brother. We'll be riding in style today."

"It needs a lot of work. You know anybody who'd want to buy it?"

"Seriously?"

"Seriously. I'm looking to sell it before I move to New York."

"How much you want?"

"I don't know. I haven't settled on a price."

Quinn thought that was the funniest thing he'd ever heard in his life and started laughing uproariously, rocking back on his heels like he'd tip over. "Far out, man. Just give it away for free. That's the righteous thing."

"I can't do that. I need the money."

"Listen up. I'll give you two hundred for it."

"Are you sure?" I interjected, knowing that Quinn was broke and that he'd come to me for the bread. And I wasn't sure I wanted to be tooling around with Quinn in the same VW van where I'd lost my virginity in March 1965. Too many memories were rolling around in the back of that van, some sweet, some not, and I wasn't sure how I felt. Plus, it needed work. Quinn didn't know anything about cars, so we'd have to hire somebody, and I'd have to pay for that, too.

"We can talk about it later," Norman said, picking up on my misgivings. Sometimes he scared me by how easily he could read my moods. No one else understood me in quite the same way. "We'd better get going, don't you think?"

Then Paul and Amanda came out. We still had to pick up Blake and Morris, and then we could head off on I-35 toward Fort Hood.

*

The van had no acceleration. Whenever we had to go up even the slightest hill, other cars would zoom past us as we puttered along at our top speed of forty miles per hour. The head cloth had ripped, exposing the bare metal in the roof over our heads. Luckily the trip to Fort Hood was short, about an hour, across dry, dusty, flat terrain, I-35, the road home to Dallas.

How often had I done this drive with Norman? Too many times to remember, but not lately. Not since the end of the summer of 1968, our junior year. That horrible year, the Tet offensive, King and Kennedy assassinated , all leading up to the Democratic National Convention in Chicago, where the pigs just went wild and ran berserk through Grant Park.

I'd watched the convention on TV with Norman, whose sanguine reaction to the horrors in Chicago frankly pissed me off. How could he not have been as outraged as I was? Were we even watching the same thing?

"I don't know why you're so surprised by any of this," he'd told me, sounding like the would-be history professor. All that was missing was the tweed jacket with elbow patches. "The same thing happened to the Wobblies after World War One. The leaders were all rounded up and tossed in jail."

"I'm not talking about the stupid Wobblies!"

"I know, but I'm trying to make a point, Louise. This isn't unusual in American history. The Ludlow massacre, Haymarket Square—"

"You're just hiding behind your books, Norman. I can't do that anymore. Not after this."

"Wait until Humphrey is elected. He'll end the war. He'll have to."

That night I decided I couldn't go on living my privileged life as a sweet sorority girl while out on the street my brothers and sisters were risking life and limb to start a real revolution in this country—which meant when I got back to Austin I'd join SDS or the White Panthers or some group dedicated to the overthrow of the corrupt and bogus and immoral system that was plunging the world into ineffable darkness. I broke up with Norman and dropped out of UT altogether, to devote myself full-time to ending the war.

*

"Are they smoking grass?" Norman asked me once the first tendrils of dope smoke reached the front seat. The windows of the van were rolled down, of course, so it wasn't a big deal, but I could tell Norman was displeased. "They should be careful. The cops around here are notorious for pulling people over."

"We'll be okay," I said confidently. "And anyway, who cares what the pigs do to us? They are a bunch of fascists anyway."

"That may be, but the last time I checked, possession of marijuana could get a person three-to-five years in prison. Or longer."

"It should be legal. It's just a plant. An herb. A flower."

"I'm not arguing that point, Louise. I've smoked pot before. But not out here among the wood choppers who hate the long-haireds."

"Do you want me to tell them to stop?"

Norman looked over at me, pained and anxious. It was hard to tell anymore that he was from San Diego. He'd become a UT frat boy, a bookish one, but still, he'd hazed pledges and went to mixers and drank too much at Roundup Week, pretending with the others like the world hadn't gone utterly insane. He was white, rich, and male, so what did he have to worry about?

"No," he grimaced. We passed a haggard billboard advertising boiled peanuts, its white letters bleached from the sun. "We'll be there soon and hopefully nothing'll happen. I've had trouble through here before, though. Georgetown, Texas. A speeding ticket, if you can believe that."

"Speeding? In this thing?"

"That's what they said. I thought they were going to arrest me. The cop was one of those stern and angry types. He reminded me of a cross between Barney Fife and Steve McQueen."

"You must've been scared shitless."

"The thing was, I'd just seen *Easy Rider*. I was sure I was going to die like Peter Fonda, gunned down by a small-town lunatic."

"Well, I appreciate you doing this." There was tenderness in my voice that surprised us both, a softness in tone that I recognized as belonging to our past when we'd been in love. I never spoke this way to Quinn. With him I used a different voice, harder and tougher-edged.

"It's the least I could do."

"How's your mom?"

He smirked and rolled his eyes. "The same."

"I know what you mean. My parents, too. Haven't changed a bit. I haven't talked to them in over a year."

"Really?"

"Fourteen months, to be exact."

"Wow, that long? I guess I shouldn't be surprised. I know they don't approve of your decisions. They've said as much to Mother, on many occasions. They're just being pig-headed and stubborn because they don't understand what you're doing. But I think what you're doing is very brave and it took a lot of courage for you to commit yourself as totally as you have."

I nearly jumped out of my seat. "That's not what you said when we broke up! You called me a child. A deluded child."

"I did not."

"In so many words."

"I thought Humphrey would win the election, and that he'd do the right thing. I didn't think turning against the Democrats would help anything, except hand Nixon the election."

"The whole system is rotten. Can't you see that? You have to see that now, don't you?"

He sighed as if in pain and gripped the steering wheel tightly when an 18-wheeler went roaring past us. It sounded like it would devour the van in one gulp. The draft sucked us toward it, but Norman managed to keep us alive with some nimble maneuvering. "Yeah, the system is pretty rotten," he admitted once the truck was clear of us.

"Are you ready to burn your draft card?"

"Maybe."

I recoiled from him, not expecting this response. He'd told me before that he'd never do something as foolish at that, jeopardizing his future to make a futile point, especially considering that his draft number was 300 and he'd never get called up. But events had conspired to push the likes of Norman Alehouse into the radical fringe circa 1970. A UT frat boy was willing to risk it all to stick it in the eye of The Man.

"Far out," I encouraged him. "That would be heavy. If everybody did that, the whole system would come crashing down right on top of Nixon's head."

His eyes stayed fixed on the highway rolling past, the flat barren tablelands of north Texas. I didn't know what he was thinking. Quinn crawled up and offered me the joint but I said no thanks.

"How about you, man?" he asked Norman, holding out the roach. Norman shook his head no. He seemed very sad, like he'd just gotten some bad news.

I had no clue how many people in Killeen would turn out for Armed Farces Day. We had leaflets ready to hand out and issues of *The Fatigue Press* to distribute around the town, but nobody was sure what kind of reception there'd be. Would a hundred of us march or a thousand or ten? We had banners to hold up, including one I'd made, FREE BOBBY!, referring to Bobby Seale, the Black Panther leader who'd been sentenced to four years in prison for defending himself in court, part of the trial of the Chicago Nine.

"Where should I go?" Norman asked once we got off the interstate onto Route 190, the road that led to Killeen.

Paul gave him directions to the Oleo Strut, the coffeehouse near the army base that served as headquarters for the antiwar movement—dozens of coffeehouses just like it had sprung up in small towns all across the country, where GI's could congregate off-base and discuss the war. An "oleo strut" was part of the landing gear for a helicopter, meaning it was a place where soldiers could go for a soft landing. What was groovy about the Oleo Strut was that Fort Hood was where GI's returning from Vietnam got stationed to serve out the remainder of their tour—and these guys could hold some heavy rap sessions about what they'd seen over there. We liked to get them together with the raw recruits so that the new guys could know what to expect—and maybe even refuse to go, which was happening more and more.

"Man, far out!" Quinn gushed when we saw that the storeowners on the main drag of downtown Killeen had boarded up the windows of their stores. "It's a ghost town!"

"They're expecting trouble," Paul, who had been toking during most of the last hour, concluded with the solemnity of a priest.

"Really?" Norman chimed in, trying not to sound nervous but I could tell he was very nervous. He was sweating profusely while white-knuckling the steering wheel.

"That's a good omen. The word must be out. I bet the Strut is packed to the rafters."

And it was. We had to park several blocks away and walk. Killeen was your typical small Texas town, with a bank and five-and-dime and a soda fountain and a feed store and pool hall and cops who looked like they roasted hippies over an open fire. But today they were outnumbered by the legions who'd streamed in from Austin and

Houston and Dallas, the freaks of the Lone Star State who were usually the ones in the minority. The ones who got singled out, harassed for no reason, beaten up, thrown in jail on bogus charges. But not today. No, today the sun was shining bright on a cloudless Saturday morning, and outside the Strut, a big crowd had formed, mingling together as someone strummed on a guitar and sang Bob Dylan's "Pigs of War."

"Can you believe Dylan recorded that song eight years ago, before anyone was talking about Vietnam?" asked Norman as we stood off to the side, digging the scene.

"He was a real visionary back then, before he went electric," I needled him. He took the bait, same as always. He shook his head back and forth as if swatting away my words with his chin.

"No, you're wrong! He sounds better with the Band behind him."

It was one of our long-running disputes and it felt comfortable to be having it with Norman, like slipping on a familiar pair of jeans. But it quickly ended when Quinn started waving frantically at me, gesturing for me to come over. I was hesitant to go, to leave Norman alone. I felt like I had to protect him, maternal instincts that I grew to resent while we were dating but old habits die hard. Quinn, however, was getting impatient, like I should've been by his side and wasn't. It was hard being around someone who was tripping and you weren't. They had a different energy, and it didn't make it easy to communicate on every level.

"I'll be right back," I told Norman. "Wait here. Hold this."

I gave him my Bobby Seale sign. He held it up over his shoulder so everyone could see, the UT frat boy turned revolutionary for the day. "How's this?" he asked, smiling toothily.

"Right on," I enthused, patting him on the shoulder. "I wish the members of the country club could see you now."

"They'd think it was Halloween or something."

For some reason I kissed him. Not on the mouth, but on the cheek. His eyes got wide and his mouth dropped a little, and I winked at him before I walked over to see what Quinn wanted. I was pretty sure that Norman was still in love with me, and even though I didn't feel the same way about him, I couldn't help fanning the flames—after all, Quinn didn't own me or my body, and I was free to explore any dimension I pleased. Besides, Quinn had slept with Amanda and almost every friend we shared in common—and so I was only too willing to test him, to see if he meant it when he said that we'd never tie each down—because honestly sometimes it hurt inside when he was with someone else, despite my best efforts to rid myself of such bourgeois notions—jealousy was just another form of slavery.

Quinn introduced me to someone named Sally, an activist from Waco who had an American flag wrapped around her body. She stopped yelling, "Fuck the army!" long enough to shake my hand.

But I kept looking back at Norman. The march was getting ready to start and he was standing there all alone and so I split and went back to him. Quinn was talking to Sally anyway about people they knew in common and I figured he could take care of himself.

And so I marched with Norman, and we took turns holding the Bobby Seale sign I'd made, and we dug the scene of a thousand people all gathered together for the same holy purpose of doing right by the world. I'd never get tired of these marches, because the energy generated by them renewed me and my faith in humanity.

"Isn't this great?" I asked Norman as we strolled with our arms linked to perfect strangers, most young but some not, white, black, brown, men, women, all shouting and singing and unafraid of the pigs gathered in their riot gear, standing ready to pounce on us. "Imagine if there were ten times as many people—or a hundred times. Then we'd show them that we could change the world."

"Woodstock was kind of like that."

"Yeah, I bet."

"I didn't enjoy the rain, to be honest. I spent most of my time in the van, sleeping and talking to people who wondered past. It was quite pleasant, actually."

Norman never cheated on me, not once. He was a faithful and loyal person, dependable and square, so very square. Quinn demanded attention with his manic energy and endless appetites, for drugs, women, music, politics—it was easy to see how I'd gotten lured into his orbit, drawn in by his sparkling brown eyes and cowboy swagger, the Lone Ranger ready to take on The Man by any means necessary. He'd been to Berkeley, gotten beat up in Chicago, took acid at the Haight, served on the national board of SDS only to see it all break apart last year—and now he wanted to wage real war, make real bombs, and blow up real buildings—he wanted to join the Weather Underground and he wanted me to, as well. Bonnie and Clyde.

"The mob was very effective during the lead-up to the

Revolutionary War," Norman explained nervously, the pigs now growing in number. "Especially in Boston. Never underestimate the power of an angry crowd. Certainly the British didn't. Or John Adams for that matter. You know, he defended the British soldiers who were involved in the Boston Massacre."

I finally saw Quinn. He was with Sally, and she had a hand on his ass and he had one on hers. And for some reason I thought about the first time Norman kissed me—that day the VW van had been vandalized in the school parking lot, when some idiots had spray-painted it. We drove to Biff Burger and got something to eat, and we talked and laughed and I knew then that he was different—he understood me and he didn't care that I didn't fit in at Highland Park High School—because he didn't, either, and we kept each other company for the next two years until we could escape to UT—and it had all started with one sweet kiss when we said good-bye that day in 1964—his breath had smelled like onions from the hamburger—my first kiss.

"I'm glad I called you," I said, looking away from Quinn and up at Norman. The love beads around his neck had gotten tangled up and it looked like he was going to choke, so I fixed them. He had the Bobby Seale sign resting back against his shoulder and held it with both hands like a club.

"I know you just needed my van. That's cool. I don't care. It was about time I did something besides complain."

"I didn't think you'd do it."

"I still can't believe I'm here. Honestly."

Someone passed us a joint and we both took a hit and then shared it with the guy next to us. We both started chanting "Fuck the army!" with everybody else, our voices growing louder, as if we wanted Nixon to hear us at Camp David.

90

Big Flat, Arkansas
1972
57148

The van is dead.

It won't start. I sit there staring out at the meadow where the children are playing, naked and brown and happy, faces smeared with dirt and no teachers to corrupt them, no school to thwart their curiosity. This is how I wanted my son to grow up, but Louise has other plans.

Louise wants to leave. Today.

But the van is dead.

*

"What's wrong with the van, Quinn?"

"It's got a broken heart."

"Come on. Level with me. What's the deal?"

"I don't know. I'm not a mechanic."

"Is it the battery?"

"No, I replaced it before we came."

"What is it then?"

"I don't know. I can't deal with this right now, dig? I've got some heavy crap I'm delving into and I just don't need this kind of head trip."

"Well, sorry to bother you, Quinn, but don't you think we ought to get the van fixed?"

*

Louise is still clinging to outdated notions of attachment. She hasn't grown much as a person the past two years while living here at Freedom Farm. She insists that our son see a doctor, for example, so that they can inject him with poisons instead of letting Nature tend to him. She always thinks he's sick. But he's just being himself. A gentle soul, filled with loving righteousness, who lives at peace with the world. But Louise says there's something wrong with him.

*

I named him Pranya, referring to the Hindu notion of life-force, the Absolute Reality that linked us to Cosmic Consciousness.

*

"You promised me. You promised me that you'd get me out of here when I wanted to go."

"I said I'd try. And I tried. But the van won't start."

"So let's get Lucas to help us get the van started. When's the last time you drove it?"

"I don't know."

"I want to get out of here, Quinn."

*

Pran starts to cry, probably because of all the hostile energy Louise is pumping out. Pran has that kind of sensitivity—all children do, but him especially. So what if he's just one year old—he possesses deep insight—he can tell when Louise's head was in a bad place—like right after he was born, and Louise's midwives handed him to her—and he had trouble nursing—and Louise kept asking what she was doing wrong and the baby kept crying—and then she said he wasn't gaining weight. He was sick. He was frail. His eyes seemed wrong. He wasn't crawling. She couldn't just let him be.

*

"He's my son, too. And I don't want to go."

"You promised me, Quinn. When I wanted to split, you'd help me get out of here."

*

In the distance, back at the Great House, I can hear the drummers start up, as they always do right before lunch. They'll sit in a circle and get a good rhythm going, one with a deep resonance that reaches the inmost parts of your soul. I'd love to join them, because I really want to go work on my breathing. I need some fresh energy to help me get my thoughts together. I have to get back in touch with Absolute

Reality, discharging the illusions swirling inside me, the falseness and fakery that trick us into believing lies and distortions. I know some people are planning a pilgrimage to Heber Springs later, where they are going to spend the two or three days in silent, holy meditation. I really want to join them. We can all go, me, Louise, and Pran. It would cure what's ailing Louise, if she would only expand her consciousness.

*

"I just—I don't know. I can't take this anymore, Quinn. Now all these new people are here—they're not good people. They're freaking me out. That one girl is fourteen and pregnant—have you ever heard her utter a rational thought? Somebody raped her—it was probably that guy she's with—the Shaman or whatever it is you call him—he makes me sick. Literally sick to my stomach. He's always over here, not a stitch of clothing on, ever. Like I won't be able to keep my hands off of him. He's gross."

"What do you want me to do?"

"Get the VW fixed so we can leave!"

"What if we can get the Shaman and the girls to leave? Would that help? I can talk to Lucas."

"I don't know. It might help. I just want to get out of here."

"I'll talk to Lucas."

*

Back in Austin we'd sworn to each other never to get jealous or never to take away our freedom so that we could explore sexual happiness with whomever we wanted. We came out to Freedom Farm to escape all the repression and stifling of creativity that went on in the straight, uptight world. And I felt like I'd been making good progress into understanding where I fit into the universe—this simple life, where we all pooled our money together and ran around naked whenever we wanted—where the land was free for whoever grabbed a piece of it. Out here I didn't care about the criminals running our government—their hideous actions, their illegal war, their racist cops—nothing could touch me. I was free. We all were, as long as we stayed together.

*

Lucas lives with his family over the hill, beneath a towering sweet gum. We call him "The Straw Boss," the man everyone looks up to because he's about the only one who knows what he's doing. Lucas has an old Ford pickup truck that runs great and handles the long rocky road back to civilization about as well as a sturdy pack mule. That thing never broke down. *Because I know how to take care of it.* Damn sure he did. Lucas can do anything. He drove up to Iowa and disassembled a windmill and hauled it back and then he welded it back together so we could run a pump to get our water instead of hauling it a half-mile each way from the creek. Lucas can rig up just about anything and on the piano or guitar he had no match. But one thing he couldn't do was make the Shaman disappear. No one could.

*

The Shaman came about two weeks ago. Pulled up in a purple Chrysler Imperial with gaudy whitewall tires and the three girls in the backseat, and we all stood stiff as boards, gawking. We'd had visitors before, drifters who'd roamed to us after hearing about our free land for free people, everyone welcome and no one turned away. Usually those people stayed a few days and always pitched in to help out— hell, one even ended staying on full-time. Built himself a teepee by the Big Rock and joined us in our mad endeavor to renounce the world.

But the Shaman was different. Soon as I laid eyes on him, I felt a strange shiver, like I was picking up on a disturbed vibration, sort of how the air feels different right before the storm clouds roll in.

Greetings, brothers and sisters! This place ain't easy to find.

He spoke with a pronounced Southern accent, the deep South, Alabama or Mississippi, and he was about five feet tall, despite the fact that he was wearing black motorcycle boots and a ten-gallon cowboy hat with feathers sticking out of it. He had long, stringy red hair, like a rag doll's, with rosy red cheeks to match. His beard looked painted on, as it grew in haphazard clumps. My first impression was that he was trying to become his own Fabulous Furry Freak Brother, because he came across as a cartoon hippie, something Gilbert Shelton would've drawn.

Then the girls got out. One was pregnant. She looked like she was thirteen or fourteen.

It feels good to finally be free. Free from all the bullshit back there. We've been driving for three days. Any chance we could get a bite to eat?

No one moved or spoke for a few seconds. By now almost everyone had gathered around the newcomers, maintaining a respectful distance. We'd just cleaned up the lunch plates, and since food was a sensitive subject, the cause of many fights, we were reticent to open that can of worms—or can of anything, for that matter.

Lucas stepped forward. The Straw Boss to the rescue again.

Are you just stopping by? Planning on staying long?

The Shaman and the girls giggled playfully. *Staying long? Hell, we're staying forever, brother! Ain't no other place in the world we want to be. Name is Timmy. And this is Laurel, Katy, and Patty.*

Lucas just nodded. The Shaman kept smiling, looking around at all of us. We were twenty-one strong, including the children.

This is Freedom Farm, ain't it? Where you can get land for free?

*

That had been the dream back in 1970, when we'd all chipped in to buy this place in the exact middle of nowhere—Sally and Doug and all the other founders, refugees from the scene in Austin mostly, who'd grown tired of the hassles inflicted upon us by Hoover's G-Men and the Vice Squad pigs of the Austin PD—this was where we were going to construct an alternate reality, one built on trust and brotherhood and equality, where race and sex and class didn't matter—everyone would chip in what they could and we'd share all equally, with no hang-ups or bad vibes or negative energy. That first year, we started every meal by holding hands and staying quiet until someone would chant *Om,* and then one by one we'd all join in until we had connected to the deepest force in the universe. Only then did we eat, after we'd established that sacred bond. Each of us had a job to do: the women took care of the food and the children, and the men handled the crops and other chores. At night we all came together at the Great House, an old leftover cabin from back in the pioneer days that we'd fixed up with long tables and a big fireplace, and sing and dance and screw and get high. But then the first winter came, and we weren't prepared at all. Not enough food canned, not enough firewood chopped. We were cold and hungry that winter, and the roof in our cabin leaked and Louise at that point said she was ready to split. But I wasn't giving up that easily.

It'll get better. I'll get the roof fixed and next winter we'll know what to do.

Next winter? God, Quinn, I don't know if I can make it through this winter.

She hadn't wanted to come out here at first. It took a little convincing, but eventually she understood that the only choice we had was to step out of that perverted mainstream world. We were targets, we were in their crosshairs, and they were about to pull the damn trigger. We couldn't stay sitting ducks. Coming to the commune was our only option. So I bought the VW van from her old boyfriend for two hundred bucks and we made it here, just barely, because that old thing was on its last legs, gasping and wheezing and on the verge of conking out. Two years later, Louise was close to breaking down, too. Just like that VW van.

*

"Louise wants to go?"

"Yeah. She's losing it, man. I don't know what to do. It's the Shaman. He's driving her nuts. If we could just get him to leave—him and those girls."

"He won't leave."

"He can't stay."

"We've never kicked anybody out before. This is free land for whoever wants some. That's always been our rule."

"I dig that, Lucas, but this guy is hateful. If we don't do something, Louise'll split, man. For real. And she'll take Pran with her."

"I don't like the Shaman but he works for the common good same as we all do."

"It's either he stays or Louise goes. Which one will it be?"

"Everyone is free in this world, brother, to do what they please."

*

The Shaman is standing in the doorway to our cottage, naked. His back is to me and when he hears me coming he turns around and waves. Every day he comes over in the nude to talk to us, and he won't leave even if Pran is trying to sleep or is crying. Always the same excuse. *Just taking a break.* He has the girls working in the garden, even the pregnant one. Katy. Claims her father is Elvis Presley and can prove it. It's all she ever talks about when she talks, which isn't much. Louise is pretty sure Katy is illiterate and has been victimized sexually by men her whole life. The other two girls, Laurel and Patty, were strippers at a burlesque in Atlanta and probably prostitutes as well. Both had run away from home at a young age and had found in the Shaman a place to stay, a roof over their young heads.

Which in Louise's mind made the Shaman a pimp. A pimp on the run from the law.

*

"Just takin a break. Hot out, ain't it? I'm already sweatin like a damn pig. Louise says your van won't start."

"No."

"I can take a look at it for ya'll. I used to work on cars back in Memphis. I hear them VW engines is easy to repair."

"Lucas is helping me out."

"Okay, that's cool. It's all one big family here and we got each other's backs. That's what I like about this place. The love and togetherness. The goddamn world back there is goin to hell in a handbasket, and it don't matter none out here. Let them niggers run wild in the street."

"I was heavily involved in the civil rights movement. We both were, Louise and I. We believe in equal rights for Afro-Americans."

"You got any grass?"

"No."

"I run out last night. I could trade some reds for a dime bag."

"I don't have any."

"Who does?"

"Ask around."

"I sure could use a buzz right about now. It's hot as hell already. Louise, what's wrong? Cat got your tongue? Everything okay down there? We all fixin to go for a swim later if ya'll care to join us. Katy really likes you. She looks up to you. And that makes two of us, honey."

*

Louise's parents came out last year right after Pran was born. They stayed for about three hours, dressed in khaki like they were on a safari. It was the first and only time I've ever met them. Louise hadn't seen them in over four years, but had written them about Pran—she thought they deserved to know they were now grandparents. And something about that visit changed Louise—spending time with her mother and the baby, posing for photographs, catching up on gossip and memories—afterwards she was very sad. Just when I thought she was getting used to living here, she started wondering about life elsewhere. She even wrote a letter to her old boyfriend, the one at Columbia. She stopped meditating with me. She was convinced Pran was sickly. She made me drive into town so that a doctor could look at Pran. They stuck a needle in his little finger to draw blood and he howled in pain—the perfect metaphor for how society operates—they poke and prick and cut you until you scream in submission.

Anemia, the doctor said. A lack of iron in the blood.

*

"Well, what did Lucas say?"
"Lucas says we don't kick anyone out."
"Not even a racist pimp pedophile?"
"Not even him."
"Oh, Quinn, he's repellant! He just stares at me with a wild look in his eyes. He's disgusting."
"I know."
"Where are the keys?"
"The keys?"
"To the van. I'm going to fix it myself."
"What?"
"I'm going to get the van to start and then I'm getting the hell out of here."
"You can't work on cars."
"Why not?"
"Because you don't know how to."
"I'll learn."

"Louise, don't be ridiculous."

"I'm not, Quinn. Just because I'm a woman doesn't mean I can't turn a screwdriver."

"Don't start that."

"Start what?"

"The women's lib thing."

"Where are the keys?"

"In my pocket."

"Can I have them, please? Here, hold the baby."

*

I walk Pran down to the creek, with him stuffed into an old canvas backpack. I cut some holes for his little legs to dangle out of, and he loves it up there high on my shoulders, so he can see everything and point and squawk in excitement. The whole world turns him on. One day I'd love to take him to India so he can meet some true yogis, the enlightened gurus who have become one with the Cosmic Consciousness. I could easily give away all I have and live as a true mendicant, questing after Eternity. But what'll happen to Pran if Louise takes him back to the Straight World? He'll want all the false and fake trinkets that our parents gave us, thinking that a new toy would somehow help us grow—but that crap just made us all junkies addicted to the New Thing. I cried at Christmas if I didn't get exactly what I wanted. Would Pran end up like that, too?

*

In the distance I see the Shaman at the creek with the girls. They're swimming in the Blue Hole, which we made by damming up the creek with logs and rocks. The afternoon sun hit it perfectly in the summer, making it a warm and bright spot for a refreshing dip.

Patty gives me a wave. Rivulets of water run down her plump and curvy body, shimmering against her creamy skin like rhinestone studs. We'd made love the second night they were here. Right in the back of the VW van. Said she'd always wanted to do it in a hippie bus but had never gotten the chance. I was stoned out of my mind and went along with her. It was like falling off a cliff. I couldn't stop myself once I started careening lower and lower. *Bite me. Bite me harder. Harder!*

101

I didn't want to bite her. Love wasn't supposed to hurt. But she couldn't get off unless it did. She blamed her father, who was a high-ranking officer in the Army and a total hard-ass.

She wanted me to inflict pain on her, and I couldn't do it. We stopped right in the middle. She offered to go down on me but I was scared she'd hurt me. I had to push her away. I didn't know what the hell she was capable of. Anything.

*

"Hi, Cutie. He's so adorable. He looks just like you, you know. How are you, little man? He's precious."

"He's anemic."

"What?"

"He has an iron deficiency."

"Oh, poor thing. What do you do for that? He can't take a pill, can he?"

"No."

"You gonna come swim with us?"

"Pran likes to walk."

"Oh, too bad, the water feels great."

"Maybe another time."

"I'd like that."

*

Three days later we met up in the back of the van again. And this time I bit her. And she groaned in pleasure, and it sounded like a grizzly bear growling. A grizzly bear that hadn't eaten in months and was now gorging on a fresh kill.

*

A chipmunk is staring at us. Pran points and grunts a few times. He doesn't say many words, something else Louise is worried about. She'd like to have his hearing tested. She's worried he's partially deaf. He's not, though. He can hear footsteps. He recognizes the sound of my voice.

"Chipmunk," I tell him.

Pran doesn't say anything.

"Chipmunk," I say louder. My voice echoes through the lonely woods, faintly trailing off into the whisper of the wind. I feel Pran's little legs kicking excitedly in the backpack. Does he understand what I'm saying? He has to. Why else would he act like this?

"You're not deaf, are you, little brother?"

Silence.

*

Yesterday we all argued about food. Some were in favor of killing a chicken and roasting it. Shiva especially was against it. *That's stupidly cruel! There's no reason for it because the chickens give us eggs and the eggs give us protein.* Many agreed with her. We'd never killed a chicken before, or any other living thing. We'd tried to adhere to our nonviolent principles and practice a nurturing sort of vegetarianism, where we respected all of Nature's children.

The Shaman spoke up: *Let's just kill the damn thing already.*

Shiva exploded. *Who are you to tell us what to do with our chickens, man? We've raised these chickens for two years and you've been here two weeks.*

And everyone started yelling. No one was listening. *You eat what you want to and I eat what I want to. I thought we stood for something out here and followed a higher law. It's just a damn chicken, a stupid bird. Look who's talking.*

They ended up killing the chicken. The Shaman had a huge knife and he held the chicken down and whacked off its head. Killing seemed to come naturally to him. Patty told me that the Shaman had slain five people, guys who owed him money or had stolen drugs from him. But she swore he'd renounced violence and wanted to live a peaceful life. They all did. They were sick of the hassles and headaches. I said I understood perfectly.

*

"Mama," Pran says.

"She's at home."

"Mama."

"Aren't you having fun, little brother?"

He starts to cry. He's probably hungry but I don't have anything for him to eat, and we're pretty far away from the cottage. Thirty minutes if I walk very fast.

"We'll be home soon," I tell him but he's wailing now. Sometimes he does this, just dissolves for no reason. And nothing can get him to stop except if he nurses. Louise is getting tired of nursing. She says her breasts are sore all the time because Pran has teeth now and will gnaw on her. *How would you like it if somebody chewed on your nipple for twenty minutes?*

I wouldn't like it.

*

I don't see Louise anywhere. The cottage is empty, so I run over to the van to check if she's working on it like she said she would. The cover in back has been lifted up and propped open with a stick, and I can see the engine inside. Somebody's been working on the car. But where did Louise go anyway?

Pran hasn't stopped crying yet. "Okay, okay," I say, trying not to sound angry but I am. I know he's hungry, so I hustle him over to the Great House to see if there's anything in the pantry he'll eat, which is doubtful. It's like he's allergic to food or something. He won't try anything.

Shiva hears him and comes running out, a concerned expression on her face. She has two kids of her own, and they trail behind her to see what the fuss is all about.

"You seen Louise?" I ask hopefully.

"She went into town with Lucas to buy a new battery for the van. What's wrong with Pran?"

"I don't know, I think he wants to nurse."

"He's hungry. I'll see if he'll chew on some bread."

Sometimes that'll satisfy him, a chunk of freshly baked whole wheat. Baking day was always one of good smells. But I can't enjoy it with Pran screaming in my ear.

"Here you go," Shiva sings, coming out of the kitchen. She hands Pran a little slice of bread. "You want some?"

"No!" I hear him declare. It's one of the few words everyone can understand when he says it.

"Let me hold him for a minute."

I slip out of the backpack and carefully set Pran on the ground. His face is red and sweaty from crying, and he looks absolutely disconsolate. If Louise went into town, it'll be an hour before she comes back. I know she wanted to wean him, but this is a bit much.

"There, there," Shiva coos, snuggling Pran against her cheek. He seems to settle down some. Shiva has the magic touch, one of those maternal women who could keep up with twenty kids. She'd been a schoolteacher at one point, at a ghetto school on the east side of Austin. "Are you sure you don't want some bread?"

I stand there helplessly hoping that Pran'll take the bread. He looks at it quizzically, as if inspecting a moon rock. For a second I fear he's going to throw it to the ground in disgust. But then he ever-so-slowly lifts the bread to his mouth and takes an uncertain nibble.

"It's a miracle," I say. My ears are still ringing from his howls. I could use a few tokes off a joint and a long, cool soak in the Blue Hole.

"Can you watch him a second?" I ask Shiva. "I'll be right back."

*

There's just enough shake from my stash of dope to roll a small, pathetic joint, but it'll do, under the circumstances. I need to get my head right. It feels like everything is crashing down on me. Louise is going to get the van started and then what the hell? She'll leave. I have no doubt about that. And I'll—I'll—I'll stay? Go? Go where? Where is she going? Back to Mommy and Daddy in Dallas? She knows I can't go back to that world, not when the pigs would still love to pop me. So what does she expect from me?

Maybe she doesn't want me to go. She doesn't seem to care one way or the other.

I hear footsteps. I take one last toke and snuff the roach out with my moist fingertips. Louise doesn't like me smoking in the cottage. She hates the smell.

But it's not Louise. It's the Shaman. And he's holding a big curved hunting knife, the same one he used to kill the chicken. His hair is soaking wet because he just came from the creek, and he has an even wilder look in his eyes, which are about to bug out of his head.

*

"Where're my reds, asshole?"

"You're what?"

"My reds. My fuckin reds, man! Somebody boosted them and the only person who knew about them was you, motherfucker."

"No, you're wrong, man. I didn't take your reds. I don't do reds."

"Where'd you get the reefer? You said you didn't have no reefer."

"I found some in a stash."

"You think I'm fuckin stupid? You think I'm some stupid fuckin hick who'll buy the trash you're sellin? I ain't no hick, got that?"

"I don't think you're a hick, man. And I didn't take your reds. I don't steal."

"That's right, because you're a nigger-lover. You think the niggers don't want to kill us all. I know people like you. Think you're better than everybody else."

"No, not true."

"You took my fuckin reds and then traded them for some dope. Who'd you trade with?"

"Nobody, man."

"First you fuck my woman, then you steal my drugs. And now you're lyin to my face."

"I didn't take anything from you. I swear I didn't."

"You got ten minutes to get them reds back to me. If you don't, you'll pay. And if you ever touch Patty again, I'll cut your dick off."

*

I run back to the Great House to get Pran and also to protect myself. I'm pretty sure the Shaman wouldn't attack me in front of witnesses. But if he tries to, there are knives and cleavers in the kitchen and I plan on grabbing a few for self-defense.

This is it: no way the Shaman can stay here. I'll tell Lucas as soon as he gets back and then we'll have to come together and have a meeting to discuss the situation. It doesn't seem possible that our noble dream of freedom and equality would come blazing down in a smoldering heap of violence and insanity. All the work we put into this place—all the sweat and tears—the babies like Pran who were born here—the music after dinner—the true togetherness—all a fading memory, because of the Shaman.

"There's Daddy," Shiva sings out. Little Pran's face lights up when he sees me, and breaks into a wide, loving smile—the kind that just melts your heart. I scoop him into my arms and pull him tight, breathing in his scent.

He has a dirty diaper.

"He might need a change," Shiva says.

His clean diapers are back at the cottage. I don't want to go back to the cottage, which is hidden away and secluded—and Pran with me, possibly in danger—the idea nearly makes me vomit.

"You okay?" Shiva asks. "You look rattled. You see a ghost or something?"

"The Shaman just threatened to kill me."

"What?"

"He pointed a knife at me and said he'd kill me. He thought I'd stolen some pills of his."

Shiva's face turns ashen. No one has worked harder than she has to make this place viable. She is the truest of true believers, still filled with all of that righteous energy that sustained us in the hardest of times. Midwife, chef, farmer, mechanic, mother, doctor, shrink—Shiva has done a little bit of everything around here. She's getting some wrinkles at the corner of her eyes that weren't there before, and the hours in the sun have bleached her out.

"He's got to go," she mutters under her breath so the children don't hear.

"I tried telling Lucas that, but he wouldn't budge. Free land for free people."

"This is different. He really threatened you?"

"It was crazy. I thought he was going to kill me."

"I knew he was a nut case. I guess this proves it."

Pran starts to cry and it's because of his diaper. I need to go change him, but I ask Shiva to get me a knife first. "A big one."

She recoils in horror. She is devoutly nonviolent, having participated in numerous sit-ins and demonstrations that led to her arrest—but she nonetheless goes into the kitchen and gets me what I asked for. In her face I can see a pall as she hands me the knife. A tear rolls down her leathery cheek.

"I'll bring it back as soon as I can," I promise.

*

I haven't changed Pran's diaper very often and I'm not good at it. Louise usually handled the task and knew where everything was and how everything worked. She was skilled at getting the dirty diapers cleaned out and washed, and she had everything organized to her satisfaction.

I lay Pran down on the rough-hewn floor of the cottage, positioning him so that I can see through the open door in case the Shaman decides to show up. I keep the big knife close at hand.

"Okay now, let's get you cleaned up," I tell Pran, just like Louise always did. He smiles at me and kicks his feet. This is exciting because Daddy is doing it instead of Mommy.

But this is a big, huge mess. And it doesn't go well with him thrashing around. I should just take everything down to the creek so I can wash everything out, child, diapers, rags—because my technique isn't working.

"Come on," I snap. I lift him up and carry him to the creek, careful that he doesn't soil my own clothes. He's not wearing any pants and he's still dirty, all over his butt and even down his legs. I have to leave the knife behind because I can't carry it and my kid down to the creek.

It's a couple hundred yards. I'll hurry down and back. I don't like being without the knife.

Patty sees me coming. She's still swimming with Laurel in the Blue Hole. She hops out and walks toward me.

*

"Need some help?"
"We had a little accident."
"Wow. You sure did."
"I'm gonna wash him up in the creek."
"Right on."
"I'm not very good at changing diapers."
"I'm an expert."
"Really?"
"From my days as a babysitter."
"Seen Tim lately?"
"He's all fucked up today. Don't know what's gotten into him."
"Did he find his reds?"

"The ones he thought you took? Yeah."

"That's a relief. He was gonna kill me otherwise."

"He gets like that sometimes."

"I thought he'd renounced violence."

"Me too. But it's hard for a leopard to change its spots."

"That wasn't very cool. It was a huge bummer, as a matter of fact. He had a knife a few inches from my face."

"He gets paranoid about people ripping him off."

"I didn't rip him off. And he knows about us, you and me."

"He's okay with it. He ain't my old man or nothing."

"Well, not exactly. He told me to stay away from you."

"Oh, he's full of it. He wants to bang your old lady in the worst way."

"No kidding. He comes by everyday and shows Louise what he's got."

"He's proud of it."

"She's not interested. It pisses her off. He's pissing a lot of people off around here."

"Fuck them for being uptight!"

"No, I mean, he needs to mellow out. He's rubbing everyone the wrong way."

"Fuck them. Like that bitch yesterday about the chicken."

"Shiva?"

"She's a cunt, acting all high and mighty. I wanted to slap her upside the head."

"She's actually a nice person."

"She's a bitch."

"All clean, buddy?"

"You need to dry him off."

"I got rags back in the cottage."

*

Patty comes with me although I don't want her to. She's more like the Shaman than I'd realized—hostile, mean-spirited, selfish. I was a dupe for ever getting involved with her—I'd allowed myself to be fooled by the illusions instead of focusing on Absolute Being and Oneness—because sex with her was brutal and hurtful, not the kind of act that brought a person closer to the wonders of Love. And Patty didn't see any of that. Couldn't see it, because like the Shaman she was filled with hatred and resentment and spite.

When we reach the top of the hill that leads up from the creek, I can see Louise off in the distance. She's walking toward us but then stops when she spots us. Then she stands with her hands on her hips, a sudden gust of wind kick up the folds of her long dress. She's pissed. The bad vibes make the hairs on my arms stand up. Still, I wave and get Pran to wave. Combat her negative energy with positive.

"There's Mommy," I say.

"Mama?"

"Oh, that's so cute!" Patty chimes in. But she's Maya, the ultimate illusion that only true wisdom can overcome. The eternal battle that the Hindus know so well.

"Mama?"

"She's way over there." I point her out. Pran starts squirming in my arms. He can't walk to her. He can barely crawl. Shiva has a daughter about Pran's age who was walking at ten months. Pran is thirteen months.

"Far out," says Patty. "He loves his mama."

You can go now, I want to say. But I don't. It would be awkward. I wish she'd get the hint and go back to the creek, go back to her freaky girlfriend and her even freakier boyfriend and the pregnant girl whose father is Elvis—I wish they'd all just disappear. But I don't yet possess true wisdom so I can't defeat Maya. So Patty keeps walking, her large, round breasts swaying with each stride, and I don't want to look. I keep my eyes fixed on Louise. She knows about Patty. She hasn't said anything, but she knows. I can hear it in her voice and see it in her eyes. That's probably the real reason why she wants to leave.

And it's almost like Patty wants to display herself for Louise— show off her young and ripe body as an act of vengeance—just like the Shaman always made a point of stopping by in the nude to display his own equipment—these two just didn't recognize any boundaries. They were transgressors, storm troupers of the soul. The bastardization of all we cared about. Love. Openness. Freedom. Equality. They besmirched these cherished notions that now nothing added up to nothing.

*

"I got the battery. Lucas is putting it in right now."

"Wow. Far out."

"I'm leaving, Quinn. And I'm taking Pran. You can come with us if you want. But to be honest I'd prefer it if you didn't."

"I can dig that."

"You should stay here because you belong here. I don't. This isn't my scene anymore."

"Let me drive you where you're going so I know you made it safe. Can I do that?"

"I don't know where I'm going. Where we're going, is more like it."

"Let me drive. I can always come back here if I want to. But I don't know if I want to."

"What about your new girlfriend? Won't you miss her?"

"No. I'll miss you, though. And him."

"Don't do this to me, Quinn. Don't make it harder. I'm about ready to lose it. This is just so scary. I don't have any money, no place to live."

"What about your parents? Could you go back there?"

"I don't want to live with them. Get real. That would be a huge drag."

"Your sister?"

"Maybe. I haven't talked to her in four years. She's married to an accountant."

"You still have friends in Austin."

"I'll be okay. Don't worry about me. I'm strong. I made it out here for two years, didn't I? No electricity, no running water, no washing machine. We'll be fine."

Taos, New Mexico
1974
61885

On my last night in Taos I decided to throw a party so that all of my friends could decorate my VW hippie van, each person painting whatever they wanted to wherever they wanted to, using any color they wanted to. My only request was that it had to be wild—wilder than wild. When I drove down the street, people had to stop and stare as I puttered on past. If they didn't, I'd consider the entire project to be a failure.

Standing out in a crowd mattered to me. I never had any desire to be average or run-of-the-mill. Ask my first husband. When we first got married, he wore his hair long and seldom bothered to put on shoes, but then he took a job with IBM and we moved to the suburbs of Phoenix, and for the next two years he expected me to be some kind of Mrs. Homemaker. No thank you. I was an artist and I was suffocating, and so I did what any sensible woman would do—divorce him. I don't harbor any ill feelings toward the man. We had three good years together, two bad ones, and we're still friends. But he bored me. I vowed never to let a man bore me again.

Taos was a funny town back in those days. The actor Dennis Hopper and his gang of crazed artists ruled the roost, so to speak. I liked Dennis. I didn't sleep with him, by the way, because he was married to a beautiful and sweet young woman named Daria, who was pregnant at the time. I didn't dare disturb the dark forces that controlled the universe by hopping into bed with her husband, although it certainly didn't stop many of my so-called friends whose moral compasses pointed in different directions than mine did. Dennis, as was well known, suffered from a form of depression, caused in my opinion by the poor performance of his last movie, called *The Last Movie,* which I heard was like watching someone remove wallpaper with a dull knife. The film flopped and he completely lost it, by all accounts. I'd been out to his ranch and had witnessed the depravity in person—the backyard littered with literally tens of thousands of broken bottles, the shards glinting in the bright sun. Young women everywhere, everyone tripping on acid—and his poor pregnant wife, sick and miserable. But Dennis was an artist, a painter and photographer, and so in my mind I could understand what he was trying to do—manipulate his consciousness, delve deeper into the abyss.

Maybe it was the altitude.

After all, Taos sat seven thousand feet above sea level and it took some getting used to, the continual lack of oxygen. I didn't like the feeling and in fact never got adjusted, perhaps one reason why I was always cranky in Taos. That and the fact no gallery would show my work. As a ceramicist, I'd developed my own quirky style, very much inspired by local Indian tribes whose lands I'd visited, including the awesome spectacle of the thousand-year-old Taos Pueblo—too derivative, I heard again and again.

So I was leaving. There was nothing that I couldn't live without in Taos. I'd enjoyed the year I spent there, especially the skiing that first winter. My advice to all women who get a divorce is simple: head for the slopes! I'd never had more fun in my life. And the men—ski instructors were a dime a dozen, and I was a free woman, beholden to no one. There were some wild nights involving me and more than one man. Yes, cocaine was involved.

I wanted to go out in style, and the idea came to me—why not have everyone over so they could add their own personal stamp to my 100% genuine Volkswagen hippie van. There was still a peace sign affixed to the front! It was adorable. I'd bought it in Austin, Texas, when I was visiting my sister, whose husband was attending medical school. I'd just filed for divorce and was feeling pretty unsure of myself—I just knew I didn't want to be anyone's hausfrau.

It was basically karma, how I came to buy the van. I was driving down the street in a seedy part of Austin because Karen had told me that was where some art studios had opened up, and I saw the FOR SALE sign in the window of an old VW microbus. There was a phone number and so I pulled over and wrote it down. I was sick and tired of driving a Mercedes, which had been a wedding present from my father, and since I was making changes in my life, I figured why not.

I called the number and spoke to a woman named Louise. I could hear a young child crying in the background. "I just want to get rid of it," she explained over the din. "It doesn't run very well and I can't afford to get it fixed, and I don't like the memories associated with it, either."

And so we talked a little more and eventually agreed to meet at a coffee shop near her house. She showed up and I was surprised by Louise's appearance. She didn't look like a hippie at all. She was dressed in casual slacks and a mock turtle neck sweater, dirty blonde hair pulled off her face, no make-up. She was a single mother, apparently, taking classes at the university to finish her degree in sociology.

"I can't stay long," she explained. "Someone's watching my son and he's a handful."

"How old is he?"

"Three."

"Oh my."

"Do you have children?"

"No, and I don't have a husband anymore, either. I'm just free as a bird these days."

"Must be nice."

"So far, so good."

"Well, I'm asking four hundred dollars for the van. It still runs, but just barely. It needs work, and as I was saying on the phone, I can't afford to dump money into it. And anyway, my parents got me some more reliable transportation. So it's time I said good-bye to the van."

"You sound sad."

She stared glumly down at her mug of black coffee. "I am, a little, I guess. A lot happened to me in that Volkswagen. Ever since 1964, when I was sixteen years old. It was my high school sweetheart's."

"Seriously?"

"Funny, huh?"

"Did you buy it from him?"

"Not exactly."

"But you still have it?"

"It's a long story, but I ended up with it when I left the commune in Arkansas last year."

"Commune?"

"Farm, was more like it. But all the land was free for whoever wanted some. Idealistic of us, huh?"

"I'll say."

"We didn't know what the hell we were doing. Oh, listen to me. Do you want to see it? Take a test drive?"

To be honest, I was ready to write a check on the spot after hearing the story of the van. As a collector of treasured objects, I had to have something that came with such a wonderful pedigree. And I'd forged such a powerful connection with Louise—two women alone in the world, trying to find our way.

Still, we walked down the street to where I'd seen the van parked in the first place, the FOR SALE sign in the window. I could feel the energy radiating from the exterior of the van, which was rather gnarled looking. Dented and scratched and mauled in places. It was singularly beautiful.

"I'll take it!" I gushed.

"Oh, far out. Sold."

We went back to the coffee shop and I wrote her check from the Merrill Lynch account. Then she handed me the keys and said, "She's all yours," her voice cracking with emotion—I could only imagine the wild times that had gone on in that van, and wondered if I'd ever get to experience half of what Louise had.

I hugged her when it was all over. Never before had a perfect stranger made such an impression on me. Louise had lived in ways I'd longed to but hadn't, for one reason or another—but never again would I miss out on life's poignant moments.

I had the hippie van towed back to Phoenix so that my mechanic could work on it and get it in tip-top shape, which cost over a thousand dollars, but no problem, because I sold my Mercedes for that amount to one of my friends in Scottsdale. Then the divorce became finalized, the house got sold, and I was adrift in the world—but not for long—because I packed up that VW hippie van and headed directly for Taos, having heard from my artist friends about the scene there.

*

For my going away party, I had invitations printed up that had illustrated palm trees with my likeness sitting beneath one, throwing clay on a potter's wheel. *SAY FAREWELL TO FAIR MAGGIE AND DON'T FORGET TO BRING YOUR PAINTS AND BRUSHES!!!*

I sent out over a hundred, to every artist in town. To Dennis Hopper and his gang. To everyone I'd befriended in Taos. At ten o'clock, exactly five people had shown up. I had food and drink enough for thirty times that number, figuring there'd be crashers—Dennis alone might bring twenty people or more. I wasn't worried, because I knew in Taos parties tended to start late and go on for days. At midnight, we'd grown to ten merrymakers. I was deliciously drunk and ready to commence the decorating.

"Okay!" I shouted. "There's just one rule. That rule is: there are no rules! Do whatever you want to it! Make it stand out!"

At first everyone was very hesitant. They looked at each other, they looked at the VW hippie van, and they looked at me for reassurance.

"Get to work!" I cried. "Hop to it!"

Someone first passed around a joint and I took a hit, ready to enjoy the festivities. Simon and Bob had come, two mad Jackson Pollack types who worked mostly in abstract forms. Neal was more representational but had a vivid palette and a unique flair; his paintings went for two hundred bucks or more and he was developing a local following. I also had a crush on him, although he never looked twice at me. Of course, my closest girlfriends were there, Mustang Sally, Jane Doe, and the Biker Babe, Lorissa, who drove a Harley—and they were the first to get to work, while their husbands stood back and watched them, muttering to themselves.

And it was magic—as soon as everyone got started on the van, the floodgates opened. More and more people came and immediately joined in the fun, and paint was flying in thick gobs all over the place. I'd been sure to put down a big tarp in the driveway, so that the asphalt wouldn't get coated. I'd wanted to make sure I got my security deposit back, but this was art! And making it was often very messy.

Within an hour I was stunned to see what my van had become: a patchwork of splashy colors and intricate designs, expressionist doodles and Pop Art cartoons. Someone had painted the outline of Florida to resemble a drooping penis. Another had painted a grotesque monster wearing a wedding dress. Yet another had put the caption "Artist On Board" beneath the peace sign in front.

It took all my strength not to break down and cry. "This is the most wonderful thing I've ever seen in my life!" I croaked, trying to hug everyone at once. I even started to doubt whether I should go or not; perhaps I'd misread Taos and the people there. "We'll miss you!" everyone was saying, and their voices sounded sincere.

"Come visit me in Key West."

"First chance!"

At about two o'clock in the morning the party started to break up. The last good-byes were said and the last promises to visit made—and then Dennis Hopper showed up, with about eight other guys, all on loud motorcycles. Dennis looked like he hadn't slept in a week, with his hair black greasy and matted and stubble covering his sunken cheeks. He was deeply tanned and attired in jeans and frayed western shirt, very cowboy-looking, complete with a pistol.

Which he brandished as he made his way to the bar and poured himself a slug of rum. "Hi, Dennis," I said, maintaining my poise. I knew better than to act flustered around him. At least he didn't have the machine gun tonight. "I'm glad you could make it."

"Wouldn't miss it for the world! What's your name again?"

"Very funny, Dennis."

"We should go fuck."

"Not tonight."

He staggered away from me and over toward the hippie van. He listed a little as he stared at it. The man possessed an incredible eye for art. He was one of the first people in the country to buy a Warhol— supposedly he picked up a Campbell's Soup Can for $75, now worth several hundred thousand dollars.

"You know what your transporter needs?" he asked me, gesturing toward the van. Transporter? What was that, I wondered.

"What, Dennis?"

"This."

He aimed the pistol and fired five times, putting five holes in the side door. The holes didn't form a straight line, but sort of trailed downward as his hand grew unsteady. The pattern resembled a wave or a gently sloping hill.

"Now it's done." Dennis Hopper gazed over at me, the smoke from the gun still swirling around our heads like misty fog. "We really should go fuck."

Key West, Florida
1975
63002

The First Part

—I've got to get out of here quick, Gordo.

Cali is standing on Caroline Street holding a tattered suitcase. The trucks are rolling out of the ice plant so I can't hear her too good. But I don't need too long an explanation. Her face tells me the whole story: something bad has happened. Real bad. Sweat's pouring down her face because the September heat is scorching. No woman eight months pregnant needs to be out in this oven. Not carrying a suitcase.

—What's going down?

—It's Manny.

—Did that bum throw you out? I told him he'd better not or it's his ass.

—No, it's worse than that.

I was just getting off work. I cook breakfast, so I'd been up since four o'clock in the morning, the hour most everyone in Key West is calling it quits for the night. Suits me, though. I like the daylight. I seen enough of the dark to last me the rest of my life. Plus, I like drinking in the afternoon. That's when the pros hone the art.

—Worse how?

—He got busted.

—Ah hell.

—He told me if he ever got busted I had to get out of here and go stay with his cousin in Miami.

—I'll buy you a bus ticket.

—No way! No bus! The pigs'll be crawling all over the station. I'm seriously about to flip out, Gordo.

That's Cali, always on the brink, always needing something from someone. What a sap I am, I used to think it was me who'd rescue her. She was barely twenty when I first saw her singing at the Full Moon Saloon on United Street. That was a tough bar, a place sometimes I was afraid to stay too long at because you never knew when there'd be a fight. Drunk deck apes would slash each other with boning knives while at the back tables the dope smugglers would settle up the latest haul, and in the middle of that craziness one night I saw a pretty brown-haired girl with bright eyes and raspy voice singing her heart out, strumming a beat-up guitar hooked to a puny box amplifier.

—You know I don't have a car.

I'd driven my Chevy Impala all the way from Buffalo and the thing died right when I crossed the bridge into Key West. I rolled it into the parking lot of the Holiday Inn and just left it there, because I had no desire to drive a car ever again. Took the New York plates off of it first, though. They're still hanging on my wall, like the way some guys have trophies of animals they've shot.

She thinks I'm a magician and can pull a car out from my top hat. She cocks her head back and lifts her chin up, giving me one of her get-real stares.

—Can't you borrow a car from someone?

—You make it sound easy.

—I told you you shouldn't have ditched your wheels.

—No, you didn't.

—Don't you have a friend with a car? What's his name? Marvin?

It takes all my strength not to pull my hair out. She knows Marvin doesn't have a car—doesn't have two goddamn nickels to rub together. He's a dishwasher and he lives at the Key West Trailer Court and he doesn't even own a bike. Couldn't ride one anyway because he weights about three hundred pounds.

—Come on, Cali. Marvin? You can't be serious.

—Shit, man. What about Bob?

—Captain Bob? He lives on a derelict sailboat. Don't you remember? He took us out there on his dinghy and made us dinner. Remember how his little TV was hooked up to a car battery?

—Captain Bob?

—Yeah. You watched that game show. *Hollywood Squares.* You don't remember?

—Stop ragging on me, because I'm freaking out, okay? I just got to get the hell out of here right the hell now. Isn't there somebody? There's like a million cars on this island.

—I'm thinking. I'm racking my brains. Rick doesn't have a car.

—Who?

—Rick. The other cook at work. Do you remember anything we ever did together?

—What about that crazy artist woman who lives next door?

—Maggie?

—Doesn't she own that VW bus with the bullet holes in it?

—She might let me borrow it. But to drive it to Miami? I don't know about that.

—We got to do something, Gordo. The fuzz is hunting me down! I don't want my baby being born in jail.

She drops her suitcase and grabs her stomach.

—What's wrong?

—Nothing. I felt something.

—Felt what?

—Something! A kick!

—Just calm down, okay? I'll figure this out.

She's not looking at me anymore. Her eyes are fixed on the shrimp boats, fewer and fewer of which could make a living anymore these days. First the navy closed its base on the island, and now the shrimp haul is in steep decline. Plus it cost a fortune to truck the catch up to Miami, and so many of the guys have turned to fishing for what they called "square grouper," the bales of marijuana that wash up on shore, jetsam tossed overboard when the Coast Guard got too close. Other captains are working with the Colombians smuggling in coke. The whole town is knee deep in dope, including Cali's current boyfriend, Manny, who apparently just got busted.

—They're gonna bust me, man, if we don't do something fast.

—That ain't gonna happen. I won't let it. I promise.

—I'm scared, Gordo. I'm really scared. My head just isn't right and I feel so sick.

She's not lying about that. One look tells me all I need to know about her physical condition. If she hadn't been pregnant, I would've told her to take a hike. But I can't do that under the circumstances.

Cali fishes a pack of cigarettes out of her beaded shoulder bag. I glare at her as she lights it. She blows the smoke directly into my face.

—It's the first one today.

—Bullshit.

—It's true.

She inhales a few more times and then stamps it out with her bare feet. She knows how I felt about her smoking with a baby on the way.

—Have you been boozing, too?

—No. Not really.

—That means yes.

—What's your deal? Who elected you sheriff of my body?

—You're not supposed to drink and smoke while you're pregnant. You promised me you wouldn't. You promised me all kinds of crap and broke your word, so what else is new.

She frowns bitterly and for a second I think she's going to turn around and walk off in a huff. But she doesn't, which meant she's really desperate and running out of options quick. I'm her last lifeline and we both know it. If I turn her away, she's screwed big-time.

We were going to get married. That might sound crazy, but it was true. And it was all my fault. I fell for her hard, as only a man approaching thirty-three can fall for a twenty-year old. She reminded me of what life had been like before I'd gotten drafted, when we all giggled through the day without a dark cloud in the sky. My girl then had been petit and brown-haired and tough as nails—my first love, my only love, who didn't wait for me to come home from the war like she said she would.

When I asked Cali to be my wife, I knew she'd say yes but the wedding would never happen. I wanted to pretend that she wasn't using me for a place to stay, and she was more than willing to play along, at least until she grew tired of the game. I knew that, when she told me she loved me, she didn't mean it. Or that she wanted to mean it, but she couldn't, no matter how hard she tried. She did try. I had to give her that much credit. For two or three months, she rattled the pots and pans and caressed me at night and connected some of the dots of my life. She wrote a few songs, fixed up an old table, and gained some weight. She looked strong and healthy, and for the first time in a long time, I was happy.

But then they started filming a movie, *92 in the Shade*, based on a book by a guy named Tom McGuane who lived right down the street from me. Cali was so excited about that, and vowed to get hired as an extra, which she did. And that's when she started to slide, because that movie crowd just binged the entire time—there were parties where you could've filled up a U-Haul trailer with pure powdered cocaine straight from Colombia. Peter Fonda, Harry Dean Stanton, Margot Kidder—this was the fast Hollywood jetset right smack in the middle of the smuggler's paradise that was Key West, and Cali got lost. She started snorting the Florida snow and spending nights away from me. She always had an excuse, like "we were shooting late," but I knew better. She was pulling away, high on the drugs, sure, but also by the idea of fame—that somehow a Hollywood big-shot would turn her into Janis Ian or Joni Mitchell—if she just slept with the right person—because that's how everyone made it in show business.

But Cali got knocked up.

At first she told me that the baby was mine, but then I had to fill her in on a little secret—I'd gotten a vasectomy right after I got back from Nam, determined never to bring another human life into this miserable world.

Her face dropped. Probably for the first time in her life she was speechless. "Don't lie about that, man," she finally managed to sputter.

"I'm not. So maybe you ought to explain what happened."

I could almost hear her rummaging around in her brain for the right comeback. But not even she could turn the table this time. She'd just assumed I'd buy her story and accept the responsibility of fatherhood, not counting on the snip job. So she was fixed and she started to sob, the one thing she knew I was powerless to defend against.

"I screwed up, man. I'm so sorry. I was so wasted I didn't know what I was doing. It didn't mean anything, I swear. I don't love him at all. Can you forgive me, please?"

It didn't hurt. I loved her, but I didn't feel any pain. I'd figured this day was coming and I wasn't surprised or caught off-guard. When something breaks, you fix it. That was all I understood about life. You had to get the right part, install it, and keep on driving.

"How pregnant are you?"

"I don't know. Two months."

"What about seeing someone, a doctor, who could help you out?"

"No way, man. I won't do that. I'm keeping this baby."

"Fine. Just be prepared for what's coming. You have no idea."

She filled in some of the details. She'd started up with one of the lighting guys on the set, a local named Manny. I didn't know him very well. I'd seen him around town a few times and knew that he was a drug dealer like everyone else in Key West. That was how he'd gotten hired onto the movie—to hold a spotlight and score the blow.

"Does he know?" I asked, and Cali shook her head furiously.

"I haven't told him yet. He's gonna wig out, man. I promised him I had everything taken care of."

She'd told me the same thing, but because of my surgery, it was a moot point. "That's a problem," I said.

"Can you do it for me?"

"No. Not on your life. This is your problem, Cali. I can't help you with that one."

"He'll be so mad at me." She closed her eyes and I sat back and wished I'd never gotten involved—but her stuff was all over my pad, and now she had to pack up and move. I didn't want her to go, but she couldn't stay. She didn't realize that, however. "I need to go crash for a while," she said, and started off for the bedroom.

"Whoa! What're you doing?"

"Crashing, man. I feel like shit."

"Go crash at Manny's."

"Seriously?"

"Cali, come on now. Do I have to spell it out for you?"

"I don't feel good, man. I'm gonna puke!" She ran off for the bathroom and I heard her retching horribly, and I knew I'd never kick her out in this condition. Most men would've been beyond angry—but I just didn't have that in me anymore. I'd hurt enough people—killed mothers and babies, too, as easy as throwing stones into a pond. So I just let her lie down and sleep, which she did, and I went for a walk to think.

The hippies were gathering at Mallory Square for the sunset celebration, and I could smell the pungent aroma of Panama red from the joints getting passed around. The local cops often came down here to bust up the musicians and performers and vendors, including the Noodle Man, who sold steaming bowls of Chinese food from a cart he'd built. I nodded to him and he gave me a friendly wave, and I almost stopped to ask him what I should do. He always struck me as a decent guy, but I didn't feel like talking, so I kept on walking.

I ended up at the Green Parrot on Whitehead Street. I sat at the bar and ordered a beer, but I wasn't in the mood to drink it. Everything inside me felt sour, like my guts were made of spoiled milk. For the first time in a long time I thought about going home to Buffalo, where the snow would be melting and soon green leaves would sprout from the bare branches—the best time. The promise of summer. Daylight until ten o'clock. Uncle Jerry's party on the 4th of July out in Elma. I missed everybody.

And it pissed me off. This whole scene with Cali had made me weak.

Finally I knew what I had to do. Alone was what I wanted to be, why I'd come to Key West in the first place, and alone I'd stay. I marched right back to my little cigar worker's shack I called home, and I was going to tell Cali that she had to leave.

I expected to find her sleeping in my bed. But my bed was empty. All her stuff was gone. She'd already moved out.

The Second Part

—Wait here. I'll go talk to her.

We're standing right in front of Maggie's VW van all painted funky colors, with the bullet holes in the side. I set Cali's suitcase down on the sidewalk. We're both panting from the six blocks we walked up William Street toward Solares Hill, the highest point in Key West, eighteen feet above sea level. I can tell Cali isn't feeling well—she's pale and sweating, and I notice how dirty her clothes are. Like she hasn't done laundry in a month.

—Hurry up, will ya?

Right across the street is a small grocery store. I reach into a pocket and pull out a crumpled five-dollar bill.

—Go buy yourself something to eat. You look weak.

She takes the money from me without saying thank you. And then something hits her, and she smiles and mutters something under her breath that sounds like *You're sweet.* I can almost see in her eyes the sparkle that used to be there, the shine of the person she was, now buried beneath the rubble of her life.

—I'll pay you back.

—Don't sweat it.

—No, I'm serious. I know I owe a hundred from before.

—Two hundred, but who's counting.

—Really?

—It doesn't matter. Go get something to eat. I'll be right back.

Maggie's house is an old mansion she's fixed up nice—for a price. One afternoon I got to talking to one of the contractors who was working on the place and he told me that she'd spent over a hundred grand. And it showed. The paint job was top-notch. The crew she'd hired took a month to finish. The trim was a combination of sky blue, violet, and hazel, and every detail of the gingerbread woodwork stood out. She's installed a new tin roof. Out in the back she's turned the cistern into a square pool and surrounded it with lush tropical plants. I live in a little shack next door, and at night I'd lie in a hammock and listen to the partying in Maggie's pool. She always had people over, and sometimes I'd peek through the jasmine to see what was going on. I felt bad because one time I saw her making it with some guy in the pool, but since she was screaming her lungs out, I figured privacy wasn't one of her top worries.

I open the gate and let myself in. Maggie's cat, one of the six-toes from the Hemingway House, comes purring up to me. I reach down and give it a nice scratch on the neck, and then follow the brick walkway around the house toward the back.

The voices grow louder. Maggie's having another party. She invited me to one once, just to be friendly, but it was obvious I didn't fit in with her crowd. She knew lots of arty types, and most of them were queer. Before I got to Key West, I didn't know any queers. But they're everywhere on the island, fixing up the old Conch houses and opening up businesses left and right—and it didn't take me long to learn that queer money spent just as good as straight money, and so I never really cared one way or the other. Everybody here just wants to be left alone—it's the one thing we all have in common.

So what the hell am I going to say anyway?

I stop walking, like I'd run face-first into a brick wall. With all these people around, I was nervous and I felt stupid even being here, knowing that Maggie wasn't close enough to me to do me a favor like borrowing her van so I could drive to Miami. Only Cali can get my head twisted around like this. The crap that chick put me through—and I was on the verge of falling for it again.

—Hello? Is somebody there?

It's Maggie. Somehow she must've heard me coming. Now what?

—It's just me, Gordo from next door.

—Oh, hi!

She rounds the corner and gives me a wave, spilling a drink. She's wearing a sarong that barely stays up. It looks like it's about to fall off and Maggie doesn't seem to mind. She gave me a tour of her house once and right by the front door is a statue she made of herself, of her nude from the waist up. Nipples and all. Life-size.

—Can I fix you a drink, Gordo?

—Sure.

I need to settle my nerves, now that I'm getting sucked in. My feet feel heavy, like bricks, as I trudge down the path, my face brushing past bamboo leaves—and it reminds me of a zippo raid we did near the Thi-Tinh River. We were just diddy-bopping through the AO like we were at Woodstock or something—I'd just snorted about a gram of smack and the bamboo leaves brushed my cheek like the silky fingers of a laughing girl—by the time we got to the village it was already burned down and a dog was barking and I sat down near a charred corpse and took off my combat infantry badge and planted it in the ground like a bad seed.

—Do you like vodka?

—Who doesn't?

—Hello!

A man is waving at me. He's small with white hair, with the face of an elf. He's sitting at a table with three other men. They all wave, too. Maggie pulls me aside, over to the bar by the back door.

—Do you know who that is?

—Who?

—That's Truman Capote. Truman Capote is at my house. And Tennessee Williams is coming over later.

—Those names sound familiar.

—They should! They're world-famous writers. And they're at my house.

She hands me a drink, her hand unsteady. She gives me a funny look, like she's checking me out. She's almost come completely out of the sarong. I try not to look. I got other things to worry about.

—Who's your friend, Maggie?

—This is Gordo! He lives next door. He's a chef!

—Really, where?

I feel my face growing red. I don't like getting put on the spot. The background is where I'm most comfortable.

—I'm a breakfast cook at Gilly's.

—I love Gilly's! Especially with a hangover. Your eggs and bacon can cut through a fog.

This entire plan is just plain stupid. I decide then and there to buy Cali a bus ticket. It makes the most sense. Chances are the cops aren't even looking for her, and if she freaks out about it, I'd even take time off from work and go with her if she wanted me to.

—Did you hear about the big bust today? They threw the entire city government in jail for selling dope! The city attorney, a bunch of cops, even the fire chief! They were all drug dealers. Isn't that delicious?

—How's anybody supposed to get any blow now?

—I'm sure by tomorrow the dust will settle and it'll start snowing again. It always snows in Key West. Somebody should open a ski lift.

—You should've seen the mountain of coke over at Calvin's last night. I thought I was in Aspen.

I m worried about Cali and I want to go check on her. I don't know why I feel so protective of her, but I always end up making her crap part of my life. Some habits are hard to break.

—Thanks for the drink.

—You're leaving? You just got here.

—I know, but I got something I need to take care of. I was just stopping by to…to say hello.

—Anytime. You don't need a formal invitation.

I rush out of there like my clothes are on fire, crashing back through the bamboo. I'm so scared and nervous I can barely breathe. It literally feels like someone's got their hands around my throat and I'm choking—I wish I didn't get these panic attacks but they come and go no matter what I do to try to calm down. I used to go to a VA hospital in Buffalo but since I got down here, I haven't bothered. I don't have any plans to set foot in one ever again.

When I get back in front of Maggie's house, I look for Cali but I don't see her. I think maybe she's still in the grocery store so I dart across William Street and duck inside the cool dark interior. The place is small, just a few rows of staple items, a candy rack, drink coolers. No Cali.

I race back outside, frantic now, drenched in sweat, my heart pounding in my chest so hard that it feels like it could come bursting through my shirt. Where the hell did she run off to? The suitcase is gone, so she took that. Why didn't she wait for me? I wasn't gone that long. My eyes strain looking down the length of William Street, but I don't see anyone who resembles Cali. I start running anyway, just to be sure. I make it maybe three strides when I stop suddenly and spin around.

The van is gone.

Maggie's van with the bullet holes. The parking space where it was is now empty. Slack-jawed, I stagger back toward this emptiness, groping blindly to understand why. Why? Why would she do something so stupid as steal a van painted a hundred different colors, the most recognizable car on the island? She won't make it past Stock Island before the cops pull her over, and then she'll go to jail for sure.

I grab my head with both hands and rake my matted, sticky hair with my grubby fingers. Just then a man rides up toward me on a bicycle. I stand aside as he hops off the bike before he reaches the curb. He hurriedly pushes the bike up onto the sidewalk and then leans it against the fence that surrounds Maggie's small front yard. The bike is perched unsteadily against the slats so it crashes down but he doesn't care. He scurries up to the front door and knocks.

—They're around back.

—Thanks! I think someone's stolen Maggie's van! I just saw it on Truman Avenue.

—No, she lent it out. It's cool.

He pauses for a second, like a wolf sniffing the air for the scent of prey. I don't flinch. I can see the indecision bleeding from his searching eyes. Slowly he walks down the steps. He stops at the bottom and listens.

—It sounds like she's having a party.

—She's got some people over.

—As usual. She's always got people over.

There's bitterness in his voice, and I figure he's one of Maggie's former boyfriends who was hoping to get back in her good graces. He keeps looking at her house like suddenly Maggie's going to come running out and beg him to come inside. The waiting makes my stomach churn, turning my guts into hamburger meat. If he decides to go back to tell Maggie about the van, then I'll be in deep shit. An accomplice. I could go to fucking jail. Why the hell did I try to cover for Cali? It's simple, really. I knew Cali's baby wasn't mine, but yet theoretically it could've been. The doctor had told me that vasectomies weren't foolproof and every blue moon the procedure fails. So there was a slim-to-none chance, yet just enough of a tether to keep me more attached than I wanted to be. At least, that's my excuse.

—I saw some chick driving her van. She seemed real upset. And young. I didn't recognize her and I know how Maggie is about her van. She never let me drive it, and we were—an item. For a little while. Do you have any weed, man? I'm just like freaking out. I've got this big art show coming up, and I just got fired and I don't have a pot to piss in. I just want to get stoned and have all my troubles go away.

—I don't smoke dope.

—Right on. I wish I didn't. Man, I got to clean up my act.

He picks up his bike and pushes it down the sidewalk toward me. His cut-off jeans are smeared with grease from the chain, big black steaks across his thighs. I just need him to get the hell out of here. But he keeps looking back at Maggie's house like he might double back any second.

—I should say hello at least. She might have some weed. Or knows somebody who does.

—I can get you some.

—Really? That's cool. I'll just stop by Maggie's for a second. I'll be back in a flash.

He puts the bike back on the fence. I can't tackle him. I've done everything I can to help Cali, and now I'm the one who's screwed. This can't go down bad for me. I can't let it. But how can I stop it? I stand there powerless, just like I did when I got inducted in 1968 and the U.S. Army gave me my TA-50, standard issue clothing and equipment, although there were antiwar hippie "draft counselors" who were begging me not to report—something swept me along anyway, the stupidity of being nineteen and thinking you're brave and tough and patriotic.

The guy suddenly stops.

—What the hell am I doing? I don't care if her van did get stolen! Fuck her! She wouldn't even put my paintings in her fucking gallery, even though I was her boyfriend, man. How cold is that? She's a heartless bitch, is what she is. Heartless. She said I only had one talent, which was screwing. She laid there like a dead fish. Come on, man, let's go get that reefer. I need to catch a solid damn buzz, is what I'm talking about. I need a job, too, goddamn it. Where do you work?

—Gilly's.

—I love that place. You guys hiring?

—Maybe. You should come down and talk to the owner.

—I should talk to somebody. My head's ready to explode. Think your buddy can front me the dope till I get paid? I don't got a damn dollar to my name.

—Probably. Can't hurt to ask.

He's got his bike again, and now he's on it, gripping the handlebars and ready to go. I go and get my bike. I keep it locked up against the fence that separates my yard from Maggie's. I can hear them laughing over there, hooting and hollering and happy as clams.

Tavernier, Florida
1975
63101

I think about the girl a lot. The one who stole the Volkswagen. Not sure why I bother. Maybe because old decrepit men like me have so little to keep our minds occupied. Especially old decrepit men who live alone like I do. But I can't help but worry about Cali. I wonder if she's okay, whether she's had that baby and just generally her overall condition and state of mind. My experience in such matters leads me to fear that my little pregnant visitor remains mired in deep trouble.

Serves her right, of course. No lady should ever find herself in that condition. We used to call such women names that start with "w" or "s." Had she kept her legs crossed, she never would've ended up in such dire straits. It's a lesson that seems to have been lost on this generation—and the one before that. I can safely assert, with supreme confidence, that on my wedding night, my bride, the love of my life, my dear departed wife, was a virgin. I don't need to divulge the private details, not withstanding the barbaric urge of the Great Unwashed to parade every indiscretion in a revolting and tiresome manner. To wit, any number of TV shows that portray depravity and debauchery with a wink and a nudge, which is why I don't have a TV. Hollywood hasn't made a decent motion picture since *The Sound of Music.* I suppose *Patton* had some redeeming qualities, but that was a true exception and five years ago.

No, I fish. And fishing presents mankind with the kinds of stark, powerful challenges that fortify the soul. I like to pole for bonefish in the flats of the backcountry, those myriad mangrove islands of Florida Bay. I prefer to do so alone, so that I might put myself to the test and push the limits of my instincts, endurance, and concentration. This ancient endeavor has been performed by hundreds of previous generations, and thus it's truly timeless, a bulwark against the slackening of resolve that comes with our too-easy and fatuous culture.

So when I found a pregnant young woman at my front door last week, even I was surprised at how I reacted. The first thing I looked at was her huge round belly, barely contained by the grimy dress she was wearing. She looked like she was ready to burst.

Excuse me, she said, I was wondering if you could lend me a hand. My car ran out of gas.

Of course, I told her. Would you like a drink of water? You look flushed.

Thanks. I had to walk farther than I thought.

I'll be right back.

I went to the kitchen and filled a highball with tap water, and then thought to add a few ice cubes from the freezer. I noticed my hands were shaking. I wasn't nervous, but something was obviously spooking me. Perhaps it was her youth—and the fact that the father of the child she was carrying had allowed her to drive around alone in this condition. I hadn't noticed a wedding ring. All too typical.

Here you go, I said as graciously as I could when I returned. She was standing in the same spot, eyes wide and puffy, like she'd been crying.

Thanks. I really appreciate it.

Where's your car?

Back on U.S. 1 about two miles.

You ran out of gas?

I don't have any money.

None?

Not a dime.

Really? What about your husband? Doesn't he work?

I'm not married. I'm not anything. I'm nothing. I'm dirt.

Don't say that.

It's true. I'm in so much trouble, it'd make your head spin.

What kind of trouble?

I just need some gas. I've got a place to stay in Miami. I'll be okay there. I just need to get going.

So you need to borrow money? Have I heard you correctly?

I'll pay you back, I swear! Every last penny! I never screw people over, ever. Just write down your address and I'll mail it to you the first chance I get.

When's the baby due?

A couple weeks. Please, I know I'm just barging in and you must think I'm totally nuts, but I'm not a bad person. I just need to get to Miami. Please help me.

*

Chivalry is a lost art. Men of my generation were taught to help women in need, no questions asked. We'd think nothing of stopping on the side of the highway if we saw a woman struggling to change a blown tire. Nowadays, the more likely outcome would be for some pervert to pull up and expose himself or even kidnap and rape the woman. I might sound jaded, but I served as a district court judge for twenty-two years, from 1951 to 1973, and during my tenure on the bench I saw nothing but a parade of miscreants, so I'm keenly aware of what the dregs of society are capable of. There is no bottom. No act of depravity shocks me anymore. I came to expect it. What had been rare in 1958 had become commonplace by 1968, and when I couldn't tell the men from the women anymore, I knew it was time to finally retire once and for all. Back in 1963 we'd bought some property in Tavernier, ten miles south of Key Largo, right on the water, and built our dream getaway. We scrimped, we saved, we cut coupons, we collected green stamps, we drove used cars, all so we could afford our little piece of heaven in the Florida Keys. We didn't ask anybody for anything. We did it ourselves, my wife and I. She was tough-minded, a child of the Great Depression like I was, and she knew the value of a dollar. While my colleagues would fritter money away on golf memberships and luxury cars and expensive vacations, my wife and I trusted that our reward would be the two acres of waterfront we owned, where one day we'd live in a tropical paradise, with nothing to worry about except sun-burn.

But she passed away last year, after a two-year battle against breast cancer. I made sure that she could spend time here, though. I hired a nurse to be with her around-the-clock, and each night I wheeled her out to the dock, near the chairs we'd positioned to watch the sun set. We were allowed by our Creator the chance to witness the coming of night a sum total of forty-one times. Then she just got too sick to be here and I had to drive her back home to Raleigh, so that she could spend her last days at home.

*

The first place we had to stop was a gas station, so that meant driving up to Key Largo to the Esso station across from the Chica Lodge. I kept a small one-gallon gas tank in the trunk for just this situation, in case I should ever run out of gas. I remember buying it during the Arab oil embargo two years back, when it seemed like the world was on the brink of collapse—Helen had just been diagnosed, and we were driving to Durham quite frequently so she could consult with oncologists at Duke Medical Center. But suddenly gas stations were running out of fuel! There were signs everywhere: NO GAS. *What has this country come to? Can someone answer that question?*

And Helen told me: *Calm down, Sed. We'll be okay.*

What's your name? I asked her as we drove.

Cali.

Where are you from?

Pennsylvania.

Beautiful country. I once drove my family to Gettysburg. Have you been?

No.

Oh, you should go. Every American should go.

I always wanted to.

It stirs powerful emotions. The fate of the republic hung in the balance. Quite literally. One can almost smell the gunpowder.

But she wasn't listening. She was chewing on her nails and looking out the window at the passing landscape, just like my daughter used to when I'd try to edify her about our nation's history. Janet would glance around and mutter under her breath and act as if I were torturing her—she had a rebellious streak, a stubbornness that bordered on outright defiance—and I could only imagine that Cali's parents felt the same way about her.

*

I saw the lights of the police car before I saw the van.

Shit, Cali barked, sinking low in the seat next to me. Keep driving.

What? Why?

Just keep driving. I'll explain everything.

I did exactly as she told me, cruising past the police car pulled up behind the garishly decorated Volkswagen van. An officer was standing beside it, peering inside. I read the lettering on the side: BUTTERFLY ART STUDIO. Then I glanced over at Cali, who had pearls of sweat rolling down her flushed cheeks. She looked stricken, beset by unspoken troubles that had apparently blown up in her face.

After a few minutes we were a safe distance from the police. I pulled into the crushed shell parking lot Betty's Good Eats, which had closed long ago. I stopped the car but left it running so the air conditioning could keep Cali cool. I didn't want her to overheat.

Well? I asked. What's happening? Are you in trouble with the law?

No.

Cali, why didn't you want to stop and ask the police why they were inspecting your parked vehicle?

Okay, sir. I'll tell you why. You know why? Because I stole it, that's why. I stole it because people are after me, dig? I had to get out of Key West fast and that was the only way. I wasn't going to keep it. I swear I wasn't. I was just borrowing it.

She started crying, great heaving sobs that caused my jaw to clench. I was on the verge of becoming an accomplice after the fact to grand theft auto, a serious felony. I'd sent men to prison for five years on such offenses, more than I could count. The only responsible thing I could do was turn her in. After all, the rule of law had guided me through my life, a shining beacon I never once questioned because it had never led me astray.

You've done a terrible thing, I told her. You've committed a crime.

I know I have.

Her sobs turned to sniffles. She was regaining her composure, which I was glad to see. I gave her a Kleenex so she could dry her eyes. Helen always made sure our vehicles were well-stocked with tissues, and I'd kept up the practice out of habit.

I'm a retired judge, I said wistfully. An officer of the court.

Are you going to bust me?

I should. I took an oath to faithfully uphold the law. And you've placed me in a very difficult situation. Do you understand that if I don't report you to the authorities, I myself will have committed a felony?

I'm sorry. I didn't mean to. It was just dumb luck. A retired judge. Wow. That blows my mind. Just let me go, okay? This never happened. You just drive home and I'll figure something else out. Please? I can't go to jail. They'll take my baby away from me.

I can't just turn you loose in the middle of nowhere. I couldn't live with myself.

But you could send me to jail?

I've sent thousands of people to jail. I know you'll be safe there. Maybe you'll get your life together. Do you use drugs? Is that what happened?

But she didn't answer. She was sitting there with her eyes closed, her mouth set in a fierce grimace, like she was pulling a few g-forces.

Cali?

I don't feel so good.

You don't?

No, I don't. I feel dizzy. Real dizzy.

She was grabbing her stomach and I got worried. Mariner's Hospital wasn't far away, just a few miles up U.S. 1. I knew I needed to take her there so that she could receive medical attention. Women in her condition could take no chances.

I'm taking you to the hospital, I said in an even tone. The last thing I wanted to do was cause her to panic. She'd been under enough stress. God only knew all that she'd put herself through. I doubted that she would make a good mother. Her poor judgment spoke for itself, and I thought to myself that society would benefit from Cali not keeping this baby. I'd seen many unfit mothers in my time on the bench, and she qualified for that dubious distinction.

We drove past the van. Another squad car from the Monroe County Sheriff's Office had joined the first. Had I stopped, I could've solved the mystery for them. But there wasn't time to stop. Cali was in clear and eminent danger, and any delay in getting her treatment would've been negligent on my part. In fact, protocol dictated that I not stop, and for some reason I felt relief wash over me. I even looked over at Cali and smiled.

We'll be there soon, I told her. You just hang on.

*

I waited at the hospital for over an hour until finally a nurse came out and notified me that Cali was resting comfortably, although since I wasn't listed as next of kin, the hospital could provide me with no other information. I asked if I could see her and the nurse said that she was in intensive care, which had a no visitation policy except for immediate family.

What about the baby?

The nurse said she couldn't tell me anything.

So I left. But I didn't drive home. No, I went to the spot on U.S. 1 where the Volkswagen had been. A nagging sense of guilt still tugged at me, that I'd committed a felony, that I still needed to report Cali's actions.

But the van was gone. The squad cars were gone, too. The shoulder of the Overseas Highway looked just as it always did, with clumps of mangrove growing tight against the asphalt, and the sparkling blue waters of Florida Bay hovering in the background. Tomorrow would be a good day to fish.

I turned around and headed home.

Key West, Florida
1978
75221

Maggie decided to raffle the van off, but of course she was going to do so in style, with flair, and invite everyone on the island to come join her at The Copa for her lavish going-away party. I promised her I wouldn't cry, which was going to be next to impossible because my whole world was in ruins. I'd worked with Miss Maggie at the Butterfly Art Gallery for the past two years, and we'd become inseparable, despite the obvious differences between us. But we had one thing in common: men. And the same luck with them: rotten.

I met her at her house and helped her pack up the party favors, the kazoos and the streamers and balloons, the cake she'd baked herself, and of course the raffle tickets she was going to pass out at the door and the big punch bowl from which she'd pluck the winner. The way the van was running, however, the "winner" was looking at a large auto repair bill.

"You didn't have to help me, Jamie," she said, but I told her to please shove it.

"I'll always be your loving slave, like Spartacus," I replied.

"Very funny. Didn't Spartacus rebel or something?"

"Talk about a rebel, honey. What's with the Dolly Parton look tonight?"

Maggie was wearing a white jumpsuit studded with rhinestones with four-inch platform shoes and her hair all piled up in a wild swirling mass, and I told her the truth: she looked like a drag queen from Fire Island who got lost at J.C. Penney's. "In other words, dear," I explained, "you look smashing. Simply smashing."

She smiled bravely but I knew well enough that leaving Key West wasn't her choice. Her mother had fallen ill and required care, and since Maggie wasn't married and had no children, she was relocating to relieve her bitch sister from lifting a finger to help. So Maggie had sold her business to a queer named Leon whom I didn't trust and wouldn't work for, and she was moving back home to New Jersey. I begged her to take me with her but she politely told me that I was insane. "No one in her right mind would ever leave this place," she said.

But the party was epic, as nights at The Copa usually were. I'm pretty sure that I deviated my septum doing a mountain of coke, and then running out to the dance floor to boogie to Donna Summer beneath the huge spinning disco ball. A nice boy from Miami kept following me around like a lost puppy, clutching his raffle ticket and telling me that I shouldn't wear polyester with my girlish hips. But he had an endless supply of blow, so I meekly listened to his sartorial advice that he was only too happy to dispense.

At the stroke of midnight, the music stopped and Maggie came over the sound system to tell us that the raffle was commencing. She was standing up in the DJ's booth over the dance floor, hovering above us like the regal angel that she was, holding that big punch bowl stuffed with tickets. Everybody was so blitzed that I didn't know how on earth this would play out. I didn't have a ticket, because I didn't want the van. Not at all my style, and too many dear memories within it.

"69!" she called out. "Does anyone have 69?"

There was uproarious laughter, of course, and someone shouted, "No, but I'm looking for some 69, too!"

Then this cowboy-looking man I'd never seen before started waving his raffle ticket and strutting around like he was some kind of hot shot in his faded denim jeans and lumberjack shirt. "I got it right here!" he crowed in delight. A dew-eyed brunette hung on his arm, huge loop earrings dangling almost to her bony shoulders.

I looked up at Maggie. She was squinting down, trying to recognize the new owner of her van. It was obvious she didn't know this person and probably hadn't invited him, but she soldiered on, showing her usual grace and poise, no matter what the circumstances.

"And who, pray tell, are you, sir?" she asked over the loudspeakers.

"Hugh Jardon!" he cried out. Did he say what I thought he said? Huge Hardon? No, couldn't be.

Maggie didn't miss a beat. "Well, Huge, tonight's your lucky night!"

Then the music came back on and we all crowded on the dance floor, and wouldn't you know, within minutes Huge or Hugh, or whatever his name was, and Maggie were dancing together and the brunette was nowhere to be seen. When she saw my jaw hit the floor, she gave me a playful wink. Fifteen minutes after that, Maggie and the cowboy were both gone.

I had my suspicions. I knew where the van was parked, behind The Copa in the alley that ran toward Simonton Street. I ducked out quickly just to satisfy my curiosity, and it didn't take long for verification. "Maggie, you slut," I muttered happily under my breath. "At least you're getting some." That van was rocking, and I didn't bother knocking.

Big Pine Key, Florida
1980
00000

I wished I could've pulled over. I'd been watching the odometer for weeks, waiting for this special moment. 100,000 miles and still going strong. But we were in a hurry. We had a long drive ahead of us and we were going to do most of it at night so Nirvana could sleep. She was dozing away, nestled on a little mattress we'd set up. She looked just like an angel. Six years old and sweet as sugar.

"Damn," I said. "The odometer just turned over. It's all zeroes again. Check it out."

Leah leaned over and looked at the instrument panel. "Wow," she said, not sounding very impressed.

"I guess I'm just being sentimental."

"Maybe it's a sign of good luck. Our stars are aligned. For once."

I felt sad when the straight zeroes disappeared. It was like hitting the slots or something—there should've been a big prize. A million bucks, a Caribbean cruise. Instead we were on U.S. 1, headed for Jackson Hole, Wyoming. We were pretty sure we could find jobs there, because we sure weren't having much luck in Key West. The island was dead. Almost all of Duval Street was boarded up, and the junkies had moved in. The last straw was when I got laid off. We had to do something drastic and this was it. December 6, 1980. We'd make it out West in time for the skiing season, when the restaurants would be hiring.

"We got nowhere to go but up," I said cheerfully. "The only thing that worries me is this van. It's running good, but it's old. It could quit on us. And I don't have the cash to fix if it did."

"It'll make it. I have a good feeling about this van. It'll take care of us. Won't you, sweetheart?" Leah petted the dashboard like she was stroking a purring kitten.

"Sure she will."

"Have you named her yet?"

"No. Was I supposed to?"

"I always give my cars a name. Don't you?"

"Can't say I've ever done that."

"How about Bernice?"

"What's that again?"

"I knew this tough girl in high school named Bernice. She could beat up all the boys. Even the football players."

"Bernice it is."

We slowed to drive through Big Pine Key, which was interesting because the island was home to the little Key deer that got run over by cars in large numbers. Signs were posted warning you to be on the look-out for them. It would've sickened me if I hit one. Talk about rotten karma. And they just darted out in front of you, too, so you didn't have much chance to stop. Especially at night.

"Watch it!" Leah cried. She pointed over toward the shoulder. I saw a runty white-tailed deer poised by the side of the road. I hit the brakes and waited until the deer had crossed the street.

"No wonder they don't stand a chance," I said. "They're sitting ducks."

"What happened?" Nirvana asked from the back.

"Nothing, baby. Go back to sleep."

"Did Hubert hit something?"

"No, baby. Everything's fine."

I gave her a big smile. She wasn't my daughter but she might as well have been. Her biological father had been Leah's high school sweetheart but he was a junkie and Leah had no idea where he was now. One day I'd adopt Nirvana. But first we had to see how things went with Leah. Neither one of us had had much success in relationships.

I kept my eyes peeled for any sign of deer until we finally got to the bridge to Bahia Honda, when I could relax a little and just watch the moon shining over the glittering waters I'd miss with all my heart. I came down to Key West in 1973 with nothing, and here I was leaving with a whole family.

We were just losing radio reception from Key West and since Leah hated static, she was about to turn it off when the DJ came on and said that John Lennon had been shot and killed. "Did you hear that?" Leah cried.

I didn't answer. I couldn't answer. The radio faded to static and Leah turned the dial searching for any reception, but we were literally in the middle of nowhere.

Jackson Hole, Wyoming
1984
11175

In 1984 I saw myself as the ultimate in cool, the owner of a real hippie van with a peace sign emblem in the front and half-smoked roaches in the ashtray. There were even bullet holes in one of the doors, which I found endlessly fascinating. And the paint job! Bizarre! Lots of weird designs and a mishmash of colors, most of them faded out. I loved it.

I'd paid seven hundred bucks for my van, getting it from a guy at work everyone called Chill. Chill's real name was Hugh, so I playfully called him Hubie and he didn't seem to mind. He was in his forties, one of those lean cowboy types who go gray at the temples and whose skin turns to the shade and texture of brown leather. Chill worked in the kitchen as a prep cook and I could tell he liked me because he teased me about being a klutz. I'd never been a waitress before, so at first I was making all kinds of mistakes on my orders and bringing back food constantly. The other cooks didn't like me very much because I made their jobs harder, but Chill would just smile and shake his head. "The Professor strikes again," he'd say. That was my nickname, the Professor, because I went to college. Everybody else was basically a ski bum waiting for the return of snow.

Chill told me a little about the van. He'd gotten it in Key West and had fixed it up some, and drove it out west back in 1980 when he was ready for a change. But the van didn't have what it takes to make it in the mountains during winter, so he wanted a pickup with all-wheel drive.

Before a shift I saw him putting up a flier on the bulletin board in the back by the manager's office, and as soon as I read it, I offered to buy it on the spot.

"Are you sure, Professor?" he asked me, as I clapped my hands and jumped for joy. I'd been driving the same boring car since high school and it was time for a change—and what could be more awesome than Chill's old hippie van?

"I'm totally positive! I'll write you a check. Oh, my checkbook's back at my apartment. Tomorrow! I promise, Hubie. Don't sell it to anyone else. I swear I'll write you a check."

"I guess your word's good."

"As good as gold."

I couldn't wait to tell Bret. We were supposed to meet up at the Cowboy Bar after we both got off work, and he'd be so surprised because he didn't think I was very adventurous. For example, he was positive I wouldn't spend the summer in Jackson Hole, and to be honest I almost didn't come. Daddy had arranged an easy job for me back in Denver, and normally I would've gone with the family for a week's vacation at our mountain place in Steamboat—but instead I convinced my best friend Kaki to say screw it and have a blast out here with me. Bret was the most shocked person in the world when he saw me stroll into the Cowboy Bar for the first time. We bet five bucks that I'd blow him off, and I made him pay up on the spot.

*

Bret and I always made sure to watch the sun set in Jackson Hole whenever we could. We'd drive the Magic Bus outside of town to a secluded little spot overlooking the Snake River, in the valley between the Grand Tetons and Pyramid Peak, and right when the sun would sink below the rocky crag, we'd kiss and light a joint. Then we'd crawl into the back of the van where we had a futon mattress and a big quilt, and we'd make love. I never wanted that summer to end. Bret and I basically lived together since we hung out every single night, and we never once fought. Never once. The whole summer was like a dream, the happiest days of my life. I was madly, deliriously in love with Bret, and he said he was in love with me, too. So much so that he wanted to get married. To elope. To run away forever.

"We could live in this van and drive all around the country," he told me with utter sincerity. "We'd get odd jobs for money and then move on to the next place. We could live in all fifty states. Wouldn't that be awesome?"

"Yeah, it would."

"So let's go."

"I can't do that, Bret."

"Why not?"

"What about school?"

He rolled over onto his back and stared up at the ceiling. "I don't need anymore school. I've had enough school. I want to live life, not study it."

"Couldn't we do it after we graduate?"

I tried to get him to look at me. Finally he did.

"If we don't go now, we'll never go."

It was almost as if he were testing me, to see what I was truly made of. Was I willing to take my future and trash it? Was I willing to renounce the comforts of my suburban existence and join him on his quest for limitless adventure? He was pressuring me into a big decision and not really cutting me much slack. I'd come with him to Jackson Hole, turning my back on my family, but Bret wanted more. He wanted everything, and I wasn't sure I could give him everything. I was just twenty, and deep down I still wasn't sure who I was or what I wanted.

"We could still go after we graduate," I countered bravely. "I mean, I will if you will."

"That's not how it works, Amanda. You graduate, then you get a job, then you get a car, and then you get a house, and all of a sudden, you're finished. It's over. Your life is over."

"Not for me it won't be. I won't be like that. Neither will you."

"Come with me right now, Amanda. We'll get married in Vegas. You'll have a blast, I promise. You won't regret it."

We were lying naked in the back of the van. The windows were rolled down and dark was just descending into the valley in inky jets. Somewhere a coyote started howling, and I remember feeling very scared at that moment. Bret was asking me to stay with him forever, and in my heart I knew I loved him. But something prevented me from saying yes. And nothing was the same between me and Bret again.

Denver, Colorado
1984
12099

When Amanda came back home at the end of the summer she spent in Wyoming, Paul took one look at the VW van she was driving and nearly died. I was taken aback, too. How had that thing made it to Denver? Was our daughter out of her mind? What had possessed her? Amanda was always so reasonable, unlike her younger sister who made rash decisions and drove us crazy with her antics. But Amanda? Amanda was reliable. Amanda was trustworthy. Amanda had a good head on her shoulders.

After the initial shock wore off, Paul and I tried to gather our thoughts. Amanda stood beaming, proud as could be.

"Has it been inspected, sweetie?" Paul asked as he circled around the van, eyes bugging out of his head. "It looks like it's about to fall apart."

"No, it runs great! I swear it does. It just needs a new paint job." Amanda sounded the same as always, happy and confident. But it wasn't like her to go off half-cocked. Her boyfriend must've been behind all this. That was my theory anyway.

"We should have a mechanic look at it. Just to be on the safe side. I'd hate for something to happen."

"Nothing's going to happen!"

"Amanda," I corrected her. "Daddy's right. We should play it safe. You're more valuable than some silly hippie van."

"It's not silly."

Paul went over and draped his arm around Amanda's shoulders. "Sweetie, I totally understand where you're coming from. I was around during the Sixties, don't forget. Your mother and I, we did some pretty crazy things back in the day. We took you and your sister to antiwar rallies when I was at law school up in Ann Arbor. Our best friends, the Baughman's, they drove a van just like this one. With the peace sign and everything."

"It didn't have the bullet holes," I added.

"No, no bullet holes. But they loved that thing."

"Just like I do." Amanda did have a bit of a stubborn streak in her. When she got stuck on something, she stayed stuck and it was hard to pry her off.

"But they sold it," Paul continued. "They didn't think it was safe enough. The engine's in the back and if you ever got into a head-on collision—sweetie, I've worked on cases involving those kinds of crashes. If you saw what I've seen, you'd understand. Not a pretty picture."

"Daddy, I love this car! I paid for it with my own money and everything."

"That's admirable. That's more than admirable. That's outstanding. But that makes it no less dangerous to drive."

"When your time's up, your time's up," she replied in what I considered an insulting tone of voice. Since when did she become so fatalistic?

"Amanda, now come on. That's ridiculous." I hated being cross with her, considering she'd been away all summer and was headed back to school in a few days. Soon enough she'd fly the coop for good, and at the rate she was going, she'd probably never come home to visit.

"I'm not giving it up," she said angrily. "No matter what. Case closed."

"Sweetie, let's get it inspected," Paul tried again. "Will you do that? Can we at least establish some basic facts? And what about the title? Do you have that?"

"The what?"

"The title. The document that shows you have clear ownership of the vehicle."

"I don't know. Maybe. I haven't looked."

Paul raised his eyebrows in consternation. Amanda hated disappointing him. Even as a baby, Paul was usually the one who could get her to stop crying. "Okay, okay," she finally relented. "Let's have it inspected. I'll get it registered in my name and make sure it's legal and all that."

"That's a good idea, sweetie."

Well, the inspection turned up all kinds of issues, and the repairs were going to be expensive and time-consuming, and Paul was clear that we wouldn't pay for them. But he made Amanda a counteroffer: to off-set her investment in the van, he'd buy her a brand-new BMW. A 325i. Which meant Amanda had to get rid of the van, of course.

I'd never seen Amanda so upset before. She secluded herself in her room and talked on the phone for hours with her mysterious boyfriend from California, Bret Lewis. I personally liked Bret, although to many, including my husband, he came across as, well, strange. He wore ripped clothing to make some kind of fashion statement, and his hair was very long in back but quite short in front, an odd combination that made Paul wonder about the boy's sanity. He honestly worried that poor Bret was mentally unstable, but I knew better: he was simply an English major, nothing more, nothing less. I tried to remind Paul of some of the more colorful bohemians we'd known back during our undergraduate days in Boulder.

I also had to remind Paul that Bret's parents were very successful, pioneers in the computer industry and extremely wealthy, despite Bret's ripped clothing and bizarre tonsure. He wasn't a bad catch, in my opinion. Paul remained unconvinced.

After days and nights of tears, one afternoon Amanda emerged from her room and announced that she'd worked out a solution to the problem of the van. Bret had offered to buy it. In fact, he was flying out the next day so that he could claim possession of it. "That way it'll stay in the family," she happily concluded.

"Whose family?" I asked pointedly. I lived in fear of her running away and eloping with Bret, so in love was she with him. Paul was ready to hire a private investigator to dig into Bret's background, just in case.

"Mom, you know what I mean. Bret loves the van as much as I do. He's going to drive it from here down to Tucson. How cool is that?"

"Are you going with him? What about your new car?" The BMW that Paul promised to get her.

"I'll drive it. We'll follow each other."

I couldn't object to that plan, because at least Amanda would be returning to the University of Arizona—although we'd offered her a year in Paris so that she could study abroad. Which she turned down, of course. To be with Bret. Foiled again.

And so we got Bret's room ready. He'd be staying for two nights, and I made Paul promise me that he'd be on his best behavior. No baiting the boy into arguments, no lectures on virtue, no sighs or groans or rolling of the eyes—not that Paul could ever be rude, but I wanted him to know that he was on a short leash. It was joyous just to see Amanda happy again, our beautiful but willful daughter whose smile usually lit up the entire house.

Amanda put up a Grateful Dead poster in the spare bedroom, and insisted it would remain up during Bret's visit no matter what, case closed. I didn't pretend to understand this hippie phase Amanda was going through—the incense she burned in her room, the overly pungent patchouli she wore, the tie-dyed shirts she made, the cheap necklaces she brought back from Mardi Gras—I hadn't even known about that little excursion, and I wasn't thrilled that her GPA had fallen from a decent 3.3 to below 3.0. I told her that all the Grateful Dead she was listening to had softened her brain. Two days later, she was off for Jackson Hole. To be with Bret.

*

We saw precious little of Bret during his brief visit. Amanda whirled him madly around Denver, stopping only long enough to sleep a few hours. It didn't seem she was packed and ready to head back to school, but Amanda always surprised me by how quickly she could pull herself together in a pinch.

Then it all collapsed.

Bret got in the van and drove away, without saying good-bye or thank you or anything. It was a Sunday morning, and Paul and I had offered to take the kids out to brunch at the country club. After all, we hadn't seen or heard much from Bret, and we both wanted to get to know this young man a little better.

"What's going on?" I asked Amanda, who came bursting back into the house in hysterics. She was sobbing uncontrollably, and she ran away from me and up to her room when I tried to console her.

"Let her go," Paul counseled me.

"Did they break up? Is that it?"

"One would assume so."

"But they were having so much fun. Weren't they?" I was on the verge of tears myself, feeling ferociously sad on the inside in sympathy for the pain Amanda must've been experiencing—the worst sort of pain there is, the end of love that crushes the young heart. I wanted to hold her until the hurt stopped—if it ever did.

"I never liked that kid," Paul offered spitefully. "Now look what he's done."

"I can't stand this. I'm going up there."

I walked up the stairs and stood outside Amanda's room for what seemed like hours waiting for her tears to abate enough so we could talk. Finally the sobs gave way to a more subdued whimpering, and I knocked. "Amanda, honey? Please let me in."

It took a few more entreaties, but she relented and opened the door. I cradled her in my arms and wiped the moist tears from her cheeks.

"He's going to Mexico!" she blurted out. "Without me!"

"What? Bret is? What about school?"

"He's dropping out. He said I couldn't come. He had to go alone."

"You were thinking of going to Mexico, too?"

"I don't know. Maybe. I wasn't sure."

I shuddered to imagine the two of them in Mexico, getting into gobs of trouble. It scared me to think she was ready to jump off a cliff with him. "You made the right decision, honey. You need to finish college. That's the most important thing in the world."

"I never thought he'd do this to me."

"He's coming back, isn't he?"

"Maybe. Who knows? I don't care. He's a jerk. I hate him!" Then she started crying again, and Paul came into the room. When Amanda saw him, she broke away from me and pointed an accusing finger at her father. "It's your fault!" she cried. "If only you'd let me keep the van, none of this would've happened."

"Oh, honey, don't blame your father," I interjected. "The van had nothing to do with it."

"It did, too!"

"Bret wasn't the right boy for you. If he was, he'd still be here, wouldn't he?"

"Everything happens for a reason," Paul said solemnly. "Never forget that. When a door shuts, a window opens."

"And I feel like jumping out."

"Oh, Amanda! Don't even think that!"

Without another word she stormed out and into the spare bedroom and yanked down the Grateful Dead poster.

Zihautanejo, Mexico
1984
14552

The crazy American boy. I meet him on the beach, La Ropa. It was Saturday in October, no school. I was bored. Only place fun was La Ropa. I walk two miles from my house, past the basketball court where the men play each night, then up the hill and down, past the woman who made the best tortillas, over the bridge, and then the hotels on the beach.

I love swimming. Especially on weekend when there's nothing to do. I float on my back and look up at the blue sky and the white clouds streaming across. The rains had just ended, and now the sun was back. Forty days and forty nights it rained, like in the Bible. The streets flood up to my thighs, and nothing gets dry. But now it was very, very nice.

I was sixteen. I wanted to see my friends, so I go up and down the beach searching. Where are they? They said they come today. The sun has blessed us again, and a gentle breeze blowing in from the ocean. But I'm alone. Still better than being at home, where my brothers are, my brothers who tease me and pull at me, and my mother who makes me work. Alone does not bother me. I go swimming and float, but then I think maybe I should go to Los Gatos beach. Farther away. Around the point, over some rocks, no hotels.

I do not know why I go. I feel like exploring. *Intranquila*, my mother called me. Restless. True. My dream was to see the world, every inch, every rock and pebble, every mountain and valley. The adventurous one. *L'aventurera*. That was I. Unafraid. Always wanting more.

So I went to Los Gatos and I saw only a few American tourists on blankets. I was taking English class at school so I could get good job at hotel, so I wanted to practice. But I said nothing as I walked by. They were older and married and not interested in me. Lots of little Mexican kids sold bracelets on the beach, and they mistake me for them. I don't know. I left Los Gatos and went back to La Ropa.

My friends still were not anywhere. Now what? My brothers and their friends were playing soccer on small beach next to La Ropa, a beach no one went to except us locals. It was big enough for sandy field and twenty boys would play soccer on it for hours and hours. I decide to go there.

But then I saw the crazy American boy. He was in front of the Hotel La Ropa, reading a book. He looked young and was alone. I walked near him on the beach and stopped and pretended to gaze out at the ocean.

"Buenas dias," he said.

"Hello," I replied.

"Do you speak English?" he asked.

"A little."

"What's your name?"

"Lupita."

"My name is Bret."

He then asked me some more questions and I couldn't understand him. So then he tried talking to me in Spanish and I couldn't understand him much better. But he had a quality I liked, a kindness and openness that many Americans do not possess. He was blonde and very tall, unlike the short and dark men in the state of Guerrero. Prince Charming, I thought.

"How old are you?" he asked me in Spanish. I decided not to lie. Some girls would have, but I cannot.

"Sixteen."

He nodded his head. I wasn't sure he understood. But I didn't care. Something inside was bursting, becoming alive. I liked this boy named Bret. "Meet me at the plaza at seven," I said in Spanish. I had to repeat myself several times. There was a fiesta tonight and I was going to attend, and I wanted to show my friends this American boy who talked to me on the beach.

*

I put on a denim skirt and a white top, and added to my lips some glitter balm. I wished my hair was not jet black but I would never dye it like some. Too lazy for that. And I was nervous. What if Bret actually came to the plaza? What would we do or talk about? He barely spoke Spanish, and I spoke even less English. Why would he bother with me?

But it was exciting. The most exciting thing that had ever happened to me. I could have had a Mexican boy, but I didn't like the friends of my brothers. They were typical. They had no dreams beyond soccer. They cared nothing for the world. I wanted more, so much more.

The plaza was crowded. A band was playing and the entire town had come to listen and eat and dance. I kept walking around looking for Bret, ignoring my friends who asked me what was wrong. I could never explain. It would make no sense.

Right at seven o'clock, though, I checked my watch and then Bret appeared. Out of nowhere. We smiled at each other. I could tell he liked me. I was no more sweaty and dirty from the beach. I was clean and pretty.

We spoke Spanish. He must've spent a few hours studying because he had more to say. He told me he was an author and he was writing a novel. He said he lived just down the street in a small room. He said he was from California. He said these things as if he had memorized the lines, because if I asked him a question, he could not answer it.

We talked for maybe ten minutes. But what I wanted to do was kiss him. So I reached out and grabbed his hand. He appeared surprised that I would do that, but then he led me away and we walked back to his room. It was in an apartment two blocks from the plaza. A concrete building with a balcony that hung over the street. In front of the building there was a strange car, a van, with California license plates on it.

I pointed to it. "Your automobile?" I asked in English.

"Yes!" He seemed very glad to show it to me. I wanted him to take me for a ride in it. So I went to the van and looked it over carefully. It was very dusty.

"Very nice," I said in English.

"Come on," he said, opening the door for me. My heart was pounding. This American was a stranger, yet I was getting into his van! I didn't care. I trusted him. He was an author. A woman should not take risks with men, and if my own daughter ever does something like that, I would want to kill her. Yet something pushed me, a force I didn't understand—the same force that has taken me here to San Antonio, Texas—the force that led me to the van with Bret. The desire for a different life.

We drove. He didn't know where to go and I couldn't give him good directions, either. My family owned no vehicles. We headed out along the road to Ixtapa, and then turned around and came back, the windows down and the cool night air blowing in our faces.

He parked in the same spot in front of his building. Then he took me upstairs. He didn't take my virginity, though. He could have. I wanted him to. But he held back and for that I suppose I should be thankful.

Menlo Park, California
1985
18013

May 5

I'm going to install a muffler. I found one today at a junkyard in Oakland. So now I've just got to put it in. Sounds easy, right? It's not. But I've been studying my copy of the *How to Keep Your Volkswagen Alive* manual, and I'm ready to give it a shot. The time has come for me to finish something.

That's not quite accurate: this morning I watched an entire episode of *The Gong Show.* It was a re-run, but a classic, the one where two teenage chicks sit on the ground with their legs crossed and they're both sucking away on huge Popsicles like they were giving head. Man, talk about a feeling of accomplishment! If only Chuck Barris would run for president. Apparently anyone in show business is qualified to rule the free world.

The point is, after I watched *The Gong Show*, I got in my grandmother's car and drove to the junkyard. Because finally I was degraded enough that I had to actually act. To regroup. Rebuild. So there was a small amount of growth in my soul. Now I have a muffler. I have no idea how to install it. The van is a mess. Four months into this project, and I've got nothing to show for it. By now I figured I'd be back on the road behind the wheel of my retooled Type-II Transporter, the coolest guy in the whole world.

Not!

Survey says: ERRRRR!

I guess I thought that all of the garages in Menlo Park were magical places. After all, the most popular personal computer in history was basically invented by tinkerers not far from my house. I personally detest computers. I refuse to use one, despite the fact that my parents just gave me a brand-new IBM 286. Nothing gets them going like the sound of my Smith-Corona clacking. If my door is open, they'll shut it. They'll drop biting remarks at the breakfast table such as *You can type faster on a keyboard, Bret, you should try it.*

That's when we're on speaking terms, which isn't often. The simple and undeniable fact is that they think I'm crazy. They cite, for example, my decision to drop out of the University of Arizona. Not to mention breaking up with Amanda, the girlfriend everyone in the family loved. Or the trip to Mexico I took in the van. And now my latest project, the restoration of a 1964 Volkswagen Type-II Transporter, aka Microbus or Hippie Van or Magic Bus—the van, I call it. Not to be difficult, but it's just easier because if you tell people that you're restoring a VW bus, they'll picture something else entirely and then you'll have to have a tiresome conversation about VW nomenclature with those who really don't care about such distinctions.

You've never worked with your hands before, Bret. This is just a form of avoidance, honey. You don't want to own up to your problems. You've got so much potential and you're just wasting it.

Big surprise. He's never lifted a finger to help out around here because he's worthless.

He's not worthless.

He isn't? What else would you call a stoned college dropout who doesn't work?

Dad is right, without question. I'm worthless. Totally and utterly worthless, meaning that on the open market my value to society is equivalent to zero. I possess no real skill, unless you need a Wallace Stevens poem analyzed, and even then I wouldn't do a very good job of it.

May 6

No progress on installing the muffler. But it doesn't seem to be too difficult if you know what you're doing, which I don't. I read over the directions several times and then it took me an hour to get out the six screws that connected the intake manifold assembly to the heat riser. That was just Step One! I didn't even bother with the screws of the crankshaft pulley shroud because my shoulders were aching. And I also hit my mouth up against the tailpipe, like I wanted to breathe the exhaust fumes or something. I worried that I'd chipped a tooth. All teeth in tact, thank god.

So I'm taking a break. I need to regroup. I don't feel like typing today. My hands are very sore. My head throbs. It's Monday. No one is home. There is an eerie quiet that I much love. There is no lonelier place on earth than the suburbs on a Monday morning. Very conducive to deep thinking. I need to make progress on SOMETHING. I can't just stay like this forever. Can I?

Last night at dinner, for example.

Dad: *Bret, are you going back to school in the fall?*

Me: *I don't think so.*

Dad: *Then you'll have to start paying rent.*

Me: *How much?*

Little Brother: *Charge him a grand! He's a free-loading bum!*

Dad: *A thousand dollars a month? That sounds about right to me. The real estate market is going crazy around here.*

Me: *Make it two thousand then. Maximize your profit.*

Dad: *Young man, this is no joke. You're doing nothing with your life. Nothing!*

Me: *I'm writing a novel and restoring a Volkswagen. I guess that doesn't count for much.*

Dad: *What novel? Is there a novel? I haven't seen a novel.*

Mom: *Tom, please.*

Dad: *I haven't seen a novel. And the garage is a mess! You've got used parts all over the place, screws and bolts and God knows what all—that is no way to go about restoring anything. I don't know what you do all day. When I was your age, I had to work two jobs and go to school full-time. Nobody gave me anything.*

Me: *I know, I'll just kill myself.*

Mom: *Bret! Don't say that! Don't ever say that.*

Later I told Mom I was sorry. I know she loves me, always has. She defends me, slips me cash every once in a while, asks me about the book.

I don't know what the hell I'm doing. Why did I even come back here?

May 7

I give up on that stupid sumbitch muffler. I thought I was making good progress. I'd actually made it to Step Four, Remove Muffler Clamps and Muffler. I'd loosened the nuts holding the muffler clamps, and then the rusty clamps just broke off so now I can't attach the muffler until I get a muffler connection kit, which will take a few days.

I'm supposed to be enjoying this. I'm supposed to be learning Deep and Eternal Truth by Immersing in the Realm of the Inanimate. But mostly I just get totally <u>PISSED OFF</u>. Because let's assume I do get the muffler installed—I still have the engine to deal with, and I know for a fact that there's major shit involved in getting it fixed.

I've got to calm down.

But here's the deal. I hate driving my grandmother's old car. She died last year, but I can still smell the menthol cigs she smoked like a chimney—they're what killed her. So each time I got into the 1973 Buick Century, I get a whiff of death—and it's not pleasant.

I miss Grandma, don't get me wrong. She was a tough old broad who drank whiskey until the day she died. In high school I'd drive over to her house in Marin and visit her, and would leave with a fifth of Southern Comfort. She bought her booze by the case and if she suspected anything, she never said a word. She got her revenge, though. In her will she left me and my brother some sweet loot, around two hundred large each, but we can't touch it until we turn 25. She knew if I got my hands on that dough today, for example, I'd piss it away in a few months. But in a couple years, who knows? Where will I be when I'm 25? Five years from now. 1990. Married? No way in hell. <u>Never</u>. Look at my parents. They make each other miserable, but they stick it out like they're playing an insane game of chicken. Who'll blink first?

Not Dad. No no no. Dad doesn't lose at anything. He never let me win a single game when I was growing up. Not a single one. Didn't matter what. Monopoly, basketball, putt-putt—he had to kick my ass each and every time, and then he'd spend the next hour ripping me to shreds, telling me how much I suck. For my own good, of course. So I could learn a few hard lessons. Because I've got it so easy.

And my little brother is just like him. Swear to God, Clay is a clone of Dad. They both can be arrogant pricks. Clay's going to Stanford in the fall, following in Dad's footsteps, so he's the big hero around here, the golden child who loves computers and never brought home a B and volunteered to work on Reagan's re-election—they both started calling me Mondale—it was pretty sickening. But Clay knows I can beat his ass to a pulp so he stopped when I told him to shove it. At least I was in Mexico for election night and didn't have to endure the nauseating coverage on TV. Another win for the Gipper.

What had I done to stop it? Did I vote for Mondale? No. Did I join in any protests? Hell no. Burn my draft card? Ha! I'd registered for the draft, just like all my friends, as ordered to by the Gipper himself. I didn't write my congressman—I didn't know who that prick was anyway. No, I'd done nothing.

And now I can't install a muffler. The two are related. I'm not sure how, but something is <u>holding</u> me back. Something internal. A desire to obliterate myself. A total lack of energy. No one I know gives a shit about anything. Honestly.

May 8

Mom left me a list of chores on the counter. Of course, she prefaced the list with a very polite *If you have time*, as if there were other pressing engagements on my calendar. Out of spite I actually went directly to my Smith-Corona and started typing, although after about an hour I realized that my novel is terrible. Why did I think I could write a novel anyway? Because I was a lit major? Because my father detested fiction? Oh, we're getting closer now, doctor.

Lit major? Are you kidding? Tell me you're kidding.

I'm not kidding.

What do you do with a Lit degree? Teach? Work at a restaurant?

I'm going to write books.

Novels?

Yes, novels.

What kind of novels?

I'm not sure yet.

You mean like Tom Clancy? He cleans up for himself. The man is printing money.

I'm not going to write books like Tom Clancy.

No, of course not. Why would you do that? He's successful and world-famous. You shouldn't emulate him, Bret.

He's a hack.

He's hacking his way to the bank, is what he's hacking. What about economics? I thought you were leaning in that direction.

I changed my mind.

Economics required too much work, huh? Too much effort?

That's not it.

You don't have to explain it to me, Bret. I've heard this song before. You always take the easy way out. The path of least resistance. All the lit majors I knew in college didn't amount to squat. None of them made it very far in life.

That won't happen to me.

It already is.

Milk was item #1. Easy enough, except there was no money to pay for the milk. Usually for household goods Mom would leave me a twenty, but not this time. I'd spent the last of my cash on the muffler connection kit (and the used muffler), so I was broke again.

Item #2:clean out Grandma's car. That I could do.

Item #3: clean out the gutters. No thanks.

Item #4: wash the dishes.

I looked over to the counter by the sink and saw a few bowls and juice glasses from breakfast, including Clay's soggy bowl of cereal. Wait a second. Since when did I have to clean up after my little brother? I'm not his maid. On ethical grounds I decided to wash all dishes but Clay's. I felt like Gandhi or something. Thoreau. Finally I was taking a stand.

Then I got to Item #5:

Smile!!! You're a great kid.

It took two hours to clean out the gutters, because apparently no one had bothered to do it for a century. I pulled out handfuls of rotting leaves older than I was. Some were actually covered with a coat of fuzzy grayish hair, not unlike Dad's, who was turning gray and going bald. It was hard, tedious work, the kind of drudgery that deadened the soul. And as soon as I'd finished, I smoked a huge bowl and found a stupid movie on Cinemax, *H.O.T.S.,* about a battle between college sororities that involved a flag football game where all the players got nekkid. There were some interesting camera angles when the girls were in the huddle. The best part, though, was seeing the cameo by Danny Bonaduce of *The Partridge Family.* I smoked another bowl in his honor and ate a bag of potato chips. By the time the movie was over, the clock had struck three.

Soon enough I found myself in the garage, where I hadn't been all day. The bare light bulb illuminated dust particles that floated in the air like tiny snowflakes. Scrap lumber from a project my dad had started a decade ago still stood in a far corner. At one point he liked making furniture but his job now didn't allow him much in the way of leisure. His tools, which I was now using, were scattered all over the floor, whereas he'd always kept them neatly stored. The tools were an obvious metaphor of my life: scattered and unorganized. There was the muffler, waiting like an obedient pet for its owner. But even if I were to install the muffler, what came next? The engine? Right. I couldn't lie to myself anymore. I wasn't close to getting the van fixed and I never would be. At some point I had to wave the white flag and admit defeat. No one would be surprised.

I climbed inside and sat in the driver's seat. The windshield remained grimed with dust from the Sonora Desert. I opened the glove box and saw the maps I'd used to guide me on my trip. It was exactly a year ago that I'd decided to change my life, because that's what the poet Rilke said we all must do. And I'd taken his words seriously. I'd stayed up one night and read all of his *Letter to a Young Poet*, where he defined what it meant for one to live as an artist—one must feel the burn to create—it must give you no peace—<u>then and only then</u> will you know whether you're destined for the life of a poet.

<u>May 9</u>

This morning I took an ad out in the classifieds of the *San Francisco Chronicle:* my 1964 Type II Transporter was for sale. I put a price of $500 on it, but I'd take the first offer I got. After hanging up the phone, I went back to bed and slept for another two hours. At exactly 11:11 a.m., I got up again. 11:11 is a good time to get up, since all the numbers on a digital clock are pointing to the heavens, like four index fingers commanding you to rise.

No To-Do list from Mom today. She'd done the breakfast dishes herself. The kitchen was clean, and the house quiet, except for the hum of the fridge. I cooked a couple of eggs and burned some toast, but ate it anyway because *Swamp Thing* was starting on Cinemax and I didn't want to skip any of it. I put my plate on a TV tray and was careful not to spill. Mom's one rule was no eating on the sofa, ever. But the sofa was closer to the TV, and I didn't want to miss Adrienne Borbeau emerging from the swamp, topless. She reminded me a little of Amanda, and the more of the movie I watched, the closer the resemblance between them grew.

I almost called her. I had the phone in my hand. My excuse for calling was to tell her that I had the van for sale, the one she'd gotten from the freaky cowboy in Jackson Hole. The one that we drove everywhere and screwed in constantly last summer—but I didn't want her to know where I was, at home, or what I was doing, nothing. I wanted her to think that I was off on my adventure, having the time of my life. After all, nobody in Tucson knew I'd come home, because I hadn't called anyone or written, except for the postcard from Mexico I'd sent to the frat house back in October.

An hour later the muffler connection kit arrived via UPS. I looked at it like someone had just dropped off an unwanted newborn baby. I cradled the package in my arms and dutifully carried it out the garage. There was no purpose trying to put the muffler on now. The new owner would attend to that chore. What I had to do was box up all the parts I'd disassembled in my ineptitude so that the new owner could do what I couldn't—namely, restore the van the way it deserved to be.

I couldn't help comparing myself to the way I'd been last summer, when Amanda and I were headed off to Jackson Hole, the first leg of what I'd hoped would be a lifelong journey, an endless adventure. Here I was, a year later, wondering what movie was coming on Cinemax. Meanwhile the van sat in rigid solitude, rebuking me with its silence.

Maybe Mom is right. Maybe I need to see a shrink.

<u>May 12</u>
I just sold the van. Got $500 for it. A tow truck backed into the driveway and hauled it away, and now there is a great big empty space in the middle of the garage. Dad told me to clean up his tools and put everything back just the way it was before I started "screwing around."

But now it's over. The guy who bought the van restores VWs as a hobby. He lives over in the East Bay and was very excited about finding a 1964 Type-II Transporter. I tried explaining to him that my intentions had been pure, that I'd wanted to teach myself how to make repairs, but that I just didn't have it in me. He nodded his head thoughtfully and appeared to understand. His name was Phil. I'd guess he was in his 40s. I had no idea what he did for a living. Didn't ask him and he didn't offer.

He asked about the holes in the side door. I told him I'd heard those were bullet holes and he laughed.

"I guess I'll have to keep them then," he said. His face resembled an owl's. Big round eyes and round face. A double chin and protruding gut. But he seemed at peace. He'd found his true calling—a devotion. You could tell by the way he'd examined the van, painstakingly going over every inch, muttering to himself as he did so, that he poured his heart and soul into it. I always respected people like that.

Milpitas, California
1987
18014

On his fortieth birthday, Phil bought himself a beat-up VW van. I was going to take him out to dinner in San Jose, but the next thing I knew, a tow truck showed up hauling a broken-down bucket of bolts.

"What's going on?" I asked him, standing outside with a sheer scarf covering my nose and mouth. The winds were out of the northwest again, which always blew in a rancid smell from the sewage treatment plant. Back when the city of San Jose built the plant, Milpitas had been a little crossroads town. But now it was growing because of all the technology companies moving in. Phil worked for one, International Imaging Systems. They were involved with processing images from satellites in outer space. Very cutting-edge stuff.

"I got a new project," he explained, grinning like a little kid as he helped guide the tow truck into the driveway. I was worried they were going to run over my zinnias or smash the lemon tree I planted last year.

"I can see that. Careful, please. He's awfully close to the lawn."

I waited until the van was in the garage and then went back inside because I couldn't stand the stench. They really needed to do something about the sewage treatment plant. Milpitas was a bustling city now, not some cow pasture. It didn't make any sense—we could beam images from satellites in outer space and build semiconductors the size of a nickel, but moving a sewage treatment plant was beyond our grasp, apparently. I kept hoping that one of the geniuses around here would come up with some big idea on how to make the smell go away. Fat chance.

*

The year Phil turned forty, I was twenty-five. I was a customer service manager for a small brokerage firm and after work I was going to aerobics five evenings a week. People said I still looked twenty. When I bought wine at the grocery store, the cashier asked for my ID.

I really wanted Phil to spend more time at the gym. He was getting a beer gut and joked that he wanted to play Santa at the office Christmas party. But I told him I didn't marry Santa Claus. When we first started dating, Phil had had a nice build, with perfect posture.

Now he was starting to stoop over. If only he spent more time on his physique, he'd look the way he used to.

But the van ate up most of his time. Drinking beer took up the rest.

*

I bought tickets to the Cindy Lauper concert but I ended up going with a girlfriend from work because Phil said he didn't want to see Cindy Lauper. I reminded him that we hadn't been to a concert together since the Eagles and they were broken up. And he said, "You know what we should do one weekend? We should drive to Big Sur and just camp out and watch the stars. That's what we should do."

"I hate camping," I told him.

"But you've never been camping. Not with me."

"My parents took me and it was horrible."

"Where'd you go?"

"I don't remember."

I was angry and didn't try to hide it. He knew that camping was a sore subject between us because I was well aware that he'd gone camping multiple times with his ex-wife, who was like this Amazon woman, able to clean fish and skin deer and play the guitar. A part of me suspected that Phil still had feelings for her and always would, since she was the one who left him, so that she could move to Mendicino with her new girlfriend. And for the past eight years of our relationship, Phil had never expressed a desire to go camping. Until now, when he was restoring an old VW van. Very curious.

*

Francine went to the concert with me. She was my age and single. She lived alone and was actively dating. Everyone thought we were sisters. We both had our hair permed the same way, so that it was kind of frizzy and wild. We both liked stone-washed jeans, Jordache or Calvin Klein, and we collected cheap costume jewelry. Francine would think nothing of putting on ten necklaces to go with fifteen bracelets.

I didn't want to complain about Phil. But when she asked how he was, I wasn't going to lie. I had to confide in someone. "All he does is work restoring an old Volkswagen van," I said on the way to the show.

"I mean, he's obsessed. It's been a year now, and he says he's half-way done."

"Lots of guys like cars," Francine offered, trying to be helpful.

"I know, but it's not just the car. It's other things, too."

"Like what?"

"I don't know. He started making his own beer. He's never made his own beer before."

"What's so wrong about that?"

"Nothing. It's just not like him. He's changing so much." I paused, thinking about Phil sampling his own ale, which he made me taste and I didn't like. I hated beer, and he knew that. I couldn't see what point he was trying to prove. "He shouldn't drink beer anyway. He's getting soft and round. And he's letting his hair grow long and he's starting to wear this little ponytail, and I don't like it very much."

I couldn't believe I was bringing up my personal life with Phil. I didn't want anyone to think I wasn't happy. I'd been with Phil for six years. But our relationship wasn't the same, and it really hurt and confused me.

"How are things in the bedroom?" Francine lifted an eyebrow and then gave me a wink.

"Fine, I guess. It's just, I hate it when his stomach rubs all over me. I have to use a pillow so I don't feel him." I sighed forlornly. "He's getting fat."

"You go to the gym, right? Why can't he join, too?"

"He says he will—but then he doesn't do it. He drinks beer and works on the van."

"That's a tough one. It sounds like he's having a midlife crisis."

I changed the subject, because I didn't want to reveal too much. Francine was a gossip and I didn't need everyone at work knowing my business.

*

Then I started to think that the reason Phil worked so hard on the van was so that he could ignore me. He wasn't obvious about it. It's not like he went out of his way to avoid me or pretended like I wasn't there. Plenty of wives complain about their husbands not listening to them, but Phil didn't do that, either. There was a different sort of quality to Phil's withdrawal into the garage, something I couldn't quite put my finger on.

Then once a month he started going out, alone, to have dinner with the Milpitas VW Club. He never offered to take me—no spouses was the rule.

"That's a stupid rule," I said. "We barely see each other as it is. What if I started going out with my friends once a month and you weren't allowed to come? How would you like that?"

"I wouldn't care. You should do your own thing. Everybody needs a hobby, an outlet."

"So you wouldn't care if my hobby became going to clubs with Francine and dancing with strange men?"

"Is that what you want to do?"

"I don't know. It might be."

"I'm not going to judge you. As long as you're not, you know, sleeping around, go for it."

I didn't want him to tell me to go for it. I wanted him to say that if I so much as looked at another man, he'd flip out. I wanted him to take me out to dinner more than once every three weeks. I wanted to go to San Francisco like we used to, and shop and eat and enjoy the good life. I wanted to buy pretty clothes and wear them to the coolest places. He used to take me to the trendiest boutiques on Nob Hill and let me pick out whatever I wanted. But now he wanted to "simplify," which meant live like a miser apparently. He'd even started meditating. Each morning he'd wake up early and go out and sit on the back porch with his eyes closed, incense burning at his feet, and it was starting to freak me out. What was next? Would he buy me a sarong or something?

But the van looked incredible, compared to what it had been. Phil had put all of his heart and soul into it. While I admired his dedication, I couldn't help think about his motivation. Why was restoring this van so important? Why did he have to put it back together exactly the way it was?

He said it was karma. I told him I didn't believe in that nonsense. And he said he was keeping the bullet holes in the side door. Like that was some kind of political statement. Good for you. That was my attitude. Good for you, Phil.

*

One night, Phil went off to meet up with the Milpitas VW Club at their usual haunt, the Gasthaus Restaurant where they could gorge themselves on strudel and wieners and beer, of course, the darker, the better. So I was stuck home again. I decided to give Francine a call.

"Let's go out tonight," I said. "I feel like having fun. You don't have plans, do you?"

"Nothing too serious. What do you feel like doing?"

"Dancing."

"Really? I could be up for that, totally."

"Awesome. Let's go."

*

Francine pointed to a guy across the bar. "See him over there? The tall, muscular guy?"

"Of course. He's hard to miss."

"I dated him."

"You did?"

"A long time ago. He played for the 49ers."

"He looks like a football player. What happened between you two?"

Francine smirked and took another sip of her drink. "We went out a few times. No big deal."

"Is that so?"

"Just some harmless fun."

Then the guy saw us and waved. He came over and joined us, first giving Francine a friendly hug and kiss on the cheek. She introduced us and we shook hands, and he asked if he could buy us a drink. His name was Colson, and he had a mellow laugh. He didn't seem like a football player, but a down-to-earth guy who worked in commercial real estate and liked to go hang-gliding.

"I've always wanted to try that," I said. "It looks like so much fun."

"It's great, being up in the sky and just floating like a cloud. It's totally awesome."

"I bet."

"You should try it sometime, Gigi. Don't deprive yourself."

"Okay, I will. You're all my witnesses. This year I'll go hang-gliding. But you have to teach me. I don't want to break my neck."

"It's a deal."

"So what do you do for fun, Gigi?"

Francine had gone off to talk to someone else, leaving me and

Colson at the bar. I deflected the question by saying this and that, but the truth was, I didn't know what to say. I got married young to a man much older than me, and now he's going crazy and I'm very lonely. Not much of an answer. But then I remembered Phil's advice to me: *Go for it.*

"Fun? I don't know. Go to aerobics class, stuff like that."

"What gym do you belong to?"

"Body in Motion."

"I've worked out in there. It's nice. I like the towels. I know that sounds pretty dumb. But you can't beat a good towel."

"Totally! They're so soft. I've taken a couple home. Don't tell on me. I don't want to get into trouble."

"Oh, so you're a bad girl, huh?"

"Not really."

"Don't worry, your secret is safe with me. I won't blow your cover."

We got another drink, my fourth, which was already way past my limit. My head was starting to get fuzzy, the way TVs got in the days before cable. Colson started talking about his business, how he was in the middle of putting a big deal together and he didn't have as much time anymore to work out. "You look like you're in good shape to me," I said.

"I can't even bench 315 these days. I'm getting soft, I swear."

"You're full of it, mister."

"I used to bench 450, no problem. I could run 4.7 40. Not anymore. Those days are over."

"I think you look great."

"Yeah? You look great, too."

"I do?" I felt my face growing warmer, like I'd been in the sun too long. It had been a long time since I'd heard a compliment like that, even though I worked hard on my appearance. I was the same size 4 I'd been the day I turned eighteen. Phil didn't notice. At least, he never said anything about my body. He pretty much took it for granted.

"I want to dance," I sang out. "That's why I came here tonight. And I love this song!"

It was Madonna. I had all her albums and listened to them while I cleaned or cooked, I tried to imagine being her, so strong and independent. She'd been through so much in her life, yet had overcome every obstacle in her way. I really respected that.

"Let's dance then," Colson said, taking me by the hand. Francine shot me a surprised look, and I waved at her to come join us. She was a good dancer and knew how to move her body.

*

The next day was Saturday, and I literally couldn't get out of bed, except to make it to the bathroom. Phil brought me glasses of water and aspirin, but nothing helped this hangover. It was epic, the absolute worst of my life.

"I'm never doing that again," I croaked to him once I was able to speak, at about three in the afternoon.

"Did you drink a lot?"

"Never again, I swear to God."

"Francine called and left a message."

I groaned and rolled over and put my head under the pillow, where it was black. I wanted to crawl into the blackness and never come out.

"Where did you guys go?" he asked. The pillow muffled his voice. It sounded like he was a thousand miles away.

"Hondo's."

"Was it fun? You got in late. After two o'clock."

"I know, don't remind me. I'm never drinking again."

"You were pretty drunk."

"I'm sorry."

"Hey, don't worry about it. You're allowed to go have a good time. It's just I was hoping we could go out and celebrate tonight."

"Celebrate what?" I rolled over and looked at him. His hair was combed and he wasn't wearing his usual ratty shop clothes. He actually had on his jogging suit. Had he gone for a run?

"I'm finished."

I didn't realize at first what he was talking about. A thick fog encircled my head, and my brain was like an airplane stuck in a holding pattern. "You're finished?" I repeated unsteadily.

He grinned and nodded and beamed with pride. "The van. It's done. I did it."

"Oh my God, congratulations. That's totally awesome."

"Thanks. And you know what I want to do now?"

"What?"

"Drive it across country."

"Today?"

"No, not today. But eventually. I want to take a month or two and just go everywhere. How does that sound?"

"Nothing sounds very appealing right now. Can we talk about this later? I feel like crap."

*

I changed into my aerobics outfit to head to the club. There was a five o'clock class, Advanced, taught by Kelli and she worked us hard. But it hurt to walk. I was sore from all the dancing. The class was probably too much for me, but I didn't care. I needed to sweat out all that I'd done last night, the drinks and the peanuts and the nachos. It felt like I'd gained two pounds and I needed a good burn and then a hot shower, and for dinner maybe a big salad. Lots of water to rehydrate.

But Phil had other plans. He saw me come downstairs and he stood up. "Don't you want to go for a ride?" he asked hopefully. I knew I should indulge him, since he was officially done, but the class was starting soon and I didn't want to miss it.

"I've got aerobics."

"I can drive you there. And then I'll drive you home."

"You could work out, too."

"I've already showered and I don't want to get all sweaty."

"Okay. Let's go."

*

I got into the van. Phil held the door open for me.

"Well?" he asked as I settled into the passenger's seat in front. "How does she look?"

"It's amazing, Phil, it really is."

And it was. The paint job sparkled. He'd picked out a gorgeous shade of brown, close to chocolate, or even café au lait, to go with cream for the bottom half. The seats were gleaming white, the tires a shiny black, almost like patent leather. Everything about the van looked brand new, unreal considering the thing was over twenty years old. But you couldn't tell.

And of course the bullet holes. He'd left them there just like he'd promised. Except he'd painted each one white, almost like tear drops.

"I completely rebuilt the engine," he announced before putting the key into the ignition. "New differential, new transmission, new camshaft, new crankshaft. New cylinders and compression rings." He paused, eyes roaming through the interior. It was like he was searching for pieces of himself he'd hidden inside.

"Let's see if it starts," I quipped.

"Oh, she'll start right up," he purred. He turned the key and the engine came on and the van started to vibrate. He put it in reverse and backed out into the street, very carefully and very slowly.

"Should I take a picture?" I asked. This was a big moment, after all. It deserved to be commemorated. "I can go get a camera. Just wait here a second."

"You don't have to."

"No, I want to. With you behind the wheel."

There were two shots left on the roll of film in the Kodak. The lighting was perfect, because it was July and the sun was just starting to sink down low in the western sky, casting a luminous glow on all objects. I focused the lens and waited for Phil to smile. But he never did.

"Smile, honey!" I shouted.

He flashed a peace sign and gave me a funky-looking grin, like he was taking a huge bite of something. I snapped off a shot and then we drove to the club.

Point Reyes, California
1989
27331

Mom told me to go decorate Phil's van during the ceremony. She gave me some car wax and other junk, and said I should write JUST MARRIED all over it. I was like, "Car wax? What about shaving cream?"

She said shaving cream could hurt the finish. Car wax would dry white. These were some serious VW people, apparently.

So I waited with everyone else out near the cliffs, and then Aunt Sharon came walking out in her funky wedding dress and this hippie guy playing the lute broke into "Here Comes the Bride," which was my cue to cruise. I grabbed the bag and slipped away, pretending like I had to go use the can or something.

I hustled back to the parking lot. There were literally about fifty VWs gathered together, and for a second I sort of panicked because I couldn't remember what color Phil's van was. There were like six others just like it, and I walked around confused and pissed at Mom for not getting this straight but she'd blame me for not listening. It was like I was in a time warp with these old Volkswagens everywhere. They were all in mint condition because basically everyone at the wedding belonged to some kind of restoration club and they all geeked out on VWs, like Aunt Sharon. She drove a red Beetle, which was easy enough to find because of the Nuclear Freeze bumper sticker.

And next to it was a brown-and-cream van—Phil's! I was so excited that I skipped down to it. I wasn't going to screw up after all. I got out the car wax and started decorating it, and then I heard this voice coming from out of blue:

"What's up, cuz?"

It was Vince, my cousin, Aunt Sharon's son. We were about the same age but the resemblances stopped there. I played sports and got good grades, and Vince hated everything and got into trouble all of the time. Plus, he was a boy and a pretty dumb one at that.

"I'm getting the van ready," I said.

"Gag me with a spoon."

"Whatever."

I kept at it, ignoring Vince, who just stood there watching me. He should've been at the ceremony, but he hated Phil, which was stupid because Phil was a pretty cool guy, as far as I could tell. Until a couple of years ago, Vince and I had been really close, but then he changed and got all angry and stopped trying, basically. Mom said that Phil made Aunt Sharon very, very happy—the best thing to ever happen to her. Vince ran away from home. It was hard to figure out.

"Let me have a turn," Vince said.

"I'm almost done. They'll be here any second."

"Come on, Liz. Don't be a tool."

"Why should I let you ruin this? I know you'll write something stupid."

"I won't, I swear I won't."

But I didn't trust him. He came over and tried to take the car wax from me, but I fought back. And I was strong, from swimming. I had a good grip on the can and he was grabbing at my arm, and the next thing I knew, I'd kicked him in the nuts. Right between the legs. He doubled over in pain, grabbing his groin. I told him I was sorry, which was a big fat lie.

"No, you're not!" he yelled loud enough I was sure they could hear him at the wedding. "You did it on purpose!"

"Stop screaming, Vince. It didn't mean to hurt you."

"I can't breathe. I'm gonna die!"

"Serves you right."

I went back to decorating the van, wanting to finish so that I could throw birdseed at the newlyweds when they came down the path. There was a big red mark on my arm from where Vince had grabbed me. I smiled, though. He knew better than to mess with me like that.

Cahokia Mounds State Historical Site
Collinsville, Illinois
1990
35209

Vince said he was staying in the van. He claimed to have no interest in learning about the Indians who'd lived at Cahokia, which was supposedly the largest city in North America prior to Columbus's arrival. It was the reason we'd come out here, braving the snarled traffic to get across the Mississippi River and through the squalor of East St. Louis, to the great American Bottom, which was what they called this flood plain where Indians had erected a great civilization.

But Vince didn't care.

"You're gonna miss out on something special," I told him, careful not to let my voice sound too angry. "I've always wanted to see this place. They think forty thousand people used to live here. There's over eighty different mounds, and the biggest one is a hundred feet tall."

"My feet hurt," Vince shot back. "You made me walk for like a thousand miles yesterday and now I've got blisters."

"Monks Mound is the tallest man-made earthen structure in the country."

"Are you serious? The tallest? Wow, Phil. Amazing. Awesome. I'm having a heart attack because I'm so pumped up about it."

"Enough of the sarcasm, Vince," Sharon scolded him.

"No, no," I interjected. "That's fine. I'm a grown man. I can take it. I was a smart ass when I was his age."

"Mom, tell him to leave me alone, okay? I'm tired of seeing stupid old stuff. I thought this trip was supposed to be fun."

I could tell that Sharon was about ready to blow her lid, so I gently took her by the arm and led her a few feet away from the van. Tears were welling in her eyes, and she brushed them away as she glared back at her son.

"We'll leave him here," I said softly. "He'll get bored and then he'll learn his lesson."

"No, he won't, either. You saw the trailer parks we passed by getting here. And the seedy little bars. East St. Louis is a rough city, Phil. The whole thing is a crack-infested ghetto."

"It's a long walk down a busy road. We're safe here."

"I don't trust him."

"What should we do?"

Sharon knew how badly I wanted to visit Cahokia, which I'd read about in the *Smithsonian* a couple years ago—It struck me as the kind of magical place that few attractions on earth could match. That was the point of this cross-country trip—to explore every corner of our great nation, to experience all of her majesty and splendor. We had three weeks to go wherever the wind blew us, because that was how long it would take the moving van to ferry our furniture and other belongings from Milpitas to our new home in Clearwater, Florida. Sharon and I were embarking on a new journey together, starting our lives over from the ground up. We'd been married for less than a year, and one day a month ago we realized that we needed to make more drastic changes. So we looked around at what opportunities we had in cities like San Diego and Phoenix, but then she suggested Florida—and something about it seemed right. Amazingly enough, within two weeks we both found new jobs in the Clearwater area, she in human resources and me with a computer reselling company called Tech Data.

Florida. A fresh start. We wanted to enjoy the beaches and the laid-back lifestyle, but we also wanted to rebuild our lives. Vince was a big part of that. He was sixteen and had fallen in with a bad crowd back in Milpitas. He desperately needed to get away from the negative influences that had led him to experiment with drugs, which in turn had gotten him into trouble at school. His grades were lousy, he had no motivation, and we thought he would benefit from going to a place where no one knew him.

As for now, though, he was the same old Vince, and we didn't know what to do with him.

"I guess we should go and enjoy ourselves and leave him here," she said without much conviction. Vince had a history of running away. Once he was gone for a week and Sharon was sure he was lying dead somewhere. We'd just moved in together. I'd barely unpacked my suitcases when it happened. Worst week of my life. Worse even than having your wife tell you that she doesn't love you anymore.

"That's not a good idea," I quickly countered. "I'm being selfish. We can do something else. Maybe there's an amusement park nearby."

"No. We can't let Vince control us. That's what he wants. He's the child and we're the parents, and he has to respect that."

"We'll be in Memphis tomorrow. He'll like Graceland, won't he? He knows who Elvis is, doesn't he?"

"Phil, we're going in this park. All you've talked about for two days is how much you want to see these mounds. Vince knows it means a lot to you so that's why he's digging his heels in."

"I don't know, Sharon. Maybe he'll respect me more for listening to him and responding to his needs."

"Phil, listen to yourself. You're giving in. You can't do that with Vince. Ever. You give him an inch, and he takes a mile. We're going. End of discussion."

Sharon went back to the van to confer with Vince. I stood aside, with sweat dripping down my cheeks. It was going to be another scorcher in the Midwest. The sun wasn't even high in the sky yet and already the heat was heavy, like a huge immoveable object.

"He's staying," Sharon told me curtly when she came back.

"Are you sure about this?"

"I can't let him push me around anymore, Phil. I've taken too much for too long."

*

We were in a tour group of about ten people. With us was a nice couple from Milwaukee who had their two boys with them. They were younger than Vince, but not by much, and they seemed perfectly happy examining all of the artifacts housed in the welcome center. Pottery shards, arrowheads, copper axes—the two boys drank in these treasures with the same kind of curiosity as my own. I didn't have to point out to Sharon the irony in this, that Vince would rather sit alone in the Volkswagen while these two kids were eager to delight in all of life's rich bounty.

What had happened to Vince?

Sharon blamed her ex-husband, who was a heavy drinker and philanderer out chasing skirts instead of spending time with his family. What Vince needed was a positive role model, a man in his life he could look up to. Hopefully in time he'd let me in. But we were a long way from that.

Also joining us on the tour was an older couple who moved slowly and kept to themselves. We didn't get to know them at all, nor did we chat much with the man in the wheelchair that was being pushed by a woman, perhaps his wife or a nurse or his sister. The man in the wheelchair was overweight, severely so. His legs were giant slabs of jiggling fat and a sickly shade of white, splotched here and there with strange purplish bruises. His eyes were alert, though, a soft and delicate shade of brown, and I couldn't help but wonder what had led him to this state. Maybe diabetes. The woman pushing the wheelchair wore a perpetual scowl and said almost nothing as she moved him from one exhibit to another while we waited for the tour to begin.

I was impatient for it to get going. Monks Mound, the biggest of the Cahokia mounds, was visible from the road leading into the parking lot, and I couldn't wait to climb up the stairs to its summit. The clock kept inching closing to ten o'clock. Sharon as usual was making friends, this time with the couple from Milwaukee, so I decided that I should go over and join in.

"This is my husband, Phil," Sharon said and then introduced me to the husband and wife, but I didn't quite catch their names. "They're on a driving vacation like we are."

"Yeah?"

"It's been fantastic," the husband announced proudly. "Say, is that your VW bus out there? She's a beauty."

"He restored it himself," Sharon explained, patting me on the back.

"Did you?" The husband grinned from ear to ear. "I'll be hanged. Nice work. How long did it take?"

"Two years."

"Impressive. I always wanted to do that, but I don't have the patience. Or the time." He laughed at himself, hitching up his trousers. I noticed that he and his wife were wearing matching Mickey Mouse sweatshirts. They must've gone to Orlando and now were headed back home. They had sunburned faces and exuded relaxed satisfaction. I hoped we'd find such peace on our Florida adventure, our days spent walking on the beach looking for shells or beneath swaying palm trees that whispered in the wind.

Then the tour guide came out, by the name of Ed, according to his badge, and he gathered us around to go over a few things before we left on the walk.

"I'd like to welcome everyone to Cahokia," Ed said in a booming voice, his arms behind him at parade rest. He must've served a stint in the military, maybe as a drill instructor. He had a wiry build, with a narrow face that resembled a large shard of decorated pottery, with faint lines and slight wrinkles arrayed in an interesting pattern, ending abruptly at his squat chin. "We're getting ready to start so you might want to use the facilities. We'll be covering about a mile on our journey today, and it'll be hot out, so make sure you bring some water. We have bottles for sale in the gift shop."

No one moved.

"Okay, then let's proceed. The first mound we're going to visit is called Fox Mound and I'm sure you can guess why it's been named that."

"Because it looks like a fox!" one of the Milwaukee boys called out as we headed outside.

"Afraid not!" We all chuckled as Ed went on to explain his prank. "Many of the mounds were named after local residents or the early excavators who first tried to save the mounds from being destroyed. The fact is, this amazing place was nearly bulldozed under to make way for more development, but luckily for us, the state of Illinois purchased the land back in the 1920s and opened a park for the public to enjoy."

I leaned over and whispered into Sharon's ear. "I wish Vince could hear that people can make a difference in this world."

She nodded her head in agreement.

*

We didn't make it to Monks Mound until the very end of the tour. By then we were dragging a little from the oppressive heat. The climb up proved to be tough for the older couple, and the heavy man in the wheelchair had to wait at the bottom. Sharon and I tagged along with the couple with Milwaukee, whose sons were racing up the stairs to the top.

"The view ought to be something," I said.

"It better be," replied Sharon, whose face was red and sticky. "My legs are killing me."

"I wish they had a monorail like at Disney," the man from Milwaukee said. His name was Dan, or maybe Dave. "That would save us a lot of guff."

"And a water slide for the trip down," his wife added. "So we could cool off."

Sharon made friends so easily, because people tended to gravitate to her. That was the first thing I'd noticed about her—that and she was beautiful. She drove a 1968 Beetle that was getting moved to Florida in the big eighteen-wheeler. It was sweet. Candy-apple red with chrome wheels. She liked to take it to shows because it always got lots of attention. We were both married when we first met, and we took it slow, but eventually we realized we were true soul mates.

Finally we reached the top. Ed waited for us to gather around and then began to explain some of the intricacies of the mound. "The summit, which we're standing on, is divided into two parts. You'll notice the northern end is about five feet higher than the southern. In the middle of the first terrace, you can see down below a projection, which we think is the remains of a graded pathway. Now if we walk over to the west side, we can see the amount of damage caused by erosion from rain over the years."

We all moved as a group. I couldn't help enjoying the view. Off in the distance I could see the Arch in St. Louis, sitting astride the Mississippi. I tried to imagine the horizon as the Indians would've seen it, stretching endlessly into the vastness of the plains, filled with buffalo and grasslands. Now there was city, two of them in fact, sprawling as far as I could see to the west.

I heard two men talking nearby. They'd joined the tour in the middle. They were around my age and dressed like they were going on a safari, with vests and binoculars and canteens. And one had a detailed map he kept referring to. They seemed interesting so I sidled up to eavesdrop.

"It's hard to imagine that this city once was home to thousands of people," one said to the other. "The great mystery is what happened, why the civilization collapsed. It seems as if one day everyone just scattered, although there is no evidence that Cahokia was attacked."

"What was it then?" I asked, butting into their conversation.

"Well, some historians think that deforestation was the main culprit. There weren't enough resources to support the population, and once all the trees were cut down, erosion set in, creeks dried up and what have you. It's mere speculation, of course. We'll never know."

"So they used everything up and died?"

"Or scattered around and joined up with other bands up and down the river."

"That's fascinating. I always assumed there was a war."

"Probably not."

I drifted away and then heard Ed say that the chief had most likely occupied a home, a palace, at the summit. But nothing of the palace remained except fragments of pottery. "But it's also likely that significant looting occurred, so whatever treasures were here have been taken," he concluded wistfully.

"Have they found human remains here?" someone asked.

"Not here at Monks. But over forty skeletons have been recovered from the mounds, and some of the remains suggest that the Indians here practiced human sacrifice. And, I might add, a few victims might have been buried alive."

Too bad Vince didn't hear that. He liked slasher flicks like *Friday the 13th*.

We stayed a few minutes longer, and then Sharon said we should go check on Vince.

*

Vince wasn't in the van.

At first we were too stunned to do much more than mutter under our breath. Even though we were prepared for this, and it didn't come as a shock, we still stood listless in the heat and looked helplessly around the parking lot. More cars were pulling in, and school buses, too, carrying black kids from East St. Louis on a summer camp outing.

"Maybe he's in the bathroom," I suggested, leaning my back against the van for support. Its metal was hot, but it didn't bother me. I remembered painting it, how painstakingly I'd finished each coat, immersed in the smallest detail—I wanted it to come out perfectly. And it did. My van turned heads. People stopped and stared at it. To me it was a work of art, my soul. I pulled my sweaty body away from the finish, pulled a towel out of the van, and wiped off my residue.

"We should go check," she sighed, exhaustion overtaking the anger.

"Wait here in case he comes back."

I walked off toward the visitor's center just as a horde of campers was trooping inside. They were all wearing the same yellow t-shirt—Davis Community Center, Summer 1990—and chirping away like a flock of little black crows. I waited for them to pass by, holding open the door and smiling at the counselors who carried clipboards and whistles as they barked instructions at the kids. *Don't touch anything. Stay with your buddy.*

We'd tried to get Vince involved in the teen program at the community center back in Milpitas, but after the only field trip he went on, we got a phone call from the head counselor telling us that Vince had shoplifted and now he wasn't allowed to go on any more field trips. Vince of course denied taking anything and accused the counselors of lying. "Why don't you ever believe me?" he'd shouted at us.

I made it to the men's room and quickly my hopes were dashed. No sign of Vince. I hurried back out to the van. Sharon was sitting in the passenger seat with the window rolled down. When she saw me coming back empty-handed, she closed her eyes and shook her head in disappointment.

"He didn't come back, huh?" I asked stoically, not wanting to alarm her.

"No."

"He's got to be around here somewhere."

"He's somewhere. He's always somewhere. Just not where you want him to be."

"I'm sorry. This was all my fault. I dragged us out here, and now this."

"No, this place was great. It's no one's fault but Vince's."

I kept looking around, hoping for any sign of the kid. "Let me walk over to the path. He might be sitting in the shade."

There was a hiking trail that took visitors on a longer loop of the mounds. It was self-guided and near its head were some tall trees. I was hoping Vince got hot or bored and just went over for a break. Otherwise, I had no clue where to look. He could have gone anywhere. We'd probably have to call the police and file a missing person report. Child. Missing child. It was important to remember that Vince, even though he was as big as a man, was no adult.

I saw him sitting at a picnic table. His mouth dropped down and his mouth formed an O as he shook his head angrily, looking just like his mother. It was eerie. They shared so many of the same features—the high forehead, the thin nose, the pale blue eyes.

I waved, of course, glad that he was okay. At least now our trip wasn't ruined. Tomorrow we'd make it to Memphis and spend the day thinking about Elvis. It seemed like yesterday when I saw him on the Milton Berle Show. June 1956. I was twelve years old, and Elvis came on and sang "Hound Dog" and moved around with such confidence— confidence I knew then I'd never have.

"What took so long?" Vince fumed. "I'm starving. You guys left me out here to die without any food or water or money. I had to beg this family of goobers from Ohio to let me eat some of their potato chips. It was horrible."

"You missed a very interesting tour. I think you would've liked it."

"Whatever. Can we go eat lunch now, finally? I'm going to gnaw on this table in a minute. This has been the most pathetic day ever. So lame."

He stood up and rolled his eyes and then marched past me back to the van. I trailed behind silently, walking in Vince's shadow. His flipflops flapped against heels with each stride, making a popping sound. In the back of the van he had a pillow and a nice comfortable place to zone out while I drove. One day he'd look back on this trip with fondness. He got a chance to see our great nation, from sea to shining sea. All in a newly restored 1964 VW minibus. How many people can say that?

Sharon came running to greet us. "Where were you?" she demanded, hands on hips. Vince breezed right past her like she was a parking valet.

"I need food," he barked. "Are you two trying to kill me or something? This trip's like the Bataan Death March."

"Next stop, Graceland," I sang out to myself. Sharon and Vince were already in the van. I couldn't wait to get back on the road. The best part was driving with the windows down, with the air rushing into your face. You could really feel the country that way.

"I saw a McDonald's back there," Vince said after I got in.

"What about some local barbeque?" I suggested. "I bet there's a good place nearby."

"Forget it! I need real food. I've suffered enough today. Don't prolong the agony!"

"No," Sharon said. "Enough of the attitude. We didn't drive all the way out here to eat a Big Mac. St. Louis is known for its barbeque and that's what we're having. End of discussion."

"You don't eat meat, so what difference does it make?"

"I'll find something on the menu. Cornbread and beans will do me just fine,"

"I'm gonna die!"

Vince pretended to croak in the backseat, like he was suffocating. He fell to the floor and didn't move for several minutes. At least it was quiet.

Clearwater, Florida
1991
43775

I wrecked the van today. Phil's beloved Volkswagen. The accident wasn't my fault, but I'm still sick about it. It's two o'clock in the morning and I can't sleep. All I can hear is the squealing of tires and then the horrible bang of the crash. Luckily no one was badly hurt. We were all shaken up, though. My neck is very sore and I'm supposed to wear a neck brace but it's extremely uncomfortable and impossible to sleep in. I want to take it off because it feels like a choke collar around my neck. The doctor in the ER told me to leave it on for a week.

The other driver was not an American citizen. He didn't speak English. I don't know where he came from. I tried a few Spanish phrases but he didn't understand me and I didn't understand him. There was no insurance information to write down because he didn't have any. Or a valid driver's license. His eyes were blood-shot and he reeked of booze. In fact, he was drunk and the Tampa police hauled him away in handcuffs, but it didn't matter, because the back end of the van was still pretty much smashed.

The drunk driver had run a red light and plowed right into us. There was nothing I could have done. Even the police officer told me that. We were all lucky to be alive, and for that I'm very grateful.

*

I couldn't drive the van home, obviously. We needed a tow. But we had to wait for the wrecker or hauler in a part of Tampa that seemed very downtrodden and perhaps gang-infested, along Gandy Boulevard near the intersection with Manhattan Street. There were pawnshops and seedy bars and graffiti painted on everything. Fortunately a police officer waited with us. We stood in the parking lot of a restaurant called Hooters, which apparently featured scantily clad waitresses with large breasts. One of our group, Laura Beth, said she'd worked for the original Hooters back in Clearwater while she'd gone to college. As a feminist I found the theme of the restaurant highly insulting, but not at all surprising. "A sister's got to do what a sister's got to do," Laura Beth said in her defense.

"I couldn't agree more," I told her.

I

I had to call Phil. After the week he'd had, getting laid off on Tuesday because of the recession, this was the last thing he needed to hear. It took every ounce of my energy to drop the quarter into the pay phone. On top of everything else, this was going to crush him. He would act like it was no big deal. He'd say the important thing was that everyone was okay, but he'd worked so hard on restoring this 1964 Type II—and he'd kept it in mint condition.

No one answered the phone at home. Phil was supposed to be helping our neighbors move a sectional sofa, but where was Vince? I tried to think. It was Saturday afternoon. He could've been anywhere, except at work, since he didn't have a job and hasn't shown much interest in getting one even though he was eighteen and about to graduate from high school in a few months.

I didn't leave a message on the answering machine. I didn't feel right about telling Phil that way. He needed to hear the news from me directly, as much as I didn't want to tell him at all.

"No one home," I said glumly to myself. The others were watching me. The air was thick with the smell of grease. From the restaurant. We were standing near the entrance, all huddled together like a flock of lost sheep.

So then Paige called her husband and Daphne called hers, and fortunately both men could come get us. We needed two cars to transport us all home. That's why I'd driven the van in the first place, because it could fit the group all in.

I kept looking at the van. Some men had pushed it out the road and it sat forlorn at the edge of the parking lot, directly beneath the Hooters sign, the indecent one with an owl's eyes shaped like bosoms. From this angle there wasn't a scratch on the van. Everything looked normal. Maybe I'd just imagined the accident. My neck told me different. It was hurting but I didn't tell anyone. I didn't want anyone to worry or waste time taking me to the hospital. We all just wanted to get home.

*

Until the accident, though, it had been a glorious day. Over a hundred people had showed up for the rally at McDill Air Force Base to protest the invasion of Iraq, and it felt good to let everyone who saw us know that we were against war. Of course we got all kinds of angry honks and middle fingers from motorists as they drove past us. Sure, we got a few thumbs up, too, but not many. Not many at all, considering how overwhelmingly popular this war is with the general public. Yet we all agreed that the effort and time had been worth it. We held our homemade signs and waved them proudly, the ultimate gadflies spoiling all the fun.

And as I stood there holding my sign that read NO BLOOD FOR OIL, it felt like Florida had finally become home. A flier on the community bulletin board at a local food co-op had led me to a group of peace activists who were willing to take abuse to stand up for what they believed in. We understood that we were a distinct minority, holdovers from a different time, but we didn't care. It was a motley collection of moms, spinsters, dikes, and college students, all thrown together in Phil's VW. Eight of us strong, unafraid of being reviled.

When it was time to go, we happily all piled back into the van, storing our signs beneath the seats. Paige McKenzie sat up front next to me. She had a son around Vince's age, and so we talked about the difficulties of raising teenagers in this hazardous and confusing world. I didn't know her very well, just from the meetings I'd been going to. But she seemed like a strong woman who for fun liked to go on long kayaking trips. She was blotched from the sun and proud of her graying hair, which she refused to color.

She surprised me by extending a dinner invitation. "You and Phil should come by one night and break bread with us," she said. "My husband is a car guy, too. I think they'd get along just dandy."

"Phil brews his own beer, you know."

"Well, I like him already. And bring Vince if you want. He can spend some time with Dylan. They might hit it off."

It sounded too good to be true. "Vince could use some new friends. He's doing okay but he still misses California."

I wanted to explain to her about Vince's father and his role in Vince's problems, but we ran out of time.

Because then it happened. Just like that, in the blink of an eye. One minute you're making a new friend, and the next you're screaming and hoping no one dies. I remember watching the light turn from red to green and then easing off the clutch to get the van into gear, praying that I didn't stall out because I didn't want the others to think I was a klutz.

*

"Clearwater?" the tow truck driver grumbled. "That'll cost you eighty bucks."

"Fine. I'll give you the address."

I told him where we lived and he jotted it down on a clipboard, looking none too pleased. He was gruff, unshaven, and darkly tanned, with a big beer belly and hairy arms that belonged on a gorilla. There was still no sign of Paige and Daphne's husbands, so I had to drive back home in the front seat of the tow truck next to this man I didn't know, who smelled of month-old sweat and had teeth the color of pine bark. My neck really started killing me, and tears formed in my eyes despite my efforts to brush them away.

"Will you be okay?" Paige asked me as she reached out and touched me lightly on the arm to show support. The gesture meant a great deal to me. It was uplifting to know that I didn't shoulder this burden alone. "I can ride with you if you'd like."

"No, I'll be okay. I just hate the thought of telling Phil. It hasn't been the best of weeks for him. And now this."

"At least no one got hurt. And it wasn't your fault. That guy was drunk."

"I know. There's some solace in that. But still, I hate all the negative energy. Anyway, thanks for everything." The driver was hitching up the van to the tow truck, and it wouldn't be long before we had to go. "It was fun until this happened."

"I'm glad we did it, despite all the names we were called."

"Me too."

Everyone came over, all the women who'd driven with me, and each gave me a sisterly hug, and I couldn't stop the tears from flowing down my face. I hated leaving them alone in this nasty part of Tampa, but what choice did I have?

*

When the tow truck got across the Courtney Campbell Bridge, my heart started pounding. Not in a good way, like when you're excited about something. But I felt like I used to when I was little and the nurse was getting ready to give a shot. I knew how much it would hurt and I just wanted to scream but I knew big girls didn't act that way, so I gritted my teeth. Just like I did in the truck.

But then the traffic on U.S. 19 was at a standstill. Again. It was horrible every day of the week, and now that spring breakers were in town, the roads to the beach were jammed. We crawled along as slow as molasses, which only prolonged the trip. It took us fifteen minutes to go three miles. I reached the point where I'd rather tell Phil about the van than spend another minute with the truck driver, who had the annoying habit of changing radio stations every ten seconds. And he chewed tobacco, which meant he was constantly spitting into an old coffee cup.

Finally we turned left onto Drew Street. It wouldn't be long now. I was literally at my wit's end, disgusted and sad and miserable and ready for a long, hot shower. I wanted this day to end.

"Take the next right," I told the driver. We hadn't spoken in a long time. But he nodded and followed my directions to the house. I saw that Vince's car was in the driveway but not mine. Phil had borrowed it for the day but he hadn't yet returned. So I couldn't tell him. The agony was prolonged.

"Where do you want it?" the driver asked.

"The driveway. I'll get my son to move his car."

I hopped out and walked to the front door. It was unlocked so I proceeded directly inside. I could hear loud music coming from Vince's room upstairs, nothing unusual there. He was listening to rap, which I didn't care for because of the misogynist and often-violent lyrics, but I reminded myself that he'd made honor roll and I had to stay positive. But the closer I got to his room, the louder the music became—and the more distinct the lyrics, and I could plainly hear filth about "bitches" spewing forth—maybe it was just a phase Vince was going through. At least he wasn't running away. B's were better than F's.

I knocked on the door and yelled out his name, straining to be heard over the din. I knocked louder and called out louder, with more urgency, because the tow truck was waiting. I knocked so hard in fact that my hand ached from the pounding, and my neck felt as if it might snap in two. Still Vince didn't open the door. I was about to knock again when the music abruptly stopped. Seconds later the door swung open, and there stood Vince, wearing gym shorts and no shirt. He seemed to be breathing heavily and he was sweating like he'd just run a few miles.

"You need to move your car," I explained tersely. "Didn't you hear me knocking?"

"No. The music was too loud."

And then it hit me. The sheepish look on my son's face. He had a girl in his room. I didn't want to be a prude, but then again I didn't need strangers in my house at that moment, either. "Is somebody here?" I asked, carefully gauging his reaction. His eyebrows lifted and he forced a chuckle.

"No."

I looked around. Everything appeared to be in order. I wasn't going to peek under the bed, because I respected Vince's space, and so I was about to turn and leave when I spotted a pair of tennis shoes I didn't recognize. They were resting in the middle of the room, and they obviously belonged to a girl.

"Whose shoes are those?" I demanded, trying to keep an even keel.

"What shoes?"

"Those right there." I pointed and then walked over and picked one up. It was light and pink. Size 6, I'd guess.

"Oh. Those."

I heard noises coming from the closet. I looked at Vince and then nodded toward the closet. "I'm thinking the owner of these shoes is in there, and I don't have time to deal with this right now." Before I could even explain, I heard the horn of the tow truck. "Give me your keys," I snapped. "I have to move your car."

"Okay, okay. Don't have a cow."

Vince gave me his keys and I went back downstairs and then outside so I could clear the driveway. I could barely unlock the car door, though, because my hands were shaking so badly. There wasn't a specific rule that Vince couldn't have girls in his room. And I'd made sure Vince understood the importance of birth control. I should've been delighted that he'd met someone—but that part also scared me, because I was afraid that I'd hate this girl, whoever she was. And for no good reason. This was just a bad day for me to be introduced to her. I had no energy for fake smiles or small talk.

I backed out of the driveway and parked Vince's car on the street so that tow truck could park the van with the front end facing the street. From that angle it didn't look like anything was wrong. Then I wrote the driver a check for eighty dollars and he left. By now it was getting dark and still no word from Phil.

*

Her name was Chris. She was a junior at Clearwater High School. She seemed sweet and polite, although very nervous about meeting me. I didn't mention the closet. I just wanted her to leave. Thankfully Vince said he had to give her a ride home, and so I quickly returned his car keys.

"It was nice meeting you, Mrs. Geyer," Chris said to me, very genuinely, as if she hadn't just been upstairs frolicking with my son. I noticed she was wearing a gold necklace with a pendant of her name hanging from it. Why hadn't he mentioned this girl before? So much of Vince's life existed in a murky twilight—with staggering moments of clarity like this one, lit up by a thousand-watt spotlight. Did he care about her? Or was she just some easy lay, the class slut? Didn't I raise my son to respect women? Had I failed in that, too? Had Vince turned out to be another objectifying bastard out to use and abuse females?

"Why was there a tow truck outside?" he asked, jangling the keys. "Did something happen to the van?"

"I got into an accident in Tampa."

"Are you okay?"

"I'm fine. My neck hurts some, that's it."

"Did you go to the hospital or anything?"

"No. I don't need to."

"Your face is white as a sheet. Are you sure you feel okay?"

The fact was, my neck was hurting worse with each passing second. The pain was starting to radiate down my spine and through my arms. Even my fingers tingled by now. "I don't know," I muttered. "I need to tell Phil what happened. Has he called?"

"No. Mom, you don't sound so good. I'm serious. You should get checked out by a doctor. What do you think, Chris? You're in Honors Bio."

This young girl who'd never seen me before started looking me over, which I found strangely touching, because of Vince's concern not just for me but also for her opinion. Deep down, maybe Vince did have a heart, as hard as he tried to deny it.

"You could have spinal damage," said Chris. "You could be leaking spinal fluid. It happened to my uncle and it really sucked. He had to wear this big brace bolted to his skull for like two months."

"Mom, come on. I'll drive you to the hospital."

"What about Phil?"

"We'll leave him a note. Come on. Chris just lives down the street. We'll drop her off and head right to the emergency room."

But I didn't want Phil to find out about the van by just showing up without me here to explain. I owed him more than that. "Let me call the Houston's. That's where he went. It'll just take a second."

I got their number from the address book by the phone, the pretty one with the birds on the cover. In it was my life, all my business contacts and old friends from California and family birthdays—without it I'd be lost.

I dialed the number and Cindy Houston answered on the first ring. They lived two streets down, but we'd gotten friendly because Herman Houston had noticed Phil's VW parked in the driveway and they struck up a conversation and then we started having dinner with them, although I wasn't as fond of them as Phil was. They were a little too conventional for my tastes, two normal Americans who enjoyed watching sports on TV, which I considered the ultimate waste of time. But since they were neighbors, I did my best to be accommodating.

"Hi, Cindy," I said. "It's Sharon Geyer. Is Phil still giving Herman a hand?"

"No, they finished up and then went off to the hardware store for something and I haven't seen them since. Knowing them, they most likely found some trouble, chances are at the dog track. But Herman knows he'd better call me or he's sleeping on the sofa tonight."

"Oh. Can you tell Phil to call me when he gets in? I have something I need to tell him."

"I'm sure they just stopped off for a few beers and they'll come rolling in real soon."

"Thank you."

"Sharon, is something wrong? You sound distressed."

"No, no." I forced a chuckle, and my neck flared up so badly that I grabbed it with my free hand. Vince rushed over and put his arm around me. "I'm fine."

"Are you sure?"

"I'm sure."

*

Two hours later we returned from the hospital and still no Phil. I had the neck brace on and a prescription for the pain and inflammation. There was a message on the machine, and when I pushed play, I was surprised to hear Paige McKenzie's voice. She was calling to check on me, to make sure I'd gotten home safely. Her last words were: "Call me about having dinner. We'd love to have you guys over."

At least someone cared about me. Where was my husband? Why hadn't he at least called? It was nearly ten o'clock at night and for all I knew he'd gotten into his own car accident—but what was the chance of that? Both of us in the same day?

No, Herman had dragged Phil to the dog track. He was always bragging about the money he'd won betting on races there, but I detested gambling, especially on animals—not just animals, but dogs, man's best friend. And Phil hadn't called because he was ashamed to admit he was doing something he knew I disapproved of—was morally opposed to. Greyhounds were notoriously ill-treated, and I hated the idea of Phil supporting this corrupt industry.

I tried watching TV, but I couldn't concentrate. The drugs were making me feel very strange, sleepy and hyper at the same time. I'd close my eyes but then I'd hear a buzzing noise inside my head, like a horde of bees was trapped in there. As the clock on the VCR approached eleven, I grew frantic. Something bad had happened to Phil. In our three years together, he'd never done anything like this. I felt like a huge rock had fallen on me and now I was stuck on the sofa, unable to change the channel or even operate the remote. It rested next to my hand and all I had to do was pick it up, but I couldn't. Phil was dead. I was sure of it.

Then, just as the news came on at eleven, news that I was positive would have video of my husband's fatal car wreck, I heard him come through the front door. The hinges squealed loudly like the shrill cry of a hidden bird. Then the plodding of his feet against the terrazzo floor. I could feel the vibrations ever so slightly as he walked.

"Hey," he said quietly from behind me. "Sorry I'm so late. How was Tampa?"

Then he stepped into the den and noticed the neck brace I was wearing. His face fell and he swooped down next to me, getting so close that I could smell the stale beer on his breath. "What happened to your neck?" he asked tenderly, stroking my arm. Here was the moment of truth, the one I'd been dreading.

"A drunk guy ran a red light and crashed into us!" The tears streamed down my face and I closed my eyes because I couldn't stand to look at him and see the disappointment. I could hear the news announcer talking about a car jacking in St. Petersburg. A woman was dragged from behind the wheel and shot dead.

"Are you okay?"

I opened my eyes and saw that he was taking the news well. That made me feel better, and so I composed myself enough to explain. "I'll be fine. It's just my neck is strained. I got it x-rayed. Oh, Phil, the van got smashed. It's in the driveway. They had to tow it here from Tampa. The back end is pretty bad. I feel so sick about it! But it wasn't my fault. The guy ran a red light and plowed into us. He was Mexican or something. They arrested him and everything."

I waited for the words to sink in. He seemed to be chewing each one like he would a tough piece of steak. His mouth moved but no words came out. He kept stroking my arm and staring at the neck brace.

"Are you mad at me?" I asked.

"No! Of course not."

"You should go see the van. There's a huge dent and the wheels are all twisted."

"I don't care about that. Just so you're healthy. That's all that matters."

Those were words I wanted to hear, but the anger remained and came bubbling out of me. For hours I'd be waiting for him, needing him, and he'd forsaken me—why? I had to know. "Where were you? I tried calling the Houston's and Cindy said you'd gone off with Herman but she didn't know anything. Vince drove me to the hospital. I thought you were dead on the side of the road."

"I went to the dog track."

"I figured as much."

"It was Herman's idea. But I won a thousand bucks."

"Phil, I don't like you going there. I wish you wouldn't do it."

"I know. It's pathetic. I've got no excuses." He smiled thinly and shook his head. I couldn't stay mad at him. He was a decent person who tried to do right in the world, which wasn't always easy. And here he was, unemployed at 47, not sure about anything, and still full of dreams. He wanted us to join the Peace Corps once Vince graduated from high school.

"Go look at the van, will you?" I begged him. "I won't sleep until you do."

"Okay, I'll look at it."

I went outside with him. The night air was cool and the sky was perfectly clear, filled with distant stars. Off in the distance a dog was barking. Phil walked ahead of me. There was barely enough light from the front porch to shine on the van, but you could see the dent. Phil dropped to one knee and ran his hands over the metal the way a doctor checks for swollen lymph nodes in your neck.

"It's bad, isn't it?" I asked him.

"It's bad. Probably needs a new axel. But it's nothing I can't handle."

"Are you sure?"

"Positive. I can use the money I won at the track. How about that? Is that good karma or what?"

"Please. Give me a break. You'll spend eternity in hell."

"At least I'll get to see my friends."

Dunedin, Florida
1997
96012

Phil told me to take the van to a garage in Dunedin and get the oil changed. He gave me the name of the place, Das Auto Haus, and told me to ask for a guy named Greer. "He's the only person I trust," he said gravely, bleary eyes fixed on me.

I promised him I'd do it. The last thing my stepfather needed on his deathbed was more to worry about. The doctors told us two months ago that he could go at any time, since the cancer in his pancreas had spread to his liver and his kidneys. But not his brain. Phil was still sharp as a tack, and concerned more than anything about easing the burdens on Mom after he was gone. Being in hospice really helped. Everyone here treated us with loving support and kindness, and we knew that Phil was resting comfortably.

So I drove home to get the van. I was surprised to find Mom's car in the driveway, the red Beetle she loved like a child. I thought she'd be at work, since we both had missed so much time during the past couple of months with Phil's illness. My supervisor had been wonderful, allowing me to take care of things without eating up all my leave—co-workers had donated sick days they hadn't used, so I felt very grateful for being in such a great place. Mom had taken a job with a local liberal arts college, and they'd been very understanding of her situation.

I still had keys to the house even though I'd moved out two years ago, after graduating from the University of South Florida. I let myself in through the front door and heard my mother say: "You can't be serious!"

I saw that she was on the phone. Quietly I waited for her to get off so that I could tell her what I was doing. She gave me a helpless expression as she cradled the receiver to her ear.

"I still don't understand how pancreatic cancer can be a pre-existing condition," she muttered. "It makes no sense. None at all."

She'd been having trouble with the insurance company from the beginning, when she'd submit claims only to have them denied. Right before he got sick, Phil had taken a new job with the city of Oldsmar in the Planning Office and supposedly the benefits were good. But she'd been getting the serious run-around, with the bills coming in for the tens of thousands of dollars. Mom was ready to pull her hair out.

"Yes, I'll fill out the forms again, and I'll send them in," she said warily. "I'd appreciate a prompt response. Creditors are calling the house, so I'd like this taken care of, please."

She hung up the phone and frowned at me. The past three months had aged her three years. I worried about her own health and the stress she was under each day. "Those people," she said, standing up and coming over to give me a brief hug. "How are you?"

"Fine. I saw Phil. He told me to get the oil changed in the VW."

"Those'll be his last words, I'm sure."

"I just want him to rest easy."

"How did he seem to you?"

"The same, really. Maybe a little thinner. Has he stopped eating?"

"He's ready to go. He told me last night. So it could be any day now. Any minute."

"I don't think he's suffering. He's being well-taken care of. That hospice is an amazing place."

"I should get back to him." She looked around for keys and purse, items always eluding her. I found them by the front door and she sighed in relief, clutching them to her chest. "I'd be lost without you, Vince. Truly I would."

"Call me if anything happens. Otherwise I'll stop by tonight after work."

She kissed me on the cheek and rushed off. I went back to the kitchen and got the keys to the van. Phil kept a spare set hanging on a hook by the wall calendar, which featured glossy images of Yosemite National Park. This month's featured a panoramic shot of a valley floor filled with purple flowers—April, when the blooms return and life begins anew, the promise of summer just around the corner. Mom and Phil had become very active in the Sierra Club, so much that Mom was even talking of going to graduate school to get a master's in environmental science. Now, with Phil sick, all bets were off. Financially they weren't in great shape. Little in the way of savings, meager 401(k)s, a second mortgage on the house—they were both too engaged in other interests to manage money. Phil's mantra was "simplify" and thus he spent more time doing yoga than meeting with accountants. They were both so gentle and so caring and so passionate—and so broke.

*

I couldn't remember the last time I'd driven the van. As I sat in the driver's seat, I racked my brain trying to recall—prom night? I'd taken Chris, my high school sweetheart, and a bunch of other people, since I wasn't drinking anymore, thanks to a DUI I'd gotten about two weeks prior. Still the best thing that ever happened to me. Thankfully I hadn't killed anyone or myself, and from that night forward, I became a different person. Sometimes it pained me to think back to my days as an insufferable punk, especially the way I'd treated Phil, like when we'd driven cross-country to get to Florida and I'd been a huge prick. At least I could admit my faults. So many just lack that ability and stay assholes forever.

The van drove great. Hard to believe that it was over thirty years old, but Phil made sure it was well taken care of. He'd tried to teach me about engines and what-not, but I'd blown him off, bored by the entire subject. VWs were what he shared with Mom, and I didn't want any part of that scene. Now I wished I'd listened, because I couldn't change the oil in my own car or do anything handy—whereas Phil was a great carpenter, electrician, plumber, painter, gardener, brewmaster, chef, computer guru, and all around terrific guy.

Phil wanted me to have the van. But I told him that I didn't think I'd take care of it the right way. And honestly, considering the bleak financial picture, my advice was that they sell it, since it was worth several thousand dollars. Mom needed that cash in the worst way, but I didn't dare mention it to Phil. Or Mom. No need to open up a new wound. There'd be a time and a place for that discussion.

Das Auto Haus was located on Michigan Avenue, just across the street from the spring training field of the Toronto Blue Jays. It was funny to see Canadian flags fluttering, as if somehow the little stadium sat on foreign soil. I pulled in and parked along the side, since both bays of the garage were filled with VWs. Arrayed along the back fence was a collection of VWs in various stages of repair—some were mere husks and others looked pretty dazzling. Greer, the owner, was a good pal of Phil's. They'd talked about going into business together but it never happened. Phil was just too restless to commit to a long-term project such as opening your own business. Instead he drifted from job to job, which he called "consulting," allowing him unfettered time to pursue his hobbies and his yoga and his meditation.

Greer came out as soon as he saw Phil's van. He probably thought I came with bad news to deliver. "Hey there, I said, getting out. "I'm here for an oil change."

"Sure thing. Any updates on your stepdad?"

"No. He's in hospice. It's just a matter of time."

Greer nodded and swallowed hard, rubbing his hands with a red grease rag. He was a short wiry guy who looked like he could crawl into a tight squeeze. Tattoos covered his arms, and a dozen earrings studded both lobes. Phil enjoyed trading stories with Greer, who'd gone everywhere and done everything back in the Sixties. Motorcycle gangs, drug dealing, a few stints in jail, three ex-wives, and usually a VW somewhere in the mix. Deep down, Phil envied Greer, a true free spirit who'd defied society's conventions and marched to the beat of his own drummer.

"Tell him I'm hoping for a miracle," he said, his voice choking a little. "I was reading about this stuff they make from the barks of pine trees. You ever heard of that?"

"No."

"Supposedly it can kill cancer cells. I got no idea where you get some. Maybe the health food store. It can't hurt. If it was me, I'd take any damn drug that had a remote chance." He stopped himself, a tear rolling down his weathered cheek. "Screw that, I would've gassed myself if it was me. Seriously. I would've sat in that van with the windows rolled up and a hose pumping in carbon monoxide from the exhaust. That's what I'd do."

"He considered it," I said softly. "But my mom begged him not to."

"Ah, fudge. You can't win, can you?"

"Pine barks, huh? I'll check it out."

"You should. You seriously should. I mean, it can't hurt."

"I left the keys in there."

"Sure thing. Give me a minute and I'll get on it. Pine bark extract. That's the name."

"I'll go find some as soon as possible."

I was willing to try anything to keep Phil alive, even if the doctors said he was in the final stages of the disease. Mom had spent countless hours in the library looking for alternative treatments, and she hadn't mentioned pine bark extract. But it was worth a shot. If Phil's illness had taught me anything, it was that life consisted of futile efforts to forestall the inevitable. The beauty came from tenacity, from denying doom any room, any space, any energy. Till the last breath.

New Port Richey, Florida
1998
96453

TO: crazymomma@aol.com
SUBJECT: MY NEW VW!!!!!!

Hi Mom!

Guess what? I just bought a new car today. Actually, it's not new at all...it's a 1964 Volkswagen hippie van, just like the one we had when I was a kid. Remember? Denise and I used to pretend like we were rock stars on tour, all because of the Partridge Family. We plastered those stickers of psychedelic flowers and peace signs on it...and you got so mad at us!!! I guess I should put an annoying bumper sticker on my van, just to be fair. I'm not sure I'll ever have my own children to do it for me...okay, no whining today about my miserable love life, I promise! I'm in too good a mood. I got a great deal on the van, which is actually kind of sad btw. The lady I bought it from's husband fixed it up into primo condition but he recently passed away so she was selling it and I was the first person who called and I don't even know why I was looking through the want ads this morning...you know how Sundays often get me down...I hate waking up alone on Sunday morning and reading the paper alone and drinking coffee alone and telling myself about the interesting articles in the newspaper I'd just read alone...that gets old when you're 35 like me. See, here I am complaining and I said I wouldn't! Bad girl!

:)

So anyway I saw this ad in the paper about a 1964 VW microbus and it reminded me of ours and so I called the woman and I don't know, something in me just had to go check it out. I've been wanting a bigger car but not one of those stupid SUV's or even worse a minivan...but since I've been doing a bunch of camping and kayaking I figured why not. So I drove down there, to Clearwater, and the house wasn't far from the building where like ten thousand people come every day to see an image of the Virgin Mary that's appeared in the windows of an office building...they've turned it into a huge shrine, it's pretty amazing but some chemists tested the windows and they determined that the streaks were caused by the sprinkler system and window cleaner. Which makes sense because from what I can see, God hasn't stepped foot in Florida in decades. He's turned it over to the developers who're paving over every square inch of this place as fast as they can…which reminds me, I saw the first sandhill crane of the season! It won't be long now before the rest of them show up from the arctic. Of course, they'll have less habitat to feed on, and eventually they'll go extinct, but who cares about that? Right? I mean, isn't "the blue dress" of Monica Lewinsky much more important? I'm totally sick of the whole thing, to tell you the truth. I don't care what happened between them. Maybe Hillary watched and took pictures. Does it really matter? Does it? AAAGGHHH!!!

Back to the story. The woman was a little odd but pleasant. I called her first and she said she was on the way to church and we agreed to meet up at two. So I called my friend Jill to see if she wanted to ride down with me but she said she had to go over to her boyfriend's parent's house for brunch, but I begged her to help me out because I knew I was going to buy this van. I just knew I'd fall in love with it. Jill drove me, sweet girl, although I had to hear about how wonderful her boyfriend was, even though truth be told he's a huge loser but Jill doesn't have the highest standards…and I know what you're thinking, maybe I should lower mine. But this is Pasco County, and around here a high school education puts you in the intelligensia. I exaggerate not. I'd be willing to settle for a man with a degree from a junior college, but the pickings are slim. You're rolling your eyes, but I haven't had a date in ten months.

How is everything in your neck of the woods? I called Denise the other day but no one answered. She must be super busy with those three kids and wonderful husband. I know I would be! Not that I'm jealous of my baby sister. Is it too early for a glass of wine? Stop worrying about me. I love you. I'll be okay.

Karen

*

TO: curryrw@virginia.edu
SUBJECT: I'M IMPULSIVE

Hi Rhanna!
Today I became the proud owner of a 1964 VW microbus. Please, hold the applause.

So what's new with you? How's the dissertation coming along? Still plugging away? Do you have a defense date yet? Why am I asking you so many questions? Is it because I'm drinking wine? Is it because I've lost my mind?

I haven't lost my mind entirely. I've come close a few times, however. Life down here in Florida isn't for the faint of heart. It's hot, it's buggy, and sometimes it's very lonely, especially on Sunday night. Tomorrow I have to attend a big meeting of the Pasco County Commissioners who'll no doubt approve the permits for yet another massive development to be built on critical habitat for scrub jays and gopher tortoises, both of which are listed by the state as endangered. But as a staff biologist for the Southwest Florida Water Management District—referred to here fondly as "Swiftmud"—I'll be ignored. I can talk until I'm blue in the face about the perils facing Florida wildlife, but most of the commissioners are already in somebody's pocket, which might sound cynical except that it's true. You told me that taking a job outside academia would prove maddening, and it has. The pettiness of the bureaucracy defies description, but my boss is a decent guy. He doesn't treat me like a hysterical nag like most men around here do. He actually thinks I'm a good scientist and supports me even if I manage to piss off somebody important, which happens about every week.

And that leads me to my next topic. I'm not seeing anyone, and at this point it'll take a miracle for me to find a mate. Here are my choices: I could join the NRA or the Klan, become a born-again Christian, or date women. In all of Pasco County, there is maybe one college-educated, liberal, heterosexual, single man with a good job. Under the age of fifty, I should add. The good ones are all taken. So of course I spend nights like tonight thinking about the great times we had in grad school, when a gal like me could shake a tree and watch a dozen eligible bachelors fall to the ground. A woman in the sciences? Our department was 90% men! I had them feeding out of the palm of my hand, and yet I managed to slip out of town without a ring on my finger. Even a guy like Dave Yazzo—I barely gave him the time of day, and he was madly in love with me…now I'd drive two hundred miles to cook him dinner. He's at a small liberal arts school in Iowa, I heard, and he has a girlfriend or fiancé or something…and Paul. Paul Paul Paul. Have you seen him lately? Forget I asked.

Maybe my van will lead me to a man. Stranger things can happen. I can picture myself driving down the street and the man of my dreams will stop dead in his tracks and stare as I cruise past. He'll follow me in his car, not wanting me to escape. The fantasy goes on from there, but you get the point.

Oh, is your wedding still on for June? I'm so excited!!! Get me the date as soon as possible so I can get the time off. My best to Brad! Ooops, the wine's almost gone…

Karen

*

TO: BioProf@aol.com
SUBJECT: THE STATE OF MOI

Hello there.
I know I shouldn't be writing you, but I'm drunk…pretend like I'm not here.

*

TO: BioProf@aol.com
SUBJECT: How Are YOU?

Hi Paul,
I thought I'd send you a quick note to touch base. I'm doing great! How's your wife? Have you told her about us yet? No? Are you scared she'll slice off your privates? I wouldn't blame her if she did! I hate your guts. Honestly. I really hope you die a slow, painful death.

*

TO: BioProf@aol.com
SUBJECT: Long Time, No See

Dear Paul,
How's it going? It's been a while and tomorrow's your birthday and so I decided to drop you a note and wish you all the best. What is it, 43? Not bad. You have to tell me the secret of your success one

day…besides getting a publication in Nature (and Science). And the NSF grants.

Life in Florida finds me hale and healthy. As you might've heard, I turned down the job at Elon Univ. and accepted a position with the state as a staff biologist with the Southwest Florida Water Management District. I spend lots of time in the field collecting data on my beloved kestrels and scrub jays and pileated woodpeckers, and I have an article coming out in Field Ornithology which isn't Science or Nature but then again I don't have the same pressures an academic faces. I also don't have to contend with annoying grad students who eat up your time! Although it was a pleasure getting to work so closely with you…you taught me more than you'll ever know. :)

Guess what? I bought a car today…not just any car, but a 1964 Volkswagen microbus…it's been restored and it's just the coolest car ever and I'm so thrilled it's mine. Are you still driving that Toyota pick-up truck? Ah, I remember it well…

Let's stay in touch. I mean that. Will you be at the ESA meeting in the fall? I'm thinking of going. I've never been to Minnesota. I'll have to buy a new winter coat, though! Anyway, happy birthday. I hope Alice and the kids are doing well.

Karen

*

TO: yazzodh@grier.edu
SUBJECT: How's It Going?

Hi Dave!

Sorry I've haven't dropped you a line since we both left C-ville…how's Iowa? I bet all the students adore you, esp the females…you were always the ladykiller! God, I've had too much wine tonight…but I'm celebrating…because…drum roll, please…I bought a car today….a sweet 1964 VW van, how awesome is that? I know you must be green with envy.

Are you going to the ESA in Minneapolis? I'm planning on it, and it would be wonderful if we could reconnect there. I've been doing a lot of thinking since I got to Florida, and you're someone I think I should apologize to…basically, I was a bonehead, and there are some good (well, not good but reasonable?) reasons...reasonable reasons...why I treated you the way I did. I wish I could get a do-over on that one, but life doesn't work that way.

Come to Minneapolis! That's an order!

Karen

*

TO: DeniseW2@aol.com
SUBJECT: It's Sunday Night (Again)

Hi sis!

It's getting close to midnight and outside I can hear the distant rumbling of thunder...it's August in Florida and it rains almost every day, usually coupled with intense flashes of lightning. Last week some poor guy was killed riding his bike when a bolt from the blue nailed him.

I've spent all night sending out emails to random people because I've been drinking wine since four o'clock...I've sobered up some but still I feel like there's this incredible weight pushing against my chest. I think it's the Bill Clinton thing. It's reminding me of some very unpleasant memories...why do I even bother? What the hell is wrong with me? Why do I always fall for the wrong man? Even in high school, I went after guys who had all kinds of problems, drugs, booze, bad attitude...why couldn't I have been more like you? Why

*

TO: DeniseW2@aol.com
SUBJECT: Remember the Old VW???

Hi sis!

I thought about calling you and then I remembered that it's almost midnight and you're asleep. Guess what? I bought a VW van just like the one Mom and Dad used to have...remember that thing and the fun we used to have? I'll have to send you some pictures! It's really cool, and you'd love it. Call me tomorrow, okay? I really want to talk to you. I'll be busy until after dinner, but call me!!!

K

Big Pine Key, Florida
1999
00000

We were teasing Karen about the new man in her life, Haden, when she told us all to shut up. "The odometer's getting ready to roll over!" she cried out, quite excited, giddy even, bouncing up and down in her seat like she'd just won the lottery. "This must be two hundred thousand miles—there's no way this is the first hundred. Think about that."

We did, for about two seconds. It was much more interesting, though, to rib Karen about Haden, from whom she had to tear herself away so that she could go with her best friends down to the Keys for an all-girls getaway weekend. Long planned, way before Haden turned up on the scene—dropped from the sky, basically, and right into Karen's lap. He worked as a bureaucratic flunkie in the Department of Environmental Protection and they'd met at a conference on sustainable water use up in Tallahassee, where he lived. They were doing the long-distance romance, but Karen didn't care because she was in love. Two months of bliss. It was making us all sick.

"Come on, guys," she insisted. "We should pull over and celebrate the accomplishment of the mighty and awesome van."

"Let's go check out the Big Blue Hole," I suggested, having read about it in a guidebook on the Keys. "It's on Big Pine, where we are now. We need to find the Key Deer National Wildlife Refuge. There's got to be a sign."

"Oh, yes, let's find a Key deer!" Karen chirped. "I've always wanted to see one in person. They're so cute and little."

I read the section on the Big Blue Hole out loud so that everyone would understand that it wasn't a natural feature of the landscape, but the remnants of a quarry built to get bedrock for the Overseas Railroad built in 1935. But quickly it filled with freshwater and now it served the same purpose as an oasis, providing many creatures with water, including the endangered Key deer. And apparently a few alligators.

"Haden would love this," Karen gushed, and we all groaned at her. But what could you say? The rest of us were married or in serious relationships, and Karen had basically written off the possibility of finding someone in Pasco County—which was smart, because Haden didn't live in Pasco County. But maybe he would soon, if he could work out a transfer. Things were moving very fast between them.

"Here's to the next one hundred thousand miles!" Karen hooted, beeping the horn a few times, which sounded anemic. "I'll probably burn them up in four months driving to Tallahassee unless one of us gets relocated."

Road signs told us that so far this year there had been 23 deer fatalities, so Karen slowed the van down to a crawl.

Dade City, Florida
2000
07848

THE STATEMENT OF HADEN T. MILLINER
November 7, 2000

On Election Day, I was assigned to transport senior citizens to various polling stations in Pasco County, Florida. For this purpose I borrowed my wife's Volkswagen van and drove it from her home in New Port Richey, leaving at approximately 6:10 a.m. I reported first to Gore-Lieberman Campaign Headquarters in Port Richey, where I picked up my passenger list. I was to interface with several predominantly African-American churches in the Dade City area, namely the St. John Missionary Baptist Church, Enterprise Missionary Baptist Church, and the Mount Zion AME. Most of the passengers were frail and elderly and required assistance to reach the polling station.

Trouble began almost immediately. The lines at the precincts were long, and poll workers were not prepared for the influx of voters. Sheriff's deputies were posted in conspicuous positions near the precinct, and I saw them stop and question young men on their way inside. Once inside three of my passengers, James K. Johnson, Louis H. Smith, and Curtis W. Anderson, were told that their names had been purged from the roll of eligible voters. They insisted that they had properly registered and produced county-issued voter registration cards, but the clerk at the polling station, Georgette Stinson, said that she would have to contact the Supervisors of Elections office to get further clarification. The clerk, however, had trouble getting through as the phone lines were jammed, and after waiting for an hour, we still hadn't gotten clearance for these men to cast a ballot. The passengers I'd brought became highly agitated and began complaining of fatigue and discomfort. I asked the clerk whether the three might cast provisional ballots but a Republican poll observer objected and the clerk informed us that we would have to wait for the Supervisors of Elections to provide guidance. I objected to this ruling and was again rebuffed. Since many of my passengers were growing tired from the long lines, I decided to return them to the church so that I could pick up my next load.

Outside, however, I discovered that one of the tires in my van had become flat. I could discern no visible signs of puncture, so I concluded that someone must have let the air out on purpose. Several witnesses claimed that they had seen two white men pull up in a BMW and "mess with" the tires on the van. I went to ask the sheriff's deputies whether they had noticed anything suspicious and both claimed to have seen nothing out of the ordinary, but the precinct parking lot was very congested and the van was parked beneath the shade of an oak tree and out of the way.

I called AAA and within thirty minutes a tow truck arrived and re-inflated my tire. I returned to the Mount Zion AME and picked up another load of passengers, again mostly elderly and frail, and this time at the polling station, two men, Lucas Hughes and Rafer Collins, were told that their names had been purged from the rolls. By now the lines at the precinct were quite long and the wait exceeded an hour, and then we waited another forty-five minutes before the clerk informed us that the men were not eligible to vote, despite them having what appeared to be valid voter registration cards.

Everyone in the third group voted without interference and we left the precinct to return to the church. We were driving east along State Road 52 at approximately 3:15 p.m. when I heard sirens and saw flashing blue lights in the rearview mirror. I noted on the speedometer that I was traveling well within the posted speed limit of 40 mph. I slowed down and pulled over to the shoulder to let the emergency vehicle pass, but quickly realized that I was being stopped.

The patrolmen exited from his car and asked for my driver's license, registration, and proof of insurance. I produced all of these documents as requested, but the officer, whose name was Frost, asked me why my name didn't appear on the registration or the insurance card. I explained that the person listed, Karen Mack, was my wife but we'd just been married and hadn't yet transferred the title in both of our names. I even provided a phone number where she could be reached in case he had any questions. He took my driver's license, registration, and proof of insurance back to the patrol car. We waited for around twenty minutes. When the officer returned, he issued me a citation for failure to obey a traffic sign. I politely asked him what traffic sign he was referring to.

"Don't get smart with me," he told me in a threatening manner.

I asked again, very calmly, what traffic sign I had failed to obey. By now the other passengers in the van were becoming increasingly vociferous in my defense, and I pleaded with them to remain silent until the matter was settled. At that point Deputy Frost asked me to step out of the vehicle. I immediately complied and then he placed me under arrest, handcuffing me as he informed me of my Miranda rights. I asked him calmly why he was taking me in and he said I had resisted arrest. I said I'd done no such thing, I just wanted to know what traffic sign I hadn't obeyed.

Akumal, Mexico
2001
15666

They pulled up in an old VW microbus. A thick layer of dust covered the windshield. Florida plates. I saw a man and a woman get out. I guessed they were around forty. She was wearing a bandana around her head like a scarf, with wraparound shades, so I couldn't tell if she had wrinkles or dyed her hair—and he had on a big floppy hat that concealed much of his face. They weren't young, but they weren't old, either. They struck me as contented, two peas in a pod on some kind of adventure. They removed their luggage, which wasn't fancy— backpacks and duffel bags mostly, and carried their stuff upstairs to check in at the small office.

I kept looking at the VW. I was supposed to be reading but I couldn't concentrate. I felt the urge to get in the microbus and drive away, deep into the jungles near Guatemala. Punta Allen. I'd seen it on a map, a peninsula in the middle of nowhere.

I wondered if anyone would miss me. My mother, of course, and my sisters. But would Elena? Would she care if I vanished for three months? Yes. She would be devastated. And even if I lived alone in a hut by the ocean with cockroaches crawling all over me, she'd accuse me of cheating on her. Her therapist has been working with her on her fears of abandonment, but she has a way to go yet. A very long way.

*

I was sitting by the pool of the hotel while Elena was out diving. She was due back at any moment, as it was nearing five o'clock. I didn't like diving. It hurt my ears and anyway I didn't have the patience for important details like checking on my air supply. I'd probably forget and then get the bends or something. My therapist recommended me not to take it up.

Diving was Elena's passion, though, and we tried to schedule at least four trips per year. I'd bring my golf clubs and play a local course, but lately I'd started to dislike playing golf alone. So I usually hired a pro to play with me because I really could use the help. Yesterday, for example, I shot a 90 at a course up near Playa Hermosa. The pro kept telling me to keep my left arm straight on the back swing and my right leg still, anchored like a pole in the ground. Hammer the ball like you're driving a railroad spike into the ground.

He confused me.

There was a pro at the Blue Canyon Country Club in Phuket who gave me great advice: go slow. Don't be in a hurry. Shot a 77 that day. A Gary Player course design. Lots of water but it didn't bother me.

Go slow. Don't be in a hurry. The pro's name was Duc. He was from Bangkok and he talked with a cigarette clenched in his teeth, which were yellow like the shade of corn before you cooked it. I could've spent a month taking lessons from him but after Elena dove at Koh Dok Mai, she had a little breakdown and we had to fly home. All because I spent a few minutes talking to a woman from Alberta at the bar of the resort. About the Canadian health system and whether she liked it. She said you may not get the best care, but you won't go broke, either, if something happened.

Elena was sure I wanted to sleep with her.

*

The couple from Florida came downstairs about fifteen minutes later. I looked up from my book and they smiled at me in acknowledgement but walked past the pool and out to the beach. They sat on chaise lounges beneath a palapa and put on snorkeling equipment. There was a patch reef just off-shore in Half Moon Bay, one of the main reasons tourists come to Akumal. Elena said I should at least put on a mask and fins and swim out a hundred yards just to see the fan corals swaying in the current. I promised her I would, but I knew I wouldn't.

I watched the couple from Florida swim out to the reef. They headed straight to where there were some breakers, where part of the reef jutted up from the crystal clear water. They spent a long time meandering along, side by side, taking in the splendors of the undersea world, which I knew I should've appreciated more. I did, but on an abstract level, as an idea. I understood all too well the stresses that coral reefs around the world were under. I just hated it when water got into my mask and no matter what, water always got into my mask.

I decided it was time for another drink.

*

Our suite overlooks the entirety of Half Moon Bay, and standing out on the balcony gave me a great view. My tequila and orange juice tasted refreshing as always, and I sipped it slowly, with my elbows resting on the concrete rail. Every few seconds I thought I heard the door open and expected Elena to walk in. It was after five now. Almost five thirty. Soon the sun would set. Already shadows were dancing on the sand from the little hotels that encircled the bay.

At night green turtles came up and nested on the beach. The females would spend hours digging into the sand, with a horde of onlookers nearby holding special flashlights that wouldn't throw off the turtles. Volunteers would mark the nest and put protective tape around it. Elena got the name of the group and yesterday I wrote them a check for ten thousand dollars. They gave me a hat and a t-shirt. I really liked the hat. It had a handsome design featuring the outline of a marine turtle and the words *Centro Ecológico Akumal*. I planned on wearing it the next time I played a round of golf.

*

At six o'clock I poured another drink and headed back downstairs. I could see that the couple from Florida had stopped snorkeling and now had gone for a dip in the pool. I heard water splashing and the piercing shouts of two people having fun. Feeling like a ghost I glided into a chair and opened my book again. The words seemed to disappear on the page the second my eyes hit them. *Fast Food Nation*. Elena had insisted I read it. And I was enjoying it, but the section on meatpacking was making me sick to my stomach.

"Don't splash me," the woman playfully called out, holding up her hands to cover her face.

"Since when do you make the rules?" the man countered.

"Since you made that wrong turn in Tampico and got us lost for two hours."

"Okay, okay. No more splashing."

"Time for a cerveza."

"Is there a store nearby?"

I looked up at them. I had beers up in my room. A case. "I've got cold ones in the fridge," I offered. "I was just going up to make another drink. I can bring down a couple of Negro Modelos."

"Sure, thanks," the man said, sizing me up. "If it's no trouble."

"Not at all."

I quickly scooted away and bounded up the three flights of stairs. I passed a maid with a broom, sweeping up piles of sand. She nodded at me as I hurried by. I felt a surge of excitement as I unlocked the door. I hoped Elena would be home by now. She could come with me down to the pool and we could have a couple of drinks with the couple from Florida.

But she wasn't there. Still out diving.

*

Their names were Haden and Karen. From the sound of it, they'd been driving through Mexico for the past two weeks, with the vague of idea of heading to Canada at some point. Or Europe. Or Brazil. They weren't sure. Except about one thing: they weren't going to live in the United States anymore, if they could help it.

"Why not?" I asked them.

They hesitated before answering. "We have our reasons," Haden finally volunteered, but I wanted to know more. Maybe it was the tequila. But I also liked to get to the bottom of everything. I could spend hours on the phone with a hedge fund manager going over trading strategy—I expected the people who worked for me to explain the positions they took and argue for them.

"Such as?"

"Such as we want to try to experience different cultures," Karen blandly replied, still keeping her cards close to her chest. "We don't have children and nothing is holding us back, and we figured we didn't have anything to lose. It was now or never."

"And that's the real reason?"

"Basically."

"Are you traveling alone, Neal?" Haden asked, turning the tables on me.

"No. My wife went on a scuba diving trip this afternoon. She should be back soon."

"What line of work are you in?"

"I do a little of this and that. I used to own my own company but I sold it a few years ago."

Haden cocked a brow, as people often did when I told them about myself. "How old are you?"

"Thirty-three."

"You look like you're twenty-three. What kind of company was it?"

"A software company."

"That's it! You look a little like Bill Gates! I bet people tell you that all the time."

I forced a smile. I'd grown tired of people telling me I resembled Bill Gates. I didn't see it. We both had straight floppy hair, that was it. I didn't wear glasses. I needed to shave every day. "I've heard it before," I responded, ready with my stock answer. "He's better looking and much richer."

I drained my glass. It was getting dark now, and Karen and Haden had finished their beers and gotten out of the pool to dry off. They said they wanted to go shower and then go grab some dinner at a local cantina. I suggested the place just down the beach from the hotel. It was called the La Pura Vida and it literally had dozens of swings and hammocks hanging everywhere. The food was decent, too.

"I'll probably be heading down there when Elena gets back," I told them as they started off, towels tied around their waists. "We could meet up with you."

"Sounds like a plan," Karen said. They carried their empty beer bottles with them instead of leaving them by the pool. Very considerate.

*

At seven o'clock I left a note for Elena explaining where I was. There was no cell phone service here and thus no way of getting in touch with her. Or she with me. I'm sure there was a perfectly reasonable explanation of why she wasn't home yet, but I didn't want to spend all night waiting for her. Once in Indonesia she went on a trip to Bunaken Marine Park, which was supposed to feature some of the best diving in the world, and she didn't come home until midnight, and I'd spent hours alone in the hotel room just paralyzed with fear. My therapist wanted me to avoid situations in which I let my imagination run wild. Get out and walk, he suggested. Break the pattern.

So I headed down to the restaurant on the beach with the idea of looking for Karen and Haden. I saw them sitting at a table for two. They waved at me as I sat in a swing by the bar. Then Haden came over and asked if I wanted to join them. At first I hesitated because I didn't want to interrupt a romantic dinner.

"Seriously," he insisted. "Come over and eat with us. Is your wife coming, too?"

"She should be. She wasn't back yet when I left. I'm expecting her any minute."

"I can't wait to meet her. I love scuba diving and she sounds like she's been on some amazing trips."

So I relented and went over to their table, carrying my drink with me. I was starting to feel hot in the face, a sure sign I was beginning to catch a buzz. Elena hated it when I drank too much. She claimed it made me talk too loud, in a booming voice, with too much cussing. Plus, she was worried that the prescriptions I was taking, especially Xanax and Ambien, adversely interacted with alcohol. No argument there. It made me loopy, which was the entire point.

"Neal!" Karen called out when she saw me. "Pull up a chair and have a seat. Your wife isn't back yet?"

"She must've gone out with her scuba buddies. I'm not sweating it. Cheers." I held up my glass and they did likewise. The beachside restaurant was starting to fill up, mostly with Americans just like us—well-to-do hipsters who'd come to this sleepy little village instead of one of the splashy resorts now common all throughout the greater Cancun region. Everyone was fit and tanned and looked exceedingly happy. I kept an eye out for Elena, knowing she'd like these people, Karen and Haden, off on their great adventure. Elena liked eccentrics. I could almost hear her asking all sorts of questions in ways I just couldn't. She'd carry the conversation along and soon enough all four of us would feel like best pals. Like last night watching the big green turtle lay her eggs—Elena was talking to everyone on the beach and getting all the pertinent information, while I stood aside and observed, which was my preferred position in the world. My therapist wanted me to engage more—to fight harder against my instincts to withdraw, to depend less on others to make connections.

*

It turned out that Karen had a Ph.D. in Zoology from the University of Virginia and was keenly interested in tropical conservation issues, while Haden had worked on the Gore campaign but had become very cynical about politics and really didn't know what he wanted to do with his life anymore. It was amazing what a bottle of tequila could do. Now I was getting the whole story, and I sat listening transfixed. They were interesting, well-spoken, and passionate people.

"The world as we know it is headed for a catastrophe," Karen said with great urgency, the flame from a nearby torch flickering in her moist eyes. "And the way I see it, habitat destruction in the so-called hot zones in the world—the areas with the greatest biodiversity—is something that we can stop quickly—without waiting for technology, without taking on the oil companies—by just using effective means of communication to reach out to indigenous peoples—and by targeting certain critical regions that could be preserved and protected. Which takes money."

"Both of us are very interested in Ecuador," Haden chipped in. "There's been tremendous deforestation and what rain forests remain are in serious trouble. We're thinking of heading down there and starting an organization. I'd handle the logistics and the outreach and Karen would do the science. It's a dream we have. A pipe dream."

"I've applied for a few grants but the amounts are very small, not enough to make a dent. Even if I got one."

"We should go anyway."

"You're right. We should leave tomorrow."

"How much money do you need?" I asked. It felt like I was floating now, with the tequila acting as a cloud I perched on. Talking business at night was something I usually didn't do, and my natural instinct was to assume the worst about people. But they struck me as totally sincere. Perhaps it was the VW van that enhanced their credibility. Liars and frauds wouldn't drive around Mexico in one.

"How much money?" Karen asked, sounding confused.

"Do you have a budget?"

"No way! We just have a dream."

"Dreams require plans," I explained. "And budgets. You need to pull together a specific proposal, describing everything you told me tonight. You can send it to me and I'll take a look at it." I paused a second and let this advice sink in. They both chewed on it in silence, nodding solemnly and searching for bullshit in my face. "I have a foundation. I just set it up. I'm looking to fund groups just like yours."

"We aren't a group yet," Karen mildly protested.

"I can help you become one. If you're serious about this, which you seem to be."

"I might take half a million or more to do it right."

"That's no problem. Just get me a proposal."

"Are you kidding? You'd give us half a million dollars to do this?"

I leaned forward and rested my elbows on the table, which was a little wobbly because it sat in the sand. "I sold my company right before the stock market crashed. I got lucky. Very lucky. And I want to use some of my good fortune to make the world a better place. Maybe that sounds hopelessly naïve, but it's what I want. Maybe if I give enough of my money away, I can sleep at night."

They looked at each other and started chuckling—not at me, not in derision, but more the unsure laughter that you heard in bars when tequila was rampant. They wanted to believe me, but I could tell they were still feeling me out.

"How long will you be in Akumal?" Haden asked, sounding more serious now, sober even if that was possible.

"I have to get back to the States soon, but here's my card. My contact info is on it." I got out my wallet and handed out the first business card that featured my foundation, which Elena named Our Shared Future. They were just printed up last week. The logo was my design—a globe with rays of light shining from it. A little LSD influenced, perhaps, but I liked it.

"We can pull something together in a few weeks," Haden said. "I mean, this is unreal. Never in a million years did I see this coming."

Karen then looked me square in the eyes. "If you're lying, I'll hunt you down and slit your throat."

"She will, too," Haden assured me.

The threat didn't faze me. Life entailed taking risks and hoping for the best. "I don't doubt it for a second. But I'm not lying. Let's have a drink and celebrate."

At that exact moment, as if my magic, Elena appeared. Her wet black hair glistened in the lambent light of the torches, and her tanned skin seemed to glow. A big smile. A wave. I stood up to greet her just as drops of rain started to fall.

Orlando, Florida
2003
20472

We were lost. It wasn't my fault. The address I'd gotten was 3476 South International Drive, but it was obvious that the talent agent we'd been working with was a total and complete moron. Lev Gibbeon, who claimed he'd discovered Leif Garrett and Bo Donaldson and the Heywoods back in the 70s, and of course I'd believed him at first because I liked to think the best about people until they invariably prove their worthlessness.

So here we were in Orlando, trying to find the casting director's office in a part of O-Town where everyone drove a million miles an hour and big resort hotels dominated the landscape, and you couldn't tell what anything was. The strip malls all seemed to flow together in long endless chain of franchises, and good luck finding a street number posted on anything. Not to mention that it was hotter than hell. Even I was sweating bullets, and I was used to the heat. A Florida boy, born and raised.

"Why didn't the stupid Germans who built this stupid hippie van put in AC?" groused Nolan from the way back.

"It doesn't get hot in Germany," I snapped. "Now help me find this place. We're running late. That's the first rule of show business. Be on time. Always be on time. You can never, ever be late."

"Look, there's Sea World!" Erin shouted as we passed by the sign with Shamu leaping from the water. "Can we go? Please pretty please?"

"No, this is a business trip. What did that street sign say? Are we on International Drive? Where the hell are we?"

"It gets hot in Germany," Nolan whined, as only fourteen year olds could. Only they suffered. Only they truly understood what was important. Adults? Ha! Adults were idiots. I gripped the steering wheel hard and tried to ignore him. It wasn't easy. He wouldn't let up. "Every documentary I saw of Hitler, he was always sweating like a pig. Like he'd just stepped out of a sauna. The Germans, they never cooled off. And it drove them nuts."

"This isn't International Drive. What is this?"

"Are we going to Sea World?"

"Are we what? Oh, for crying out loud, Erin. No, we're not. We have a big audition. A huge audition. That's what we should be thinking about. Not amusement parks."

"If only the Germans had invented air conditioning, maybe there wouldn't have been a war. Think about that."

"They built this VW after the war," I shot back. "It's a 1964, ace. There's no AC because it doesn't get hot in Germany. Look at an atlas."

"Yeah!" Erin started clapping her hands and jumping up and down in her seat. "We are going! Sweet!"

Nolan had gotten me distracted with his inane comments from the back, and somehow we ended up turning into the parking lot of Sea World by mistake, and there was no way to turn around. All the traffic was getting funneled to the pay booths, and we were behind a long line of cars. We had exactly ten minutes to find this place. Lev said both kids were perfect for the parts they were casting. They needed a blonde girl and a blonde boy both around ten, and even though Nolan was fourteen, he could still pass for ten because he was so short—shorter than his sister, which he hated. I told him he'd be a late bloomer like me, but he wasn't convinced. So he set up a chin-up bar in his doorway and he'd hang from it, letting gravity do the trick for him. When he cared about something, he actually tried.

It was just a commercial, but it paid and the more work you got, the more work came your way. That was one of the ironies of the business. It was impossible to break in, but once you did, you could work forever if you handled your career smart. A guy like Mickey Rooney landed parts for 70 years. Because he could sing and dance as well as act. He could do it all. Breadth: that's what I tried to teach the kids. The need to be broad. Never put your eggs in one basket. Always have a backup plan, because you never know what life's gonna throw at you. The kitchen sink. And the toilet. At the same time. You had to be ready at all times for everything.

"Are we auditioning at Sea World?" Nolan asked in mock incredulity, just to stick it to me. He pounced on every slip up I made.

"Yeah, you're going for the part of shark bait."

"I'm sure that would be way better than some stupid car commercial. 'My daddy bought a Jeep. He's the best.' Sickening."

"Nolan, I don't need the mouth right now."

"You don't need a mouth? How will you eat and talk?" Erin started giggling so I shot her a look and she got quiet. She had what it took to make it. A toughness to go with her talent. Nolan wanted to joke his way through life but Erin had ambition. She was my girl and I knew she'd get the part if I could just get her in front of a decision-maker. Nolan had no shot. Not with his attitude.

The line was moving slow as molasses, and when we got close enough, I could see why. Each and every car was getting searched.

"Great!" I yelled. "We'll never make it now. This is insanity. Why are they searching every damn car? Because they think some towelhead's going to blow up Shamu? Come on!"

We'd need a miracle to get to this audition on time, but you had to stay positive in this business. No was the expected answer. But it just took one Yes. One Yes could change your life forever.

Finally we got to the booth. We were five minutes late. I had to hurry this up.

"Ten dollars," the attendant said. I gave him a winning smile.

"Listen, we made a wrong turn. We're not going to the park. Is that the exit over there?"

"Sir, it's ten dollars, and we're going to have to search your car."

"But I made a wrong turn! We're late for an audition—can we just pull out over there?"

He didn't reply. He stood there like a statue, with the clock ticking. I had no choice. I paid him. Just so he'd let me through. First, though, he and another security flak poked their heads inside the van and snooped around. I was ready to explode. This was just an utter waste of time. What did these two idiots know about international terrorism? They both looked like they used their fingers and toes to count. I could've had a bomb strapped underneath the van and they never would've known. They didn't even bother to look underneath! Talk about homeland security!

"You're clear," he finally announced, like he'd just cracked the case.

I sped away, my blood boiling.

"I feel safer now," Nolan chuckled merrily from the back, mocking the world as only the young can. "Maybe those guys could go to Iraq and they'd find those weapons of mass destruction in no time. Seconds flat."

But I couldn't laugh. Not when we were on the verge of blowing a golden opportunity. I needed a drink so I could settle my nerves. I didn't want Lev Gibbeon to see me all twisted up into knots. Just a nip of something to take the edge off.

St. Petersburg, Florida
2006
42156

We loaded up the van for the gig at Ferg's. But Dave was already drunk. I could see it in his bloodshot eyes, and I didn't even bother asking him because he would've lied about it. So I let it go. At least he was happy. We all were. Excited and giddy and looking forward to our big night. Even Nolan wasn't complaining, even though he hated being in the band. He wanted to quit but Dave wouldn't let him. Dave was sure this time he was on to something, and the crazy thing was, he might've been right.

Last week at Ferg's the kids killed. They absolutely killed. Erin's voice sounded tough yet vulnerable, pretty awesome for a fourteen year old. Nolan on the drums, giving it everything he had. And the pair of brothers, Johnny and Joey Little, rocked on lead and bass guitar. It was just open-mike night at Ferg's, which was a big sports bar on Central Avenue, but the place was packed because there was a baseball game at the Trop—and the kids killed. They opened with Tom Petty, and then Sheryl Crow, and everyone in the bar was on their feet and screaming. I was standing next to Dave, and I saw tears in his eyes. I couldn't help it, either. We were both crying and we hugged each other and he whispered to me: *I got it right this time.*

The Spotlights. This was the fourth band Dave had put together, with Erin singing lead and Nolan on the drums. They'd never had good luck finding a guitarist. Nolan could've done it, but he was too good on the drums and finding a drummer was even harder than finding a guitarist. The Littles, though, had talent. Johnny especially, who was just twelve but he could play. Joey was the older one, a sweet gangly kid whom Erin had a crush on. But Joey acted as if Erin didn't exist, which only made her like him even more. She was starting high school in the fall, and I was worried about the choices she'd make when it came to boys. I really hoped she wouldn't follow in my footsteps.

*

Dave had removed the back seats from the VW. He kept them stored in the garage, though, in case his brother ever wanted the van back. Haden had moved to Ecuador with his wife, Karen, a few years ago to save the rain forests—it was her van, actually, and she'd made it clear that the arrangement was temporary and that one day she'd move back and reclaim her van, so we had to keep it in decent shape.

So we drove it to gigs because we could fit all of our equipment in it. We were so excited. I did Erin's hair and used the special brush my mom had given me, the one with the pearl handle. She put on pink lipstick and a cute white top, and she looked fantastic. Just like Jewel.

Except for her teeth. Erin needed braces but we couldn't afford them just then, because Dave wasn't making much money. He was trying to get his own seafood delivery business off the ground and it was a struggle. Braces for Erin were going to cost five grand, and we didn't have it. But with things looking up, who knew what was in store for us?

"If we can start getting some regular gigs," Dave kept insisting, which he had for years but now it seemed like he wasn't deluding himself, "then I can see us pulling down a grand every week, easy."

And I thought: finally we can fix Erin's teeth. They were twisted so bad that she hardly smiled anymore. She was very self-conscious about her teeth, as all girls were about every facet of their appearance at that age.

*

"Let's go!" Dave barked once he had the van loaded. "Time to get moving!"

We were ready. Dave would drive the van and I'd follow in the Toyota. Just as we pulled away from the house, I heard the rumble of thunder. Worriedly I gazed up to the sky and saw big black clouds looming. A violent storm was on the way, the typical evening rain during a Florida summer. Except this one was even more vicious. Not just thunder, but dozens of bolts of lightening crashed from above, and gusty winds shook the trees. Who in their right mind would go out on a night such as this? I hoped it would blow over quick.

By the time we parked at Ferg's, it felt like we were in the middle of a hurricane. We waited for the worst to pass and then unloaded our equipment in a drizzle. The place was desolate. Last week's crowd had vanished, seemingly washed away by the heavy rains that now flooded the streets. Plus, there was no baseball game at the Trop like last week. Ferg's was the place to meet up before every home game since the stadium was right across the street. Still, a few people were drinking at the bar. Dave got our name added to the list. We'd be going on second, right after a trio of guys with spiked hair and lipstick smeared all over their faces. Nolan said they looked like a cross between Insane Clown Posse and Hanson.

Erin's hair got wet from the rain and she started to freak out, so we had to go into the restroom and I tried to fix her up, but I didn't have the right kind of makeup in my bag.

"Mom, but I need some blush!" she snapped at me. "How could you forget to bring some?"

"That's not my job, girlfriend. You're old enough to think of these things. Let this be a lesson. Always bring what you need."

She pouted off by herself in a corner while the first band went on. They were terrible. The few patrons who'd come literally walked out as these three tone-deaf posers jumped around and snarled and strutted and played as if they'd each had about two guitars lessons. U2 couldn't follow that act on a rainy Wednesday night. Erin wasn't her usual bubbly self. I tried to get her up for the performance and so did Dave, who'd managed to suck down about three more shots of vodka at the bar, so he was hammered. "A real pro is up for every gig," he urged her on, spit flying from his mouth. "There are no small crowds, just small bands. You don't know who's out there—the president of Capitol Records could be in town for a convention. Each show is the most important of your life!"

"The president of Capitol Records isn't out there," Nolan chimed in, clicking his drumsticks and looking bored.

"He doesn't know anything!" Dave thundered. "Don't listen to him, Erin!"

"I'm just being realistic."

"You're being a downer. A downer with a rotten attitude."

Not even being around Joey Little cheered Erin up very much. The whole band was flat, and I feared for the worst. They were supposed to open with "Leaving Las Vegas," which Erin knew by heart, but she flubbed the lyrics in the first stanza, and then Nolan missed a few beats, which threw off both Littles, and before you knew it, they sounded about as unprofessional as the first group, as if they'd never rehearsed these songs, which wasn't at all true.

Dave of course drowned his sorrows, excusing himself during the second song, "Even the Losers" by Tom Petty, to throw back a few more belts of Stoli. The second song went much better than the first, but Nolan still drummed like he just didn't care, with no heart, because the dream had long ago died for him. He and Dave fought like cats and dogs now, and I worried that in time one of them would hit the other—and then all hell would break loose. And if Dave ever so much raised a hand in anger—I'd leave him. Take the kids and never speak to him again.

"Nolan is a cancer," he told me at the end of the set. "He has talent but no ambition. He won't amount to anything."

"You don't know that."

"Stop defending him. You always take his side. Every damn time."

I didn't want to argue with him at Ferg's. Erin looked like she could cry any second, so I hurried over to her and told her she'd done a great job. She buried her head in my shoulder and we walked to a quiet spot in the back while the next act set up. The manager who'd been so nice to us last week didn't say much beyond "Nice going." No offer of a weekly gig that paid. We were like a colony of lepers and he couldn't wait until we were gone.

*

The ride home was very somber. We said good-bye to the Little brothers, and I wondered whether we'd see them again. What had started out so promising now seemed destined for failure. I wondered if we weren't pushing the kids too hard. If it wasn't the band, Dave was taking them to auditions for commercials. And the magic act he trained Nolan to do so he could make money at birthday parties. It never stopped. Dave was convinced the kids would make him rich, somehow or some way. All the pressure was taking its toll.

"He's hammered, isn't he?" Nolan observed from the backseat. We were following the van down Central Avenue. The streets were still slick with rain and mostly empty. Dave was driving faster than he should've been, considering how wasted he was and we were in shouting distance of police headquarters. "I saw him throwing back vodka shots like they were water. He's an alcoholic, isn't he?"

"Maybe he'll quit one day," I said heavily, not believing my own words. But I had to keep up the façade—at least, I told myself that. "He keeps promising us he will."

"He thinks we're going to be the Backstreet Boys or Menudo or the

Jackson Five, but I got some news for him. He's kidding himself. And I'm the only one with the guts to tell him."

"Why couldn't you just play tonight?" Erin blurted, choking back tears. "I know I messed up the first song, but we could've come back strong."

"You're the only reason I put myself through this hell," he replied with a strange tenderness. "But I can't do it anymore. Ten years is enough. I'm over it."

"Where's he going?" I wondered aloud. We could all see the van hang a sudden left, in the opposite direction of the house. "Check and see if he called," I asked Erin in a stricken voice, although I already knew the answer.

She got my cell phone out of my bag and scrolled to both Missed and Incoming calls. Nothing. There weren't any new messages, either. "No," she said. "Should I call him?"

"Let him go," Nolan barked from the backseat. "Maybe he won't come back."

"That's enough!" I snapped. "You don't have to be so rude all the time."

"I'm just expressing my feelings. It's healthier. Maybe I won't go crazy like he has."

Erin called anyway. Maybe there was something wrong. An emergency with his mother, who was very old and not well. But no one answered, so Erin left a message: "Hey, it's me. We're just wondering where you're going. Sorry I messed up tonight."

We waited for him to call back. And waited. And waited. Then we pulled up in front of our house and it was dark, every light off to save electricity. Nolan was a stickler for that. With no lights on, though, the house looked barren and even spooky. It was huge, three stories tall and surrounded by large oak trees with long limbs that looked like the gnarled arms of giants squeezing the house.

Nolan came inside and went right up to his room and slammed the door. Erin stayed downstairs with me, and I made a snack in the kitchen. Chocolate chip cookies, fresh from scratch. As we ate, we waited for the phone to ring but it never did. "Where did he go?" Erin asked, worried that something was very wrong.

"I don't know."

"Is he okay? Maybe we should call the police or something."

"No, he'll be home soon. He probably stopped by to see a friend.

He mentioned something about that." I tried to sound reassuring, but she knew I was lying. I stroked her hair and gave her a kiss. "You should get some sleep. It's getting late."

She said she wasn't tired but I made her go to bed anyway. I followed her upstairs and tucked her in. Then I took a shower to wipe off the smell of the bar, the cigarette smoke and the beer and the rain. Then I turned off the light in the bedroom and listened for the van. Its engine had a very unique sound, being a Volkswagen. I'd learned to recognize it, and once I thought I heard it sputtering down the brick street. I sprang out of bed and dashed to the window to check. It was 12:32 a.m. according to my cell phone.

But it wasn't the van. It was a VW Beetle, an old one. I crawled back into bed and pulled the covers over my head and eventually I fell asleep.

Gulfport, Florida
2007
47296

He looked normal enough. Medium build, about five-nine, blonde hair that was turning gray. I didn't suspect nothing, and I've been in the business a long time, long enough to sniff out when someone's renting a storage unit for bogus reasons. Although I don't ask too many questions, if you get my drift. Don't ask, don't tell. What I don't need is the people who try and live in one. There was this family with a newborn baby, and they just left the diapers in a trash bag. The smell! It could've peeled the paint from the walls.

But this guy, he came across as regular. He wanted one of the big units, big enough to pull a van into. "Got a 1964 VW microbus," he told me. "I need somewhere I can strip it down."

I could see the VW parked right outside the office. Everything added up. Couple years ago I had a guy rent a unit for thirteen months so he could replace the engine on a GTO. Kept to himself, mostly. His checks cleared, so I didn't care. I'm not looking for friends. I got enough to worry about as it is.

"I don't remember this place being here," he told me as he filled out the contract. "I used to live right down the street."

"I been here since 1981."

"Yeah? I don't remember it. Hell, I was nineteen, and so you can guess where my mind was. In the gutter."

He wrote me a check for the full amount and then I took him over to the unit, B17, and showed him how to unlock it. My knees were hurting bad and I wanted to go sit back down, but the guy wanted to talk. "This was a wild neighborhood back then, huh? Everybody I knew was getting high on something. Ah, we were so young, so young and dumb. I played in a band. People said we were pretty good. We got regular gigs all over town."

He kept talking as he followed me back to the office. I didn't like rock and roll music. It gave me a headache. I went for jazz, but mostly I enjoy silence. Peace and quiet.

"Thanks a million," he called out, getting into the van. "This is going to help me out big time."

For a second I thought he was crying. But my eyes are always playing tricks on me. And anyway, he was a grown man.

St. Pete Beach, Florida
2007
47305

What's he doing here?

That was my first thought when I saw the van parked in the driveway. It was Friday morning and I was going to Mrs. McNamara's house as usual, like I had been for the past fifteen years. She was a sweet old bird, just lovely in every way, and I enjoyed chatting with her as I worked. Not that there was ever much to clean up. The poor dear wasn't feeling well and hardly made a mess, but that wasn't the point. She liked the company. She knew she could count on me to run an errand for her. Or just listen to her talk about her latest doctor visit. I had three other customers who were old ladies living alone, and they all beamed happily when they saw me each week.

I had a key and so I let myself in, still unsure why her oldest son would be here at this time. I knew he and his family came over on the weekends, but never in fifteen years had he come on a Friday morning. I was worried that something had happened to Mrs. McNamara. I braced for the bad news, that she had fallen and broken a hip—or her heart was giving her more trouble.

"Hi, Georgia," Mrs. McNamara called out to me. She was sitting on the sofa with the newspaper in her lap. She looked the same. Her voice sounded strong.

"Oh, hello there." The son was nowhere to be seen. Maybe it wasn't his van, but it looked exactly like the one he drove. But I could hear the shower running. I could smell him in the house.

"Dave has been staying here," she said sadly.

"Yeah?"

"I told him you wouldn't clean up his room. He's on his own. Don't change his sheets, either. He can do that."

She was talking like her son was a teen, not the grown man he was. A man with a wife and kids. What had happened? Had his wife finally had enough and tossed him out?

"I hope he goes home soon. I really do," she continued, wanting to get it off her chest. "He belongs at home. But he really did it this time. This time he went too far."

"Sorry to hear that."

"Me too. I'm just sick about it."

The shower stopped and I went to the kitchen, where I always started with the dishes. There were more of them this time, pots and pans even, like someone had been cooking big meals. Mrs. McNamara mostly ate frozen dinners she put in the microwave. So the son must've been here for a while. And what cook didn't clean up after himself?

I filled up the sink with water and added some dishwashing liquid. "Don't wash his mess," Mrs. McNamara said, hobbling back toward me, using her cane for support. "I told him he had to do it."

"I've already started," I replied. "It's no trouble."

I saw the vodka bottles on the counter. Three of them. All empty. Mrs. McNamara didn't drink a drop because of the medicines she was taking. Her son hit the sauce hard, apparently. No wonder he got thrown out of his own house.

"He promised me he'd wash his dishes," she sighed.

"I'll be done in a flash."

"And Erin—you remember Erin, my granddaughter? She was expelled from high school yesterday."

"What on earth for?"

"Drugs! Can you believe that? On top of everything else that's been happening."

"That's a shame. She seemed like such a nice girl."

"She is. But the things that go on in that house—it's enough to make your head spin."

The son came out of the spare bedroom, his hair wet, wearing a white shirt and faded blue jeans. I smiled at him as I scrubbed out a pan.

"Hi, Georgia," he said quietly, like he was ashamed of seeing me, which he should've been.

"Hi." I scrubbed harder, trying to get off the crust at the bottom.

"I was just getting ready to do that."

"You don't have to," Mrs. McNamara snapped.

"I'm heading out, Mom."

"Will you be back for dinner?"

"I don't know. I'm not sure yet. Maybe not."

"Have you spoken to Beth? Or the kids?"

"Not yet. I was going to call them later."

"Good. Don't give up yet. She might take you back. It depends on you, though."

"I know it does."

"She's a good woman who'll forgive you if you show her you mean business."

"I've got everything taken care of."

"You do?"

"I do. Everything is in order."

"If you say so."

"Trust me on this one, Mom."

He leaned down and kissed the top of her head, and then he left. Then I got the whole story, of how his wife had called the cops after he'd gotten drunk and hit her, and Mrs. McNamara had to bail him out of jail. She could barely get through it all without sniffling and moaning, and I worried that her heart would explode then and there.

Gulfport, Florida
2007
47321

Gulfport Police Department
Narrative for Officer Jason G Mathis
Ref: 07-1035-OF

SUSPICIOUS DEATH
REPORT 07-1035-OF
OFFICER MATHIS
MAY 12, 2007

On May 12, 2007, at about 10:42am, I was dispatched to a possible suicide.

Synopsis:

On arrival I found a deceased white male inside unit B17 at the Gulfport Storage Complex. The initial investigation made the death appear to be a possible suicide.

Crime Scene:

4924 Tangerine Avenue South. This location is a storage complex. The storage unit in question is B17. This unit is located off Tangerine Avenue and is halfway down the eastern most building. The unit in question is located on the west side of this building and faces west. The door to the storage unit was open when I arrived with a paramedic inside tending to the deceased person.

As I looked into the unit there was a brown and cream Volkswagen van parked in the unit. The van was not running when I arrived. While looking into the unit I noticed a white male lying on the ground behind the van next to the van's exhaust pipe. The unit smelled strongly of exhaust when I arrived.

Officer's Observation:

When I arrived I observed Paramedic Hayes inside the unit while three white males stood outside the unit.

When Hayes pronounced the white male dead at 10:49am, I secured the crime scene. I briefly entered the scene to acquire a license plate from the brown Volkswagen van. While in the unit I observed the decedent's body. The body was located at the rear of the van. The van was backed into the unit. The decedent was lying on his back next to the van's exhaust pipe.

St. Petersburg, Florida
2007
47330

I can see the van parked on the street under the mimosa tree. Mom finally drove it home yesterday. Once she got back, she was spooked. She wasn't crying but her hands were shaking like it was cold outside. But it was hot. Hot and dry and dusty.

*

All I've been doing lately is sitting alone in my room. I'm going to go totally crazy if I don't get out of this house soon. I can't talk to anybody, either. My cell phone got cancelled and Mom was like, "Get used to it."

We don't have internet anymore. Too expensive. Or cable TV. Just rabbit ears. And the reception is terrible. It feels like I'm living in the dark ages. Nolan is happy as can be. He said one day he's gonna live off the grid so he can be free. Whatever that means.

*

It's weird seeing the van again, parked like normal. Any second I expect Daddy to come home and get set up for a rehearsal. He thought I could go solo. He said a pretty girl like me, with a voice like mine, didn't need a band. I just needed a song. One song is all it took. One song that hit big. He told me to keep a journal and write down my thoughts and maybe a song would come out. Songs hide in strange places. If you look for one, you'll never find it. Songs find you. Like stray dogs.

*

A man walking his dog stops and stares at the van. The dog sniffs at the dying brown grass. The man starts smiling like he's just heard a funny joke. And I want to yell down at him and ask him what's so damn funny. Then his dog hops over and pees on the front tire. He pulls the dog away and looks around to see if anybody saw.

That's pretty much all the excitement I get these days.

*

The van is now officially for sale. Aunt Karen and Uncle Haden called from Ecuador. Because there was no funeral or memorial service of any kind, they didn't come back. They didn't want the van anymore and we had their permission to sell it, and we could keep the money. Mom thinks three thousand dollars is a fair price. She did some research at work where she has a computer. Must be nice.

*

The mimosa tree keeps dropping its blossoms on the van. Now it's covered in white petals, kind of like a shroud. Mom thinks we're going to sell it soon. People are calling about it. People are interested. After all, it's a collector's item. It's a classic. Nolan wants to set in on fire. He really does. I'm not kidding. He wants to pour gasoline on it and then toss lit matches at it to see how long it would take to catch. He has a theory he wants to prove. He also hates the van. He said he spits on it whenever he walks outside. I'm not allowed to leave the house. But I wouldn't do that. The van is way cool. Daddy said I could drive it when I turned sixteen. He trusted me. Nolan, no way. Maybe that's why they always fought. Maybe that's why Nolan isn't sorry.

*

Nolan has his entire body inside the fridge looking for something to eat. He comes out with a shriveled-up orange. Which he tosses right into the trash. "Did you eat the last donut?"

"No. Mom did."

"What are we supposed to have? There's nothing to eat."

He looks around hungrily, rubbing his stomach. "Well, this calls for extreme measures."

He picks up the keys to the van that are hanging on a hook by the phone.

"What're you doing?" I ask him.

"Are you coming with me or not?"

"Mom said you're not allowed to drive the van."

"I guess that's a no." He stomps past me and I'm wondering

whether I should call Mom at work. Since she's selling the van, she told Nolan that under no circumstances could he drive the van, ever. Not without her permission anyway.

"Last chance," he calls out from the front door. An offer I can't refuse. I have to get out of this house.

"You promise to be careful?" I ask just to be sure. Nolan can do some real stupid stuff. Like the dreadlocks he's growing. He thinks he looks suave but he can't admit to himself that he looks like a pown.

"What, do you think I'm gonna wreck? Don't worry about me. It's your big mouth that'll get us into trouble. You promise not to tell Mom?"

"I don't have a big mouth."

"You always tell on me."

"I do not."

"Let's just keep this on the DL, okay?"

*

I wait for Nolan to get in and then reach over to unlock my door. The van is so old that it doesn't have an unlock button like new cars. The windows don't go down automatically, either, and there isn't any air conditioning. The radio only gets AM stations.

No trash on the floorboard. Someone must've cleaned it up. There was usually all kinds of brown paper bags littering the floor, the little ones people could fit cans of beer into. The way-back always had boxes and crates of one kind or another, but now it was empty, too.

Nolan puts the key into the ignition and starts the engine. It sputters a few times but then starts to purr nicely, creating that familiar sound I used to listen for.

"The engine still works," Nolan says, putting it into gear, which takes some effort. It's a manual transmission, and Nolan isn't very good at working the clutch. We stall out and Nolan has to re-start the motor, but soon enough we're off, slowly cruising down Bay Street on a bright sunny day. We have the windows down and Nolan finds a Spanish station on the radio. I rest my elbow on the door and let the breeze blow through my hair.

*

Our favorite convenience store, Shep's, is just ten blocks away. The ride is short, but the little taste of freedom goes down smooth. How long has it been since I smiled? I can't remember the last time.

"Do you have any money?" Nolan asks as we pull in and park.

"No. Do you?"

"I've got exactly one dollar and forty-six cents."

"You can't buy much with that."

Nolan gets on his hands and knees to hunt beneath the seats, but there's no hidden treasure. There's nothing, not even trash. "The cops must've gone through this van with a fine-tooth comb," he says, disappointed and sweaty.

"Really?"

"They had to. Somebody cleaned it up. It was never like this."

"Maybe Mom did it."

"It was the cops. They were looking for evidence."

"Why did they need evidence?"

"Because that's what they do. When they find a dead body, they don't assume anything. They seal the crime scene and look at every last shred." Nolan sounds very confident and knowing, as usual, but I don't understand how he could just say the words "dead body" like it's no big deal.

I get out of the van and walk into the store.

"We can split some chips," Nolan says when he catches up to me.

"I'm not hungry," I tell him. My stomach is churning and I feel dizzy.

"I'm sorry I said anything about a dead body," he mutters under his breath. We're standing in front of the snack shelves. A Chinese woman is looking at us like we're going to rob her blind.

"Come on, let's get a bag of Funyuns," he tries again. "You like Funyuns, right?"

"Sure."

"Funyuns it is."

*

The sun is blazing hot, getting higher in the sky on a cloudless day. The asphalt of the parking lot shimmers with heat. I hold the Funions while he starts the motor.

"How did he do it?" I ask. Nolan looks surprised as he tries to get the van into reverse. He has to shove down on the long shift stick and the gears keep grinding because he doesn't have the clutch pushed in far enough.

"I thought you knew."

"I know a little. But like where did he do it?"

"It was some storage place down in Gulfport."

"Gulfport?" I remember the police officers coming to the house. It was around noon and I'd just been expelled from school and was home. Mom had taken the day off from work because I guess she didn't trust me to be alone.

But the police officers didn't wear the right uniforms. Theirs were blue, and the St. Pete cops wore white and green. They were Gulfport cops.

Questions keep popping into my head, stuff I've been thinking about even though I didn't want to. "Why did he go there?" I ask.

"I don't know. That's a good question. There's a million storage places between here and Gulfport."

We're both sweating like pigs now, sitting in the parking lot of Shep's with the sun beating down on us. Nolan can't get the van in reverse. He's not even trying anymore.

"I wish I could've said good-bye or something," I say. "There was no funeral. You know? I feel like we should do something. To make it feel better. Like put some flowers by his grave except there isn't a grave."

Nolan thinks for a second. "I have an idea if you're up for it."

Gulfport, Florida
2007
49885

I pulled the van into an empty gravel parking lot. In the distance I could hear the sound of a motorbike. Then it grew louder, and a kid on a four-wheel ATV came ripping around a building. He skidded to a stop on the gravel, looked at us, and then went tearing off again, disappearing behind a rusted-out husk of a U-Haul truck, kicking dust up into the windless air.

"Is this it?" Erin asked. "Gulfport Storage?"

"According to the police report, it was unit B17."

"Oh, man. This is creepy. I don't know if I can handle it, Nolan. Maybe this wasn't such a great idea after all."

"You don't have to do this. If you want to split, we can."

"No, we have to. And then it'll be over. We'll say good-bye."

She closed her eyes and drank in the smells and sounds. In her lap was a little bouquet of flowers she'd picked from the raised beds bordering the parking lot of Shep's. Some sunflowers and lantana and periwinkle, bound together by her hair tie.

"Are you sure?" I asked one last time. She nodded and then we hopped out of the van. We walked quickly along a cracked sidewalk and passed by a powerboat perched on a trailer. The tires of the trailer were flat, so the boat wasn't going anywhere soon. Someone had left two shopping carts by the outboard engine. I couldn't figure out why, though. Maybe an old sea captain was trying to fix the boat because the crusty old goat dreamt of one day launching it and never coming back. I totally got that.

I heard the kid on the four-wheeler again. He was coming right at us, like he was going to run us over. Then he slid to a stop ten yards from the boat trailer and killed the engine.

"Hey," he said. I guessed he was seventeen. He was thin and muscular, with an Eminem fade cut and a bunch of tattoos on both arms and his back. His face was covered with dirt and he was sweating and his jeans were halfway down his ass, exposing his floral-patterned underwear. "You guys looking for someone?"

"No," I replied tersely. I wasn't in the mood for company. "We're good."

"I seen you with them flowers. They real pretty."

He smiled at Erin and I thought he was going to start macking on her, so I hurried her along. That was the last thing I needed, for Erin to fall in love with this hood rat. Yet I was also tempted to ask him whether he'd talked to Dad. After all, it was possible they'd run into each other at some point. That would've been an interesting conversation. *Don't off yourself, dog. You got much to live for, yo. Peace out.*

*

Erin knelt down and placed the flowers carefully by the brown metal door of unit B17. She remained there a few minutes and said her good-byes. I did, too, in my own way.

So this was where he did it, at a nondescript storage facility where over the office was a rundown apartment and across the street was a strip mall with stores I'd never heard of. Neo-Soul. Ruth's Fried Chicken. Queen's Beauty Secrets. The Southside Church of Christ. The parking lot in front of these stores looked pretty empty, and in fact many of them were boarded up. Just their signs remained.

The guys that found him operated a tree-cutting service and rented the space next to B17 to store their equipment. One of the tree cutters had heard an engine running in the next-door unit, and he knew there was trouble. An engine meant exhaust, and with the unit all closed up, the exhaust had nowhere to go.

I pressed my ear against the warm metal door and listened very carefully. I thought I heard an engine. Honestly. It was really stupid creepy. Was his ghost inside warning me to get the hell away? Because I didn't come here to pay last respects or lay a wreath or anything like that. This was for Erin because she needed to do it. Not me. I came to show him, that drunk bastard, who was the last man standing. He said I wouldn't amount to a hill of beans. He punched me in the face and said I was worthless.

But I was alive and kicking. And I knew one thing—never in a million years would I let my life get so screwed up that I'd rent a storage unit and then kill myself by leaving the engine of my sister-in-law's VW running in it. I might not make it far in life. I might fall flat on my face.

But I'd never do that.

Seminole, Florida
2007
49902

We were underwater. We were drowning, literally gasping for our last breath, ready to declare bankruptcy and start over, when what does he do? Brings home another toy. Another something he couldn't live without.

Don't get me wrong. I love my husband. He's a good man, kind and considerate, and funny which is very important considering that the world is totally insane. But he has a few flaws that he could work on, and the biggest one involves money. I know money doesn't make you happy. I get that, trust me. So money doesn't make you happy, but try living without any. I'm not greedy. I'm not one of those women who spend all day at the club getting massages and facials and two-hour spin classes. I just want to be comfortable. I don't need rich. Comfortable is fine.

So Kyle shows up one day and he tells me to put on a blindfold. "I'm not in the mood," I tell him. "Wrong time of the month."

"No, it's not that," he says. "Just put on a blindfold."

"Why?" I want to know. "Why am I doing this?"

"I have something I want to show you."

"What?"

"It's a surprise."

"Just tell me!"

"Then it won't be a surprise. Do me this favor. Indulge me."

So I go and get a bandana and tie it around my face so I can't see anything. And I think to myself: this is what I've been doing my entire marriage. Kyle has led me around by the wrist through the dark, always with the promise of brighter days ahead. First we bought this huge house that we couldn't really afford but he said it was a great investment and we'd make a killing except now it's worth a hundred thousand less than what we paid for it. Then he cashed in a 401(k) from his old job so he could buy a condo in downtown St. Pete and that was a disaster, too. I mean, we're belly up right now. We're belly up and we both have college degrees and good jobs and we should've seen this coming but we were wearing blindfolds the whole time, like two kids at a birthday party trying to whack a piñata. Except we ended up whacking each other in the head.

He leads me outside. The rain's just finished and there's a coolness hanging in the air that lasts about six seconds during the summer. Droplets of water plop down on top of my head and I want to rip this stupid blindfold off because I know he's done something he shouldn't have. Let's get it over with already.

"Ta-da!" he sings like a game show host. Like he's Bob Barker or something.

I pull off my blindfold.

"What the hell is that?"

"An investment."

An investment? It's a VW hippie bus that looks like it's been shot up by thugs. I mean, there're bullet holes all over it! Seriously.

"Why did you buy this?"

"I got it for a steal. Fifteen hundred bucks. We sink a couple hundred into it, patch up the bullet holes, and we can sell it for five grand. That's what these things are going for."

"We don't have fifteen hundred bucks, Kyle. We don't have a pot to piss in."

"We do now."

"How's that?"

"We stop paying our mortgage. That's two grand a month right there."

"Until they kick us out."

"So what? We'll have money to live on. We only put down one percent."

"Our credit will be in the tank."

"For seven years. We'll be fine. Trust me, it's the right move."

"Does it even run?"

"I drove it here, didn't I?"

"Where's your car?"

"Back in St. Pete. We have to go get it. This was spur of the moment. I was driving around the Old Northeast, thinking about all the shit, the money and the condo and all of it, and the next thing I know, I see this van and something just took over. I called the number and talked to the woman and she just wanted it gone. So I jumped on it. We can triple our money. You watch."

"I've heard that before."

"Just wait."

New York, New York
2008
50001

Dad was turning sixty this year, and I really wanted to do something nice for him. Something special. But it's hard to buy a gift for a man who has everything and yet at the same time really lives for one reason and one reason only—to surf. My father, dentist and eternal fourteen-year-old kid who still spent as many hours as he could at Ocean Beach. He was always trying to get me to surf with him, but I preferred ballet and gymnastics and so I blew him off all the time. Not that he cared. My brothers loved surfing as much as he did, and he had his old San Diego surfing buddies, too, guys he still hung around because Dad was as loyal as they came. Married to the same woman for thirty-five years. His receptionist, his hygienists, his office manager—they never left his practice. He still lived in the house he bought back in 1969 for twenty grand—and he said he's never going to sell it. Two blocks from the beach, two blocks from the one place on Earth he felt truly at peace.

But what could I get him? If I asked him, he'd say that he didn't need anything. Mom would say to get him a new shirt, because she wanted nothing more than to throw out all his old clothes but Dad wouldn't hear of it. A shirt? No way. I wanted to show him how much he meant to me. To everyone. Twice a year he went to Haiti and spent a week providing free dental care to children—that was his idea of a vacation. He supported a wide array of causes in San Diego, but he never wanted his donations to be made public.

He liked collecting anything and everything from the Sixties. Last year for his birthday, for example, I found a Fender electric guitar that I knew he'd love, and so I got it for him and had it shipped out to San Diego. But he had at least three other guitars, and so while he appreciated the sentiment, I knew this year for the big 6-0 I needed to pull a rabbit out of a hat.

I went down to Washington Market Park, one of the more tranquil places in all of Tribeca and just a few blocks from our condo. Here was a spot where I could do a little thinking. Mark was at work, and the kids were at school. I had my laptop with me and settled into a park bench beneath a big shady tree. I was happy as a clam, while Mark was wondering if Citigroup was going to survive—whether the entire financial system would weather this awful storm. He worked on something called a SIV—structured investment vehicle—that acted kind of like a bank except it wasn't so they could make buy and commercial paper and then lend out what they borrowed—to be honest I barely understood a word of shoptalk when it came to all matters Citigroup. I was a graphic designer and did some consulting here and there, but mostly I lived in the make-believe world of my imagination. I spent my time scribbling and sketching and combing through consignment stores in the Bronx or Staten Island, looking for things that inspired me. Lately I've been into hand-painting moustaches on old coffee mugs and selling them on-line for ten bucks each—so far, I'd sold fifty. Five hundred bucks! Not bad for a few moustaches and some black paint.

But poor Mark, the past few months had taken a toll on him. All the Wall Street folks we knew and partied with were going through the same thing—this was the worst they'd ever seen—unprecedented—frightening. Mark was ready to quit. He'd had enough. Ten years at Citigroup had turned him to mush. His words, not mine. To me he was the same thoughtful and intelligent man I'd fallen in love with, but he said he was dying on the inside, getting home ten, eleven at night, after the kids were in bed, and he was usually gone again before they were up in the morning. But last year he'd earned a bonus of two million dollars. Three million the year before that. Our condo was paid for. The kids were at the Trinity School. Each summer we spent a week on Block Island, and at Christmas we went to Park City, Utah. Not bad for two clueless people in their mid-30s.

But I understood what Mark meant. He wanted more from life than to work seventy hours per week. At night he'd ask me about rehearsals and practices and games and scraped knees and teacher conferences, and I'd try to fill him in, but he just got so down listening to all he'd missed and feeling so guilty because his father had been the same way and he'd vowed not to be but here he was, behaving the same way for the same reason. Money.

But look at all you give us, I tried telling him. Not good enough, he replied. My kids are two strangers. They barely know me.

They love you very much!

They don't know me. And I don't know them. That's got to change. So quit.

I didn't care if he worked at Citigroup or not. We'd survive somehow. I'd leave New York if that was the best thing for his career, but the kids had friends in the city and they'd hate to relocate and I'd grown up in the same house and wanted for my children to have the same kind of stability as I did. It was a confusing time. Mark was miserable. The world seemed on the verge of collapse.

And maybe that was the inspiration. The tumult and doom that pervaded our lives somehow got me thinking about the Sixties in a different way. What was it about the period that infatuated Dad so much? It wasn't just the surfing. Or the music, either, although he loved both. He still rode waves and listened to rock albums on a turntable, after all. Those were the obvious attractions, but what lay beneath the surface? What really moved him? What could I buy him for his birthday that would blow him away and at the same time connect him deeply to his passion? What?

Sitting there at the park, I did the usual web-browsing, gunning from one site to another, not liking anything. A poster from a 1967 Jimi Hendrix concert? Tickets from a Jefferson Airplane show at the Fillmore? Old hat. Predictable. Might as well get him a tie. Except he didn't wear them. Not even to my wedding.

Was there something Dad used to have but didn't anymore? Wanted but never got? It didn't seem possible, because he was so ridiculously satisfied and content. Nothing bothered him. He was happy all the time. You'd never know, looking at him, that dentists had a high suicide rate.

Hippie van.

Those were the words that came to me. The exact phrase. My skin started to tingle. That was it, the perfect gift. I'd buy Dad a hippie van. Because really, what else captured the era more perfectly? The freedom, the lifestyle, going with the flow, windows rolled down, surfboard strapped to the top—it was him. And he didn't have one.

With a huge smile plastered on my face, I typed "Volkswagen van" into my search engine and sifted through the results. There were plenty for sale, but not real hippie vans built in the Sixties. The first ones of those I saw were totally restored and the asking price was over forty grand, which I would've happily spent if Mark's work situation had been a little more secure. Even though we had money in the bank, he wouldn't have appreciated that kind of expense at that juncture.

So I kept at it. I knew somewhere in the big worldwide web was the precise thing I was looking for. Because there always was. Always. If you kept clicking on links. Links and more links. Which I did, because finally I found the perfect van. 1964. Over two hundred miles. Ran okay, not great condition. Brown-and-cream. Three grand. Cheap.

I got out a credit card and within minutes I owned it. The last hurdle was getting it shipped out to San Diego from Seminole, Florida, which proved to be a bigger hassle than buying the thing in the first place. But for the right price, you could find someone to do whatever it was you wanted.

And that same night Mark came home in a buoyant mood. The federal government was going to pump a few billion into Citi, which meant Mark was getting a bonus this year after all. Not two million, but close. So it turned out to be a pretty stellar day, all things considered.

San Diego, California
2008
50,024

I feel younger just sitting in it. Like it's 1964 all over again. Sixteen years old, a kid with a surfboard headed to the beach. Now I'm sixty, and some things never change. My longboard's in the back, right behind me, and I'm going to drive my VW van to the beach because there's a tasty break at the pier.

I've always wanted a microbus. But the opportunity to buy one never presented itself.

My first car was a 1953 Chevy, a hand-me-down from my older brother who was headed off to UCLA. And it ran without too many problems, and being of a practical mind, I never saw the value of buying things you didn't need. A paid-for car was a treasure, and I kept that Chevy going until I was done with UCLA in 1970. Lena was pregnant and money was tight, so right after we got married, we bought a used Ford wagon for a hundred bucks. Then came dentistry school and two more children, and before you realize it, a few decades have gone past, and you've made up a long list of reasons why you shouldn't indulge yourself. The college fund, parents who might need assistance, the rainy day, earthquakes, famine. Anyway, I'm not the kind of person who thinks a car defines you.

But if any car did define me, this one comes close. Yes, indeed. It suits me just fine. At first I thought my daughter had gone nuts, spending money on something I didn't need—my car ran perfectly. A Camry hybrid. Three years old, dependable, great gas mileage. The birthday gift was thoughtful and I thanked her for it, but until I actually sat in the van, I had no idea what it would do to me on the inside. The strong attachment I'd form. Like it was talking to me. Because we'd grown up together, me and the van. It was like reconnecting to a long-lost friend. The van knew my secrets, my pain, my joy.

I open the glove box because I'm curious about my new toy. I want to learn all I can about it, hoping that hidden within the interior are some clues about the journey this machine has been on. All I know is that my daughter had it shipped from Florida—all the way across the country. As if there weren't any old VWs for sale in Southern California. But she enjoyed doing unpredictable things, being by nature quirky and dreamy and impractical.

Lo and behold, the original owner's manual is still around! Unreal!

I take it out and it's a lot like me—worse for wear, a little tattered, faded and splotchy, held together with brown tape. But stapled to the inside of the front cover is the business card of the auto dealer who must've sold the van to the original owner. Damian Sincilio of Fortune Motors.

That's right here in San Diego. It's one of the oldest dealerships on the Mile of Cars in National City. Damian Sincilio? Do I know him? The name sounds familiar. I can't place it, but the incredible irony is just so mystical, really—the van has come home.

I lean back in the driver's seat, still looking down at the owner's manual. "Wow," I mutter happily. "What a long strange trip you've been on. From one end of the country and back again."

One last laugh, and I put the manual back in the glove box. Then I stick the keys in the ignition.

11063352R00181

Made in the USA
Charleston, SC
27 January 2012